**"SOMETHING WRONG, SWEETHEART?"** he asked, feigning innocence.

Blue fire glared up at him. "I would like to shoot you now."

The threat was so unexpected and said with such venom, he couldn't help but laugh. "I'd love to see you try."

"I'll more than try." She sounded so confident. Too bad she didn't stand a chance.

"Hmm." He settled more heavily on her by stretching his legs alongside hers and going to his elbows on either side of her head. Danger instincts flared through his brain while heat licked through his veins. "And then what?"

Her glare cooled as her gaze dropped to his lips. "I would run." Some of her earlier confidence seemed to have disappeared. *Smart woman.*

He toyed with the loose strand of her hair lying beside his hand. "Probably a good idea considering you'd miss and I'd be chasing you. Can you do me a favor, though?"

She blinked up at him. "What?"

"Try not to run in circles. It takes the fun out of things."

# IMMORTAL CURSE SERIES

# FORBIDDEN BONDS

AN
IMMORTAL CURSE
NOVEL

# LEXI C. FOSS

Editing by: Jacy Mackin & Jenny Dillion

Cover Design: Covers by Julie

Photography: Wander Aguiar Photography

Models: Andrew & Evan

Series Logo: The Font Diva

Published by: Ninja Newt Publishing, LLC

Print Edition

ISBN: 978-0-9985557-8-2

*To Louise, my captain, for your friendship, support, and endless humor. You keep me sane when I need it most. Thank you.*

*And to Matt, for understanding and supporting my passion for writing. I love you.*

# FORBIDDEN BONDS

## BOOK TWO

# A NOTE FROM THE AUTHOR

*Forbidden Bonds* is the second book in the Immortal Curse series and picks up right after the events in *Blood Laws*. It's strongly encouraged, but not required, to read these books in order. For those new to the Immortal world, I'm including a glossary with key terms and definitions.

Cheers,
-Lexi C. Foss

# IMMORTAL CURSE SERIES

## GLOSSARY

## PRETERNATURAL BEINGS

**Fledgling (noun):** The child of a male Ichorian and a human female, who has not yet been reborn as a Hydraian; they do not typically possess supernatural or psychic gifts until their immortal rebirth.

**Hydraian (noun):** An immortal offspring of a male Ichorian and a human female, who possesses two supernatural or psychic gifts and does not require human blood to survive.

**Ichorian (noun):** An immortal being of unknown descent who possesses one supernatural or psychic gift and requires human blood to survive.

**Immortal (noun):** A general noun designating a being who does not age and is immune to natural human death.

**Seraphim (noun):** A being who belongs to the highest order of angelic hierarchy. No known Seraphim are in existence today.

# KEY TERMS

**Arcadia:** Notorious Ichorian club in New York City that also serves as the primary meeting location for the Ichorian government.

**Blood Laws:** A series of ordinances created by the Ichorian governance board in response to the Treaty of 1747.

**Catastrophic Relief Foundation (CRF):** A global humanitarian aid organization headquartered in New York City with a secret paramilitary unit designed to destroy rogue supernaturals.

**Conclave:** The Ichorian governing board.

**Elders:** The original Hydraians who also serve as the Hydraian governing board.

**Nizari:** Ancient Ichorian assassins who hunt and kill fledglings.

**Nizari Poison:** A green substance notorious for killing fledglings and preventing their rebirth.

**Sentinel:** A soldier in the CRF unit designed to slaughter rogue immortal beings.

**Treaty of 1747:** An armistice agreement between Hydraians and Ichorians to cease fire and live in their designated areas. Those who opt to cross these boundaries do so at their own risk.

# A Soldier is Born

## 15 Years Ago...

Blood.

Death.

Unspeakable things.

Shades of red and black coated the walls, pictures, and toys, but none of that compared to the gory mess on Tom's bed. His mother's lifeless eyes stared back at him as he cowered in the corner. He tried not to cry, but the treacherous tears leaked down his cheeks, rolling over his trembling lips, to the soiled ground below.

"Come here, son." His dad engulfed Tom in a hug, holding him tightly as they grieved in silence. Father and son. A bond forged in birth and strengthened by death.

"Now you understand our purpose," his dad whispered. "Why we must fight."

Tom nodded. The monsters who did this were evil. They deserved to die.

"Your training won't get any easier," his dad continued, voice broken. "It will be brutal, and I will be hard on you, but I want you to be strong enough so that this never happens to you. I can't lose you, son. And there's only one way I can protect you."

By training to become the perfect soldier. A walking weapon designed to kill immortals. To seek vengeance for his mother's brutal murder. And to protect humanity from the evil on earth.

Tom never understood his purpose before, why his father constantly pushed him away, but seeing his mother's mutilated corpse changed everything. It shattered his heart and left rage brewing in its wake. He would channel that emotion, sharpen it into a weapon for immortals to fear, and become a man that would make his father proud.

"I'm ready, sir. Teach me everything."

# CHAPTER ONE

## Welcome Home

Tom Fitzgerald hated this place. Memories hung in the air as he searched each room for suspicious items or objects. He held his pistol low with both hands, ready to shoot anything that moved. People were always trying to kill him; an occupational hazard. And his fledgling bloodline didn't help matters.

The phone in his pocket buzzed. He knew who it was without looking. That detour he took to grab a few things from the store hadn't gone unnoticed. Fucking GPS tracker.

He holstered his weapon after clearing the guest suite. It no longer resembled the childhood bedroom he remembered due to the renovations completed after his mother's murder. His aunt stopped by weekly to keep the place up and running, which was a waste of time. No one lived here. Tom owned the family property and wanted nothing to do with it. Too many raw emotions were floating about, and no amount of redecorating would fix that. If it were up to him, he'd sell the place, but his father forbade it.

Tom hit speed dial on his phone as he walked towards the front of the cabin. His dad, who also happened to be his boss, picked up on the first ring and didn't bother with a greeting.

"Your report is late."

The days when Tom enjoyed his father's brief calls were long gone. A consequence of their last few months together.

"I didn't realize I was on a deadline," Tom drawled. "Maybe you should have been clearer." He suppressed the urge to add, *asshole*, to that statement.

"My directions were more than clear, Sentinel. Has the asset been moved to the appropriate quarters?" Of course his father would want to know this first. He was obsessed with the *asset*. Tom eyed the sedan parked in the gravel driveway through the front window. *The asset is contained and unconscious, sir.*

"Is this how this is going to go?" Tom wondered. "With you checking up on me every ten minutes? Because we both know I'm more than capable of handling this job."

"Like how you handled the Stas situation?"

The reminder of why his father sent him on this mission made him cringe. All Tom wanted was to show Stas the truth about her blood-sucking boyfriend, but that plan backfired big-time. He doubted she would ever trust him again, and now he was stuck in the middle of upstate New York on a babysitting mission. *At least she is safe here...*

"The asset and I are on site. What other information do you require, sir?" Tom learned a long time ago that

2

formality was the best way to placate his father. And he wanted nothing more than to end this conversation and go about his business. The sooner he completed this mission, the sooner he could go back to preparing for the inevitable.

"Is the asset secure?"

Tom looked at the black car outside. "Yes." *Just not in the way you want.* The unconscious woman didn't need to be restrained, which was why he removed the handcuffs the second they crossed the New York City limits. And fuck the idea of keeping her in a cage as his father wanted. This mission would operate according to Tom's plans, and that did not include locking a female up like an animal.

"Why did you stop at the pharmacy?" his father asked.

*Ah, and now we get to the real reason you called me.* "I needed a few things."

"Such as?"

Tom recognized that steely tone. John Fitzgerald's innate ability to force the truth out of others only worked in person, but that didn't stop him from attempting it over the phone. *Nice try, Dad.*

"What, you want a list? Toothpaste, shampoo, deodorant, some pain killers for the headache I know you're going to give me. Oh, and I got some cereal for tomorrow because I didn't realize Rosalie was going to stock the fridge for me." He'd noticed the abundance of food when he cleared the kitchen area. It brought a brief smile to his face. He hadn't seen his aunt in over a year. As his mother's only sibling, she felt obligated to take care of this cabin even though he told her not to. But family could be insistent.

"You'll need to keep her away from the asset, Sentinel." The '*or else*' part of the statement hung unsaid at the end of that sentence. Tom already knew what his punishment would be should he fail: Assassinate the civilian. His father wouldn't care that Rosalie was family. If anything, he'd consider it the perfect reprimand.

3

"Understood." Tom had no intention of anyone meeting his charge. If his aunt insisted on visiting, he would join her in town for a meal. He walked outside towards the car. "Anything else, sir?"

"Nothing for now, but I expect a detailed report every evening until I say otherwise. Also, Anita will likely be in touch regarding a visit. She needs more samples."

Tom eyed the female sleeping in the backseat of his sedan. He knew what samples meant, and it made his stomach roll. Arguing would accomplish nothing, and the relationship with his father couldn't be more tenuous lately. Tom needed to lay low and follow orders if he wanted his freedom back.

"I'll await her call, sir." A few blood samples never killed anyone. Besides, he'd be there to monitor. All good.

"Excellent. Do try to behave, son."

He refrained from rolling his eyes. "Yes, sir."

His father hung up without a goodbye. *Typical.* Tom pocketed the phone and opened the backdoor. Amelia's dark hair hung in unkempt ringlets over her face, and her threadbare shirt hit her mid-thigh. No pants, shorts, or anything underneath.

"Un-fucking believable," he muttered, not for the first time since this nightmare started. He was thankful for the exclusivity of their location as he gathered the woman in his arms. His father suggested keeping her in the basement, but Tom had other ideas.

He laid her slender form on the double bed in the guest room then went outside to retrieve his belongings from the car. Agent Stark said Amelia would be unconscious for a while, but failed to give a stringent timeline. Tom hoped she woke sooner rather than later, because the girl needed a shower. His father preferred she live in her own filth, but that treatment ended now. Hence his detour to the store.

Back inside, he opened his suitcase in the master bedroom and pulled out a t-shirt and a pair of gym shorts. He held them up and frowned. *Too big.* The woman needed to eat more. He swapped the shorts for a pair of boxers and added *buy her some clothes* to his mental to-do list. Grabbing the shirt and plastic bag of bathroom essentials, he ventured into the guest room and froze.

She was gone.

He dropped the items on the bed and checked the window. *Locked.* With the exception of a few boxes, the closet was empty as well. *What the hell?* The tiny cabin consisted of two bedrooms and a single bathroom. How had she escaped without his notice? He walked into the hallway, noted the unoccupied restroom and checked the living area. The front door hung ajar. So not only did she get up without him hearing her, she walked outside. That's what he got for staying up all night to drive here.

"I don't have the patience for this shit," he muttered as he headed outside. Amelia didn't have proper clothes or shoes, so she wouldn't make it far in the woods. The closest neighbor lived over three miles away, and the nearest city was a half-hour drive. Secluded didn't begin to cover it.

Keys in hand, he started towards the car. She most likely ventured down the long gravel driveway, hoping to find the road. The rocks against her bare feet would slow her down. And if she went into the grass, he'd see her from...

Movement in his peripheral gave him pause at the car door. He squinted and frowned. Wisps of dark brown hair danced in the warm breeze as his charge twirled in a circle near the lake about fifty yards from the side of the cabin. What was she planning to do, swim to her freedom? Because she would be in for a surprise when she realized it only led deeper into the wilderness.

Tom pocketed his keys and moved towards her. She didn't seem to notice his approach, too lost in the bliss of the sun shining down on her. Her smile made him hesitate.

There was no question. Despite her frail condition, Amelia Wakefield was a gorgeous woman. Her long legs, subtle curves, and angelic face gave her an otherworldly appeal any man could appreciate. He suspected that was the reason his father withheld shower privileges and forced her to wear that hideous shirt. All the Sentinels were male, which posed a risk around an alluring female. Especially one considered to be the CRF's greatest asset. Not that any of the men would necessarily act on it, but better to avoid the situation than to welcome it.

The girl paused mid-twirl to stare up at the sky and laughed. The broken sound echoed with disuse and went straight to his gut. *What the hell have I gotten myself into?*

~*~

Amelia Wakefield loved this dream. It was nothing like her usual trips into the darkness. First, she woke in a real bed, and now, she stood outside. *Fascinating.*

The sun warmed her hair and face and felt so real. It had to be the drugs. Agent Stark mentioned they were different than the normal pills he smuggled in for her during the healing process. She hadn't really cared when she swallowed them. Anything to get rid of the pain. *Then that strange girl came in, talking about my brother...* A hallucination like this one? Her mental faculties usually recovered at unnatural speeds, just as her body did, a perk of being immortal, but maybe Jonathan's beating had jarred her worse than she originally thought.

Amelia shook her head and spun around again. She didn't care to think about what anything meant. This moment meant too much to her. When was the last time she experienced the outside world? Years, maybe? Decades? Time was an elusive concept in her cement prison.

She stopped her dancing to fondle a leaf. The lifelike texture made her grin. *Beautiful.* She needed to ask Stark to give her these drugs again. It would make her next beating worthwhile.

"Amelia."

She jumped at the unexpected voice and whirled around. Of all the men she expected to visit her in this dream, Tom Fitzgerald was not one of them. But it didn't truly surprise her. Amelia thought of the man often, a side effect of him being the only decent person in her life at present. He brought her things in captivity, like food and water. She recognized his role as the good cop to his father's bad cop. Another game, no doubt. But she enjoyed playing along. It wasn't like she had anything else to do.

"Hello, Tom." Her voice came out softer than she expected and hurt a little. Almost as if she hadn't spoken in days. *Could this dream get any more realistic?*

"What are you doing?"

"Enjoying the fresh air." She twirled, wishing her shirt would transform into a sundress. One would think she would have more control over her dreams. Maybe she could build a bonfire and burn the offending fabric.

"When do you suppose I'll wake this time?" she wondered aloud. "Stark warned me the drugs were laced with a sedative. Perhaps I'll sleep longer than expected?"

Tom's hands were in the pockets of his jeans as he studied her with those intense brown eyes. *So much like his father.* But the cruelty in his father's gaze didn't linger in Tom's dark depths.

"Stark gave you drugs?" he asked with an arched brow.

"Mmm," she murmured and faced the sun again. "He always gives me something, but this is definitely the best. It feels so real." She knelt to touch the lake again. The water was cool against her palm. "I want to stay here forever and never wake up."

Silence met her reply, making her wonder if Tom disappeared. Then his boots appeared beside her at the water's edge. He crouched down and rested strong forearms on his knees. The grey shirt he wore stretched across his broad chest and strained over impressive biceps.

If he wasn't the son of a monster, she might call him handsome. As it was, she would kill him—and all the others—at her first opportunity.

She touched the metal choker around her neck and grumbled, "This bloody thing follows me even into my dreams." If she ever got it off, she'd make Jonathan Fitzgerald eat it.

"Amelia," his deep voice rumbled, "this isn't a dream."

"What?"

"You're not dreaming."

She smiled and shook her head. Of course she was dreaming. What else could this be? There was water, sunshine, and trees. "I wish for you to go now." No need for the handsome Sentinel to spoil her temporary reprieve from reality.

"I wish I could, but I'm stuck here for the foreseeable future." Tom rose to his full height beside her and held out a hand. "Let's get back to the cabin. You need a shower, and I need to get some sleep."

She frowned at his long, masculine fingers. He wiggled them once in an impatient gesture that matched the tick in his square jaw. When she stood up, she found the top of her head barely met his chin. The heat radiating from his broad chest felt very real, so real that she pinched her thigh to test his theory. A slight pain radiated up her side, making her eyes widen. "I'm not dreaming?"

He gave her a small smile. "No, Amelia. You're very much awake."

She stumbled back and nearly lost her footing over a rock near the pond's edge. *What is this?* A new CRF illusion? A simulation of some kind? She scanned their surroundings for a clue, but saw none. Where were all the researchers and Sentinels?

"What game are we playing?" Because this was obviously another one of Jonathan's tricks. A manipulation meant to drive her insane. That seemed to be his favorite pastime of late.

Realizing she had no intention of taking his hand, he dropped it to his side. It drew attention to the pistol on his hip. "Not a game, Amelia. Just a new location."

She peered up at him. "A new location?" What did that mean? She was no longer in the CRF basement? *Impossible.*

He palmed the back of his neck and blew out a breath. "Yeah, it's a long story, but in summary, we're staying here for a while."

"In the middle of the woods," she added. Where serial killers took their victims to dispose of them. Had Jonathan finally gotten what he wanted through all those tests? Was she no longer of use to them? *Am I here to die?*

She stared into those dark eyes that gave nothing away. Tom looked so much like his father, but more muscular, and taller. She took a careful step back, which had him raising a blond brow.

"I'm not going to hurt you, Amelia."

*Said the wolf to the lamb.* She had trusted Jonathan once, and he'd done unspeakable things to her. Why would Tom be any different? They were in the middle of nowhere, where no one could hear her scream. She moved another step back while evaluating her options. If they were indeed away from the CRF, that meant she had a chance of escape. She just needed to take down the armed Sentinel in front of her. *Easier said than done.*

"I can see what you're thinking, and..."

She didn't wait to hear the rest of Tom's statement, but took off in the opposite direction through the woods. Her bare feet screamed as she stumbled over rocks and uneven terrain, around the lake and towards whatever was on the other side of all those trees. She ducked and swerved to avoid branches and heard Tom's muttered curses following her in the wind as she moved aimlessly through the wilderness.

He was too close for comfort, making her push harder and faster. Her lungs screamed for air as she tore through the underbrush as fast as her body would allow. Her size was an advantage, allowing her to move between the trees at an angle he couldn't. *I'm finally escaping. Maybe this is a dream after all? Why else—?*

Her thought was cut off as she slammed into the trunk of a tree. She started to fall, but a pair of sturdy hands caught her before she could hit the ground.

"Ow," she mumbled as she massaged her bruised nose. Peeking between her fingers, she realized it wasn't a tree at all, but Tom's muscular chest. He'd somehow gotten in front of her.

"Are you done?" he asked, his voice patient.

Amelia's breaths came in heaves from the mad dash through the woods, and he wasn't even panting. He hadn't even broken a sweat. Realizing her body was pressed far too close to his, she pushed away with a huff and stumbled when he let her go.

"Don't…" She paused for a necessary inhale and started again. "Don't touch me."

"You ran into me, sweetheart."

"Because you… you… teleported or something." She waved a hand, like that explained it all.

"You were running in circles around a group of trees, Amelia. No teleportation required." His condescending tone made her want to hit something. *Like his face.* Deciding that sounded like a sound back up plan, she launched herself at him. If she could get ahold of his gun, she could shoot him. It didn't matter that she'd never used one before. How hard could it be? She attempted to slap him, but found both of her wrists caught in one of his sturdy hands.

"Seriously? Who taught you how to fight? The Three Stooges?"

She had no idea who or what that was, but sensed he was making fun of her. She brought her knee up as hard as she could and hit his thigh. It felt like kneeing a steel wall, but the abrupt shift of his legs to protect his sensitive parts doubled as a distraction. Twisting a wrist free from his grasp, she curled her hand into a fist and aimed for his defined cheekbone. It connected with a hard thunk that sent pain shooting down her forearm.

"Christ, Amelia!" He grabbed her again, but this time pressed her up against a tree with his legs braced on either side of hers and both of her hands in one of his. Despite the aggressive hold, he maintained a gentle touch as he examined her throbbing knuckles. The pain was minor compared to what Jonathan had done to her over the last few years, but her ego was bruised. Here she was bleeding, broken, and out of breath, and Tom wasn't even fazed. She wanted to crawl into a hole and hide. *I'm hopeless.*

"Doesn't look broken," he murmured after moving the thumb of her right hand. It was the one she used to punch him. *Unsuccessfully.* "Next time, curl your fingers like this, and put your thumb on the outside." He demonstrated with his free hand. "If you were stronger, you would have sprained or broken your thumb doing that. Now, are you done?"

She glowered up at him. It wasn't like she could move with his big body pressing her up against the tree. What choice did she have?

"Look, even if you get away from me—which you won't—that metal collar around your neck is tied to an object in the cabin. You get more than two miles away and it explodes. And don't get any ideas about me taking it off of you. It's not going to happen." He pushed away from her with those final words and dropped her hands. "Now, do you prefer to walk or be carried?"

She eyed the pistol on his hip again, making him smile.

He folded his arms and cocked a brow. "Try it. See what happens, sweetheart."

"Stop calling me that."

Tom chuckled and turned away from her with a shake of his head. "Suit yourself, *asset.* I'll be making breakfast."

She stared at his muscular back as he walked towards the cabin. It was still within eyesight, which meant she hadn't run nearly as far as she thought she had. A glance down at her bloody feet told her maybe he was right about running in circles. Could anyone blame her? She'd been a lab rat for who knew how long in a tiny room without windows. Exercise hadn't been part of her daily regimen.

*Why am I here? Why move me now?* She wondered if it had anything to do with the blonde woman who visited her cell after Jonathan's beating.

*"He'll come for you. Even if it means burning this place to the ground."* Were those words real? Did Issac know she was alive? She pressed her palm over her aching heart. Was her brother finally coming for her after all this time? Jonathan showed her articles and photos of Issac, a way of confirming that her brother had moved on and no longer mourned her. It hurt at first, filled her with both fury and hopelessness, but she understood. Everyone thought she was dead. She couldn't blame them from moving on with their lives. But what if that woman hadn't been a hallucination? Did her brother know the truth? Would he save her from this hell?

The hope blossoming in her chest hurt. She didn't want to trust it. But why else would Jonathan move her if not to hide her? If she was here to die, surely Tom would have killed her already. *Unless he wants me to suffer...*

She stared after his retreating form as he entered the cabin. He hadn't bothered to turn around once. Whatever his purpose, he was confident she would follow.

*The damn choker.* She pressed her fingers to the cold, abnormal metal around her neck and sighed. She didn't doubt for a second the truth of his statement. The CRF's technology was far superior to anything she had ever seen, and the simple metal necklace repressed her immortal gifts. She couldn't shift while wearing it. She couldn't even impart wisdom.

The tears welling up behind her eyes disappeared with a blink. One gift Jonathan had given her was the ability to hide her emotions. She was an expert at deception, something that could be a benefit in this situation. Fighting Tom physically wouldn't get her anywhere, but mentally? She was up to that challenge. And if they were truly alone out here, that gave her an advantage.

*Issac's searching for me.* She could feel it. All she needed was to gain Tom's trust, and then she could use it to garner her freedom. Men were easy to manipulate, especially when it came to sex. She shivered. Seduction was a weapon she never contemplated in captivity, but with Tom? She could consider it. He was the only thing on this planet Jonathan cared about other than himself, which made him an ideal candidate. She would use Tom to escape and enact some semblance of revenge on the man who ruined her life. It wouldn't be easy, nor would she enjoy it, but it would be worth it to escape this hell.

She gazed at the sky, hidden above the cloud of trees, and closed her eyes. *Eli.* He would understand this sacrifice and forgive her this sin. He had to. She didn't have a choice. Then she could avenge him properly by murdering Jonathan.

Decided, she started towards the house and stubbed her toe on a rock. The pain reminded her that she was not dressed to impress in the ratty old shirt and bloody feet.

"All right, so I'll shower." She regarded her scrawny legs and thin arms and pursed her lips. If her limbs looked like that, what did her face look like? She hadn't seen a mirror in, well, forever. But her hair was tangled, not smooth, and her skin felt dry and chapped.

Good thing Tom said they were here for the unforeseeable future, because she would need some time to ready herself for this task. Not only to improve her appearance, but to figure out how to entice the Sentinel. All of her experiences were tied to Eli, but she'd seen other women seduce men. How hard could it be?

# CHAPTER TWO

## Doctor's Call

Tom's white lie about Amelia's collar worked like a charm. It contained no explosive, only a mechanism that disabled her psychic abilities. Was it a kind lie? No, but he preferred it over locking the woman in her room. And it ceased her foolish escape attempts. She needed some serious training, and the last thing he wanted to do was accidentally hurt her.

They fell into a quiet routine during their first week together, which suited Tom. He preferred solitary work, and he suspected Amelia wanted her space. They only spoke when necessary, and mostly during meals. The first few times he gave her food, she watched him eat his half before tentatively nibbling on hers. By day four, she started eating like a normal person, which he took as a sign that she was somewhat trusting their situation. Tonight, she opted to dine with him on the couch while he enjoyed a baseball game.

He wasn't sure how to react to the change in her pattern. She usually ran back to her room after finishing dinner, but she set the dishes in the sink and joined him in the living area instead.

Having a woman dressed in his shirt and boxers played tricks on his mind and made it difficult to focus on the game. Her dark hair held a healthier tint thanks to the daily showers and the brush he had given her, and she had it piled in luscious waves over one shoulder. He swallowed thickly as she curled her finger around the strand dangling against the side of her breast. The innocent gesture provoked all manner of inappropriate thoughts, making him regret not locking her in the guest room.

*This mission better end soon.* And not just because of the alluring woman beside him.

Tom finished his beer and went to the fridge to retrieve another. He'd offered one to Amelia their second day together, and she gave him a look of such grave offense that he didn't bother again. Apparently, she wasn't a beer girl.

"I don't understand the purpose of this sport," she said as he returned to the couch. He intentionally put an extra foot between them. Attractive she might be, but she was still an asset, and dangerous. "At least football has a defined timeline of two halves. This nonsense goes on and on, and nothing interesting happens. How are you not bored to tears?"

Her English accent was sexy, but the same could not be said about her words.

"Okay, first? We call it soccer here." He took a swig of beer before continuing. "Second, have you not heard of the Yankees? Nothing boring about them, sweetheart." He inwardly cringed. *Why do I keep calling her that?* The endearment just seemed to roll off his tongue every time she walked in the room, and he couldn't seem to stop it. The look she gave him said she liked it about as much as he did.

"I told you not to call me that."

*Yes, and I told myself not to call you that, either, but you see how well that worked out.* Clearly, his mouth had a mind of its own.

"Yes, ma'am," Tom replied. He gave her a mock salute with his bottle to loosen his tense muscles and went back to enjoying the game. Or trying to anyway. He loved baseball, but her presence absorbed his focus. Feeling her eyes on him, he glanced sideways at her. "Yes?"

"You never answered my question."

"Regarding?"

"How are you not bored by this? It's mind-numbing."

He set his bottle down on the end table and turned towards her. "What would you prefer to watch, Amelia?" Not that he would change the channel. The one benefit to this new assignment was all the free time, and he planned to use it appropriately.

"Hmm, let's see. I haven't had the opportunity to watch a television in, honestly, I have no idea how long. But there has to be something better than this."

"You realize you're insulting one of New York's proudest accomplishments, right?"

"Should that matter to me?"

He snorted. *It was so much nicer when she stayed in her room.* He opened his mouth to say just that when his pocket buzzed. Time for the evening check-in with dear old dad. Picking up the controller, he muted the television and answered the phone with a "Yo."

"Very professional, son."

Tom grinned. "You know, Dad, I try. I really do." Amelia tensed beside him, her blue eyes going round at the device in his hand. Yeah, he could imagine she wasn't very fond of his father. *Join the club, sweetheart.* "To what do I owe the pleasure, *sir?*" He couldn't help the sarcasm on that last word.

These nightly conversations only seemed to further drive the wedge between them. His father used to call when Tom had done something to impress him, but now he only phoned to remind him how much he'd fucked up. It hurt to an extent, but it also pissed him off. Hence his attitude. The sooner his father disconnected, the sooner he could continue his discussion with Amelia. Someone needed a lesson in why insulting the Yankees was poor form.

"Have you been drinking?" his father asked.

"What, no status update first? The asset is fine by the way. And, yes, I am enjoying an adult beverage. Anything else before I hang up?"

The silence on the other end of the line told him he'd overstepped. He envisioned his dad's expression turning darker by the minute. The familiar look used to terrify him, but now it only served to irritate him.

When Tom returned from the Special Forces to work for the CRF, his father had been so proud and excited to show him the ropes. They worked well as a team at first, managing the Sentinel unit and discussing future plans. As they delved into his father's pet projects and the company's secrets, however, Tom's respect and admiration dwindled. Then he discovered Amelia in the research wing, and everything changed.

Her kinship to his biggest enemy didn't detract from the fact that she was an innocent woman in captivity. He'd made his feelings known that day and openly disagreed with his dad for the first time ever in his life. The heated argument fractured their father-son bond, and their relationship had yet to recover.

His stomach hurt with the memory as his blood boiled. The convoluted response left him unsure how to feel, furious or guilty. He spent his every waking moment trying to please the only person in his life who loved him, and he betrayed that over a disagreement. But looking at Amelia now, with her wide eyes staring at the phone by his ear, he couldn't help but feel a tiny bit of pride for sticking up for her. Not that it had done any good. Here she sat, a prisoner in a new outfit, awaiting her fate.

He ran a hand through his hair and blew out a breath. *Time to play ball,* he thought. If his father pulled him from this mission out of anger, he would send him somewhere worse, and he didn't want to know what mind fuck his father would throw at him next. Tom intended to survive, with or without his father's help, but his contingency plan wasn't ready yet. He needed freedom to complete it, which meant he had to obey. For now.

"I'm watching the Yankees game," he said, voice devoid of humor. "And enjoying a beer, yes. Sorry, sir."

"I see." His father fell silent for too long. *Something bad is coming.* "Please be advised that Doctor Patel and her team are five minutes out. Prep the asset and await further instructions." The line went dead.

He stared at the phone. "Well, shit." An hour warning would have been great. "Yeah, I'm going to need you to follow me to the guest room."

Her eyebrows shot up. "Excuse me?"

"Doctor Patel is coming for samples, and I doubt she'll approve of you hanging out with me in the living room."

The indignation in Amelia's expression fled as her face paled. "Anita's coming?" Her soft voice sounded nothing like the stern woman of ten minutes ago.

"Yeah, and she'll be here any minute." He made a shooing motion towards the hallway. "Come on. I need to ensure the guest room looks un-lived in."

Some of the color returned to her cheeks as she puzzled over his statement. "What? Why?"

"Because I'm supposed to be keeping you in a cage in the basement," he muttered as he started towards her room.

"There's a basement?" she asked as she followed.

"*That's* your question? Seriously?" He took in the guest

room's immaculate appearance then glanced around for anything personal. Their clothing routine consisted of him leaving fresh shirts and boxers in the bathroom, and Amelia leaving folded laundry in its place. "Nothing incriminating. Go ahead and sit on the bed."

He didn't wait to see if she obeyed, but went into the bathroom to stow the feminine items, like her brush and deodorant, under the sink. If Anita's team noticed them, he would say they belonged to his aunt. Then he would take on his father's persona and ask why they were snooping. Sometimes it paid to remind CRF employees who he was destined to become.

Grabbing the laundry basket and Amelia's towel, he moved into the master bedroom and tossed everything in the closet. The telltale sound of tires over gravel greeted him as he returned to the living area. Rocky driveways were a good warning system. He flipped off the television, picked up his beer, and relaxed against the wall with one ankle crossed over the other. His favorite pistol rested in its permanent spot on his hip, and there was a knife hidden in his left sock. Just in case. He only disarmed when he was naked, and even then, he had a weapon within arm's reach.

Agent Stark entered first in his trademark jeans and t-shirt.

"Thanks for knocking," Tom drawled. He should have known his father's favorite Sentinel would lead Doctor Patel's entourage. "Aren't you supposed to be training Stas?" That was the whole point of this babysitting assignment. Tom guarded the asset while Stark trained the CRF's first female Sentinel. Another punishment from his father, because he knew Tom wanted to manage his friend's training. He loved the woman like a sister, and it hurt not to be there to help her.

"I gave her the night off. She has to maintain her cover with Wakefield."

"Ah." Tom sipped his beer to hide his grimace. Issac

Wakefield made him want to play target practice with his favorite handgun. "And how's the training going?"

"I didn't come here to chat, Fitzgerald. Where's the asset?"

Stark stopped two paces in front of him and lifted a blond brow. They were similar in size and stature, but the stoic man lacked a sense of humor. Something was very wrong with the Sentinel, his ability to heal with touch notwithstanding. Whatever he was, he wasn't human.

"Why the late-night visit?" Tom wondered. "Why not wait until tomorrow?"

"Because I was in the middle of a case study when your father decided to move my asset," Anita Patel announced from the doorway. The tiny woman boasted a no bullshit attitude. Tom supposed she had to be that way to lead the CRF's research wing. She managed multiple assets at headquarters, most of which were rogue immortals who committed heinous acts. Amelia was the anomaly, a victim of circumstance.

"Doctor Patel." He nodded a greeting to the dark-haired woman. Two male researchers entered behind her with bags and averted their gazes. Typical behavior from CRF employees. Not only was Tom a Sentinel, but their future CEO.

"Hello, Tom." The doctor bowed her head in a gesture of respect, something she also did with his father. "Where's my test subject?"

His hand tightened around the beer bottle—a bizarre reaction to an innocent question, as was the knot forming in his gut. Playing warden meant guarding the asset from potential escape and discovery. It did not mean protecting her. But his fingers twitched like they wanted to caress his favorite gun. *Not a good sign.*

"What are you planning to do with her?" It wasn't like him to pry, but he couldn't help himself. Anita clasped her hands in front of her and pursed her lips. She didn't seem to care much for his interest. *Well, too fucking bad.* "I only ask because this cabin isn't exactly built for extensive lab research, and I don't have a lot of supplies on hand."

Understanding brightened her dark gaze, and she gave an approving nod. "Of course. I have all the supplies I need to run my routine tests and obtain a few samples. But it may take a little longer than usual, so I'd like to get started."

"Right." Tom shrugged to loosen his stiff shoulders. What she said seemed legit, but something about this situation didn't sit well with him. Ignoring the strange vibe, he gestured to the hallway behind him. Better to get this over with as soon as possible. "She's in the guest room." At Anita's raised eyebrow, he added, "I didn't think you'd want to do this in the basement. Bad lighting." Growing up around a human lie detector made him skilled at telling half-truths.

The doctor nodded, pleased. "Excellent. We'll let you know if we need anything." She snapped her fingers at the researchers who trailed after her like obedient dogs.

Stark didn't follow, his expression void of emotion. Tom eyed the man over his bottle as he took another swig. *Yeah, definitely not mortal.* Not Hydraian or Ichorian, either. He suspected Stark was one of Anita's pet projects. That would explain his ability to heal through touch and his bizarre demeanor.

"Are you providing protective detail for Doctor Patel and crew?" Tom asked.

"No." Flat response with no elaboration.

"Okay, then." He finished his beer and tossed it in the kitchen trash bin.

He paused near the hallway to listen for any signs of struggle coming from Amelia's room, but heard nothing. Doctor Patel administered his medical exam last year and was a complete professional, but something about her always struck him as dangerous. Morbid curiosity lurked in that woman's gaze, which was a typical trait for a researcher, but it rubbed him the wrong way sometimes.

And tonight was one of those occasions.

The instinct to grab his firearm hit him again. Hard. "Any idea how long this is going to take?" he asked, ignoring the sensation. *What the hell is wrong with me?*

"Why?" Stark's light green eyes flicked towards him. "Do you have somewhere to go?"

Tom gaped at him. "Did you just make a joke?"

"Some might refer to it as a taunt."

"Or a joke."

Stark shrugged. "Sure. I'm going for a run."

"A run?"

"Yes. We're going to be here a while, and it was a long drive." He rolled his neck and shoulders while he spoke. "And I'm bored."

*Because that's normal.* "Okay. Have fun."

Those eerie eyes looked Tom up and down. "You know these woods better than me. Show me around, and I'll tell you how the training with your friend is going. And maybe we can talk about what I have planned."

Tom started. "You want me to go running with you?"

"That's what I said, isn't it?"

If it was any other Sentinel, he wouldn't have batted an eye. But Stark, the lone wolf on the team, asking him to go running? He never expected that. Maybe he really was bored.

*Or maybe he's up to something.*

His instincts warred. Leaving Amelia alone with the researchers felt wrong, which was ridiculous. His father was the one who enjoyed beating the shit out of her, not the researchers. She was safe here, away from the lunatic CEO of the CRF. And so far he hadn't heard any sounds coming from her room to indicate distress.

*I'm overthinking this.* A run would be good for him, and he wanted to know what Stark had planned for Stas. She might be pissed at him, but that didn't keep him from caring about her.

"Yeah, okay." The June heat would be hot as hell in

jeans, but if Stark wasn't putting on jogging shorts, neither would he. Part of their conditioning was to train under unnatural circumstances. Sounded like they would do just that tonight. Together. He laced his tennis shoes and met Stark by the door. "After you, Agent."

~*~

*Sadistic bitch.*

Whatever nerve agent Anita stuck in Amelia's arm made it impossible to move or utter a sound. But she felt every single poke and prod as they explored her nude body with cold instruments.

The doctor loved testing the limits of Amelia's immortality. Pain management didn't exist in their sessions. It was all about seeing how much she could take before passing out, and she was on the verge of it now. Hence the smelling salts beneath her nose.

Time eluded her.

*Minutes, hours, days...*

Everything hurt.

The burning sensation crawling up her spine consumed her and fractured her thoughts into incomprehensible pieces. She wasn't sure how much longer she could win this battle against insanity.

Darkness loomed, waiting to take her to that place where she stopped feeling. She created it for moments like this where the pain became too much.

Her own personal drug.

Addicting.

Sating.

One day, her mind would go there and never return.

*Would that be so bad?* she wondered.

*Yes... Jonathan can't win.*

Anita's stern voice floated from above. Something about containers. Amelia couldn't be sure.

She screamed internally as someone inserted a knife

between her ribs. Tears fell of their own volition from her unblinking eyes. This was what Anita wanted, and knowing that made her sick to her stomach.

One of these days, Amelia would kill her. She wondered what Eli and Issac would think of her violent fantasies. Kindness and formality were traits of her past. They wouldn't recognize the woman she'd become through this experience.

Ice hit her chest, followed by fire, as one of the research minions shoved a needle into her heart. She both craved and hated this part. It hurt like hell, but it meant her torment was coming to an end, and she would be able to move soon. Then the vomiting would start, followed by brief rest, and the inevitable mental countdown of when this would all start again.

She thought being in the cabin meant she would have a break from this torture. But no. Just hope playing another evil trick. She hated that tormenting emotion.

"Three, two..." Anita's voice grew louder with each number. "One."

Amelia gasped in a much-needed breath and shuddered against the plastic sheet beneath her.

"There, that wasn't so bad, right dear?" Anita's smile was pure evil.

A litany of curses lined up in Amelia's mind, but her mouth refused to expel them. If she ever got her hands on the sadistic doctor, she would paralyze her then pump her heart full of adrenaline and see how she handled it. A cough worked its way up her burning lungs to her throat, and the researchers rolled her to the side as she expelled the contents of her dinner.

No mortal could survive this treatment. As an immortal, she barely did. Amelia hated her minds' ability to heal in a fraction of a second. It held her on the edge of insanity during Anita's sessions, while keeping her lucid.

*Unless I venture into the darkness...*

*Not tonight.*

"Go fetch Agent Stark," Anita said after several agonizing minutes. The command was unexpected. Usually, she requested Stark's presence later in the process. Maybe Amelia needed to be healed before they began another round of testing?

"Ma'am." Stark's deep voice soothed her on a deep level. She craved his healing touch more than she wanted to breathe.

"I assume you've distracted Tom?" Anita asked.

"Yes, ma'am. He's on the phone outside talking to Stas."

"Good. Take the asset into the bathroom and clean her up. We'll take care of this mess."

So clinical and detached. *I hate you.*

A sturdy arm slid under her knee while another wrapped around her shoulders. She didn't look at the man as he carried her into the bathroom, nor did she meet his eyes as he set her in the bathtub. He kicked the door closed before kneeling beside her with a bland expression.

"Here." He held out one of his famous pills, and she opened her mouth without question. This was their routine, though she suspected he wasn't supposed to give her pain medication. There were a lot of things Stark seemed to do that he wasn't supposed to do. Like disappear into mist. He did that during their last healing session, much to her shock. She knew he could heal, but had no idea he could disappear. Or was that a hallucination?

He grabbed a cup from the counter, filled it with water, then brought it to her parched lips. "Drink."

She swallowed the cool liquid and the pill before closing her eyes. Her immortal genetics healed her mind faster than her body, but Stark's touch would help the latter along. It would hurt, but she welcomed the eventual reprieve. Unless Anita planned to start all over again, in which case, this would be a long night.

Heat enveloped her as Stark pressed his palm to her

shoulder. The energy exchange always tingled at first then grew into an inferno that had her crying out on instinct. He pressed his opposite hand over her mouth to quiet the screams as he poured his power over her. Last time, it knocked her out, but her injuries weren't as substantial this round. Jonathan enjoyed inflicting internal damage. Anita preferred exterior pain. The woman loved to make Amelia bleed.

"Almost done, Amelia." His deep voice was a sweet caress, despite its lack of emotion. She couldn't figure him out. He did things that seemed counterintuitive to the CRF's goals, like letting that girl walk out of her room the other day. Assuming that conversation was real.

*It had to be. Issac's coming for you...* The conversation in her cement prison was bizarre to say the least, starting with the way Stark vanished into thin air just before the blonde woman opened the door. Then all that talk about her brother romancing the girl with a dance? That sounded very unlike the Issac she knew, though the speech was right. But if the woman meant what she said about breaking her out of the CRF basement, why did Stark not intervene?

*Unless...*

Her eyes flew open as she met his glowing green gaze. "You're—" She couldn't speak because of his hand. *You're the reason I'm here*, she accused with a look. But why hide her in a cabin? Surely it would be easier to dispose of the girl who found her.

"Not everything is black and white," was his cryptic reply. "Go ahead and shower when you feel up to standing. I'll find your clothes."

He closed the shower curtain before she could say a word.

# CHAPTER THREE

## Target Practice

Tom hung up the phone as the researchers walked out of the cabin. They were grinning about something, but their mirth died upon seeing him. He rolled his eyes when they averted their gazes and scurried over to the car with a set of containers. *Blood samples. Gross.*

Stark exited next with their equipment bags. It didn't escape Tom's notice that it took two men to carry all that in originally. The assistants weren't big guys, but they weren't scrawny, either.

"The asset is taking a shower," was all Stark said as he passed him. He tossed the bags in the trunk like they weighed nothing before leaning against the massive jeep with his arms folded. The bulky man had changed his shirt. It was black before, and now it was red.

*Why?* They hadn't worked up that much of a sweat on their five-mile run. Instincts prickling, Tom started towards the cabin, but stopped when Anita walked out. That fucked-up gleam was back in her gaze, making his gut churn.

"The asset is ready to be returned to her cell. Do you mind taking over from here? We need to get these samples back to the lab, and the clock is ticking."

"Sure." He kept his stance casual as his mind raced. The run had done little to dispel his nerves, though his conversation with Stas had given him a temporary reprieve. He hated to admit it, but he felt an inkling of admiration for Stark. The stoic Sentinel had created a masterful training plan, and Stas sounded happy about it.

He didn't call her often, but this situation warranted a verbal update. She thought he was on a mission overseas, something he didn't bother correcting. Then her roommate stole the phone to give him a piece of her mind. Lizzie Watkins was a close family friend and daughter of a CRF employee. She went off on a tirade about Stas becoming a Sentinel, of which she did not approve, and then lectured him about being safe while abroad. He had hung up with a grin and a shake of his head. She had no idea that immortals existed, and he intended to keep it that way.

"Fitzgerald." Stark gave him a nod. His version of a goodbye.

"Stark." He returned the nod, and the team disappeared into the jeep.

A wave of loneliness hit him as the headlights disappeared down the driveway. He considered calling the girls back for a longer chat, but decided against it. As much as his friends cared, they didn't truly know him and never would. A man with his background wouldn't be around long enough to experience such connections. Death loomed at every corner and haunted every dream, and every person in his life was a liability.

*I should have stayed in the Middle East.* At least there he had a true purpose. Just a man, a rifle, and his target. Peace.

With a sigh, he walked back inside. The bathroom was empty, and the guest room door was shut. He knocked and waited for a reply, but heard none.

"Amelia?" He didn't like the way his arm hair stood on end. Violent memories tormented this cabin, and he suspected some fresh ones were made here tonight. When she didn't reply, he knocked again and cracked open the door.

"Are you all right?" He realized the stupidity of that question the second it left his mouth. Of course she wasn't okay. The woman was a prisoner of war.

His father kidnapped her as an act of revenge, but rather than use her to bring their real enemy to justice, he kept her in the research ward.

*"You have to see that she is useful, son," his father had argued after Tom first discovered her. "Think of what we could do with her genetics."*

*"This is wrong," Tom had replied. "You have to know this is wrong."*

The CRF wanted to replicate her unique gifts. The heated debated ended with a promise that Amelia was well cared for, despite the way she might appear. That lie crashed and burned when Tom found her beaten to a pulp earlier last week. When he confronted his father about it, he was reminded yet again that he didn't have any choice but to go along with it.

*"Where would you go, son? The Ichorians want you dead, and the Hydraians won't protect you. Not after everything you've done. We're all you have. I suggest you play ball."*

Shoving the vile words from his head, he pushed open the door to find Amelia curled in a ball in the corner of the room. Her damp hair sprawled around her frail frame and clung to her shirt. He wondered if Stark or Anita noticed she wore his clothes. If they did, he would no doubt hear about it from his father later.

A spot on the floor near the foot of the bed caused him to frown. He knelt to get a closer look, and his heart skipped a beat. *Fresh blood.*

Flipping on the overhead lights, he investigated the room and found more blood on the furniture and walls. They resembled tiny specs to the untrained eye, but Tom recognized them for what they were. *It's even on the ceiling...*

"What the hell did they do to you?" The anger in his voice couldn't be helped. Seeing blood—in this room of all rooms—made his head spin.

*His mother's mutilated body sprawled out on his childhood bed... Screams that he later realized belonged to him...*

"Fuck." He staggered backwards out the door and into the hallway wall. With his hands on his knees, he took several deep breaths to calm the nightmarish images. This was why he refused to visit this place. Hell lived here.

He stumbled into the kitchen to grab a bottle of water and guzzled it. With each gulp, the memories subsided, and reality resurfaced. A friend once told him he had unresolved issues surrounding his mother's untimely demise. *No shit.* There was a reason he hunted rogue Ichorians, but his father wouldn't let him take out the one responsible. Issac Wakefield was too valuable alive, so his dad settled on taking Amelia instead. It seemed unfair to punish the woman for her brother's sins, but here they were.

Exchanging his bottle for a fresh one, he headed back towards the guest room with renewed purpose. His charge hadn't moved from the corner, but her blue eyes were bright with curiosity when he reentered the room. He sat beside her and held out the water without a word. She accepted it with a suspicious look and examined the seal. Finding it unbroken, she opened it and took a sip. He leaned his head against the wall and closed his eyes. It'd been a long fucking day, and he was exhausted.

"For what it's worth, I'm sorry." He wasn't sure what

else to say. Who knew what horrors this woman had endured at the hands of his father. Tom used to idolize the man, but he wasn't sure how to feel anymore. The man he grew up loving and admiring did awful things behind closed doors for reasons that remained unknown. Like beating the shit out of a female hostage. His father never justified his actions and instead reacted by assigning Tom as Amelia's babysitter. A test of loyalty? Punishment for disobeying orders? Only his dad knew the answer.

Amelia shifted beside him. Her leg brushed his, making him hyperaware of her actions. He could tell what she was planning before she moved. Eyes still shut, he caught her wrist an inch away from his firearm. "Even if you got a hold of it, would you know how to use it?"

"Maybe."

*That's a no.* He peeked at her through one eye. "First rule of firearm safety, make sure you know how to handle a weapon before you play with one."

Her frown was cute. It puckered between her brow and gave her an innocent appeal. "How hard can it be?"

He pulled the firearm off his belt and held it out for her. *I'm so going to regret this.* But it would be a fun diversion. Maybe.

"Show me what you would do with it." She stared at him like he'd grown three-heads. *An accurate assessment.* He had no idea why he was showing her this, but it seemed the least he could do considering their situation. "Go on. Show me."

"Is this a trick?"

"No trick. Show me how you would use it."

"You're not worried I'll shoot you with it?"

"I know you won't." And even if by some miraculous measure she did, it wouldn't matter. His immortal genetics would kick in after he died, and he'd wake up tomorrow as a Hydraian. She had to know that.

Long, slender fingers slid over the metal in his hand as she gingerly took what he offered. He made no move to stop her, even when she moved back and pointed the pistol in his direction. By his calculations, if she pulled the trigger, the bullet would graze his ear and hit the wall. And that was only if she managed to hold the handgun steady, which she wasn't.

"What's next?" he wondered.

"You tell me where the device is that controls my metal collar."

He smiled. "No."

"Then I'll have to shoot you."

"Works for me." He rested his head back against the wall and closed his eyes again. "Let me know when you're done playing, sweetheart." There's that word again. A slip of the tongue. He never called anyone *sweetheart*, but it suited her.

Cold steel met his temple. "I told you *not* to call me that."

"And there's mistake number one," he replied.

"Excuse me?"

He grabbed her wrist in one hand and the barrel with the other, and disarmed her in a swift move, all with his eyes closed. *Child's play.*

"Never get within arm's reach of someone who knows how to handle a gun, especially when you yourself don't know how to use one." He held out the sidearm in his open palm. "Try again." She snatched it from him and scooted away. He stretched out his legs and crossed them at the ankles. This was an excellent distraction from the memories threatening to overwhelm him in this room.

He heard her try to pull the trigger and grinned.

"As mentioned earlier, know how to use a weapon before you try to take one. Which, coincidentally, would be mistake number two. While you're trying to figure out how to shoot me, I'd be disarming you." He paused for a dramatic yawn. "Oh, and if you managed to shoot me, you still wouldn't have the device to remove your collar." Not that there was one for her to find. "Which means you'd have to wait for me to wake up tomorrow, and I probably wouldn't be too thrilled with you."

A low noise emanated from her throat, causing him to peek at her. "Did you just growl at me?"

Her next move was not one he expected. Instead of aiming the firearm at him again, she threw it at his head. He caught it reflexively with one hand and gaped at her. "Well done."

"Oh, let me guess, *mistake number three*," she did a poor representation of his voice, "giving the predator back his weapon. You're a right arse, you know that?"

"A right...?" He trailed off on a laugh. She looked so indignant, glowering at him like that. What a pair they made, sitting in a room full of horrors where she'd undergone God knew what in the last few hours. He shook his head and holstered his favorite toy.

"For the record, throwing the gun at me was your smartest move, because it was what I least expected. And since you couldn't use it for its intended purpose, you might as well create a weapon out of it. I'll consider this lesson a successful one." He pushed off the ground and started towards the door. Then he paused and met her blue eyes over his shoulder. "Everyone should know how to use a firearm. If you're interested, I'll show you tomorrow."

Probably not the wisest move on his part, but who the fuck cared anymore? This mission was a joke. He might as well have a little fun with it. And if he died in the process, it wouldn't be the end of the world. He'd just wake up immortal the next day.

~*~

Amelia studied the woman in the mirror. The bone structure was right, if a little hollow, but the eyes were all wrong. They looked haunted and darker.

She finished combing her damp hair and used a rubber

band she found to pull it up into a ponytail. It felt good to have it off her back. The researchers occasionally cut her hair, but they were not proper hairdressers. She slipped on the shirt and shorts Tom left for her on the sink and eyed the socks and shoes. Those were new. Did he intend for her to meet him outside? She recalled his offer from last night and frowned. Was he serious about teaching her how to fire a weapon? Why would he do such a thing?

The Elders never let her near the armory on Hydria, and Eli's weaponry in the house was off limits. No, that wasn't quite right. They would have let her in if she asked, but she never had a need. She was surrounded by some of the most powerful immortals in the world. Why would she learn how to fight? No one expected a close family friend to betray them, least of all her.

She slipped on the socks and shoes and was surprised to find that they fit. The sneakers definitely didn't belong to Tom. No way would his over six-foot frame fit in these tiny things. She hopped once and half-grinned. Stilettos had been her go-to footwear in the old days, but she could get used to these. Even if they did look a little worse for wear.

Stepping into the hallway, she moved towards the music playing in the living area. It sounded grungy with a heady base and growly voices. Not her preference. She meant to continue her journey to the fridge to grab a bottle of water and a snack, but froze upon spotting a shirtless Tom in the main room.

*Oh, wow...*

She didn't know bodies could move like that. It was some bizarre variation of a push-up that involved clapping behind his back and moving from side-to-side in rapid succession. When he popped up into a standing position, she assumed it was because he noticed her watching. She was wrong. He grabbed hold of a bar hanging over the doorway and lifted himself with ease into a pull-up. Amelia stood hypnotized by the muscles flexing along his back.

Eli had been a sight to behold in his own right, but had a burlier frame. Tom's athletic form was leaner, more refined. *A human weapon.* He went back to the floor again to begin another series of exercises that left her mind boggled. She couldn't keep up with his reps or positions, but she enjoyed the way his body moved. No wonder he disarmed her so quickly. His reflexes weren't human.

After another set with the bar, Tom switched off the music and picked up his water. He turned towards her with the bottle in hand and paused mid-drink. Surprise flighted over his features at finding an audience. She tried to look away, but his rippled abdomen was even more impressive than his back. Her throat went dry as he squirted water in his mouth and swallowed. Oh, this wasn't good.

*You cannot be attracted to him. Ever.* But what woman in her right mind wouldn't fancy a man built like Tom? *A woman being held in captivity against her will.* Right, well, there was that. She'd blame the drugs Stark had given her last night for her lapse in judgment, but those wore off hours ago.

Giving herself a mental head shake, she forced her feet towards the kitchen. She grabbed a bottle on autopilot and noted the sandwiches in the fridge. One plate each. She chose the closest one and made to go back to her room with it, but a half-naked Tom stood right behind her. His skin glistened with fresh sweat, making her lick her lips.

*All right, no. No, no, no.* She would not be attracted to him. Gorgeous he may be, but he was Jonathan's son. And her guard for crying out loud. *I will not be tempted by this… this… God of a man.* Especially not less than twenty-four hours after Anita's torture session. *So wrong.*

"I see the shoes fit."

"Hmm?" She followed his gaze to her feet. "Oh, yes. Thank you."

He shrugged and reached around her to open the fridge. "I think they belong to Rosalie. She's about your height and occasionally stays here." His arm brushed hers as he snagged the other plate.

"Rosalie?" she repeated, ignoring the butterflies fluttering in her stomach.

"Yeah, she maintains the cabin for me." He shut the fridge behind her. "That's where the food came from, but I'll need to run into town to get more." He paused to study her. "If you give me your measurements, I can get you some clothes, too."

"Measurements?"

His gaze went to her breasts. "Yeah, for whatever." He hesitated a moment too long and turned around. "Just let me know what you need."

She followed him to the couch. "Are you offering to buy me essentials?"

"Essentials?" he repeated as he sat down. "Is that a fancy word for undergarments?"

"Like knickers?" She had a fetish for silk in her previous life, but doubted she would fancy it now. It would be too soft.

His gaze darkened as he looked her over again. "Maybe it would be easier to let you shop online and have it delivered to town." He focused on devouring his lunch while she considered his statement.

*Shop online?* What did that entail? She had shopped in a store, but never online. "Do you mean the world wide web?" she asked after taking a few bites of her own sandwich. It was turkey and cheese, and much better than anything the CRF ever gave her.

"Uh, yeah. The internet."

"You can shop online for clothes?"

The look he gave her was a mixture of shock and pity. "Yes."

"But how do you try them on?"

"You don't. You shop based on your size."

"Size, like measurements." She gestured to her breasts on instinct, which made him choke on his food.

He took a long swig of water and stared up at the ceiling. "Yes."

"I have no idea what my American sizes would be, and I doubt my English sizes are still accurate." She regarded her scrawny form with a frown. She missed her natural curves.

"Exercise."

She blinked. "Pardon?"

"We'll exercise together. It'll help you put on a few pounds, and you'll feel better." He spoke so easily, like it was the most natural decision in the world. "As for the sizing, I'm sure there's some measuring tape lying around somewhere. You can use it and order some clothes."

"With a computer."

He finished off his sandwich and cast her a sideways glance. "Yes, with me sitting beside you."

She almost laughed. If he thought she was going to reach out to someone using his machine, he was crazy. She barely knew how to type. "You'll have to show me how it works," she warned.

"Sure. But first, I'm teaching you how to use a firearm." He snagged their empty plates and took them to the kitchen. She ate the rest of her sandwich and trailed after him.

"You mean you were serious about teaching me how to operate your weapon?"

"Yes." He finished loading the dishwasher and grabbed another bottle of water. She supposed he needed it after all that working out.

"Not that I'm ungrateful, but why would you do that?" It seemed counterintuitive to keeping her here. Although she couldn't shoot him until he removed the device. Was that the reason for his confidence?

He shrugged. "Because we have nothing else better to do, and maybe I'm up for a challenge. Besides, it's not like you'll ever get the chance to shoot me, right?"

*Arrogant arse.* "Care to test that theory?"

His smirk said he wasn't worried. "I'm ready when you are, sweetheart."

"Now sounds good."

"Then I better teach you how to shoot to even the odds a little."

Her eyes narrowed. If her Hydraian gift for imparting knowledge could work in reverse, she'd steal all of Tom's gun skills and use them against him. Oh, and she would use her other gift for shifting and choose a huge male humanoid form to kick his arse. Brilliant.

*Even if that was possible, you'd need to remove the collar first,* her unhelpful conscious reminded. *And there's also that tiny matter of not being able to shift anymore.*

That day when Anita blocked her ability to shift without the collar would forever haunt her.

*No. I will not think about this right now.*

*Eventually...*

*No.*

"Let's go before I change my mind," Tom said, interrupting her mental gymnastics.

*Yes, let's do that instead.* Thankful for the diversion, she nodded. If he wanted to teach her self-defense, she wouldn't stop him. Even if she did find it a bit odd.

Grabbing his shirt from the back of a chair, he tugged it on, picked up a bag by the door, and led the way outside. Distracted by all the muscle on display, she hadn't noticed the handgun strapped to his side. *Did the man ever go without it?*

"We'll start with the basics," he said as they walked. "The safety."

"Rule one, know how to use a weapon before you handle it," she parroted. That's what he told her yesterday.

Tom's warm chuckle provoked a shiver from deep within. *Oh, that's... pleasant.*

"Right, but that's not what I meant." He stopped under the shade of a tree, dropped his backpack, and removed the pistol from his side. "You remember how you tried to pull the trigger last night and failed?"

Her cheeks warmed at the memory. His eyes had been closed when she tried to use his weapon, so he didn't know that she'd aimed away from him when she pulled the trigger. "Yeah, it didn't do anything."

"Right. Because the safety was on. Here, see this?" He pointed to a tiny switch looking thing towards the top of the handle. "Switched this way means it's on. If you switch it this way, it's off."

"So you're saying I could have killed you if I switched it off."

"Sure. If your aim was right."

She folded her arms. "I was three feet away from you."

"Yes, and holding the firearm with one shaky hand. Had you hit me, it wouldn't have been fatal. But it would have hurt like a son of a bitch."

The cocky arse made her want to try shooting him again. And this time she would use proper aim. "Go on."

"Let's master rule one first." He handed her the gun. "Turn the safety off and back on."

She did as he asked with very careful fingers and kept the barrel pointed away from them. "Next."

He grinned. "Rule two, always aim the firearm at the ground unless you intend to shoot something."

Pointing the metal at the ground, she raised an eyebrow. "Better?"

"Yes. Let's talk about stance. Do you see that tree over there with the bullseye setup?"

She followed his gaze to the circles in question. Apparently, he'd prepped for their training while she'd slept. Intriguing. "Yes."

"Okay, I want you to put your left foot forward with your toe pointed down the range or, in this case, toward that tree. Good. Now bring your right foot back and angle it a bit. Uh, not so much." He kneeled to grab her ankle and moved it where he wanted it. "Do you feel stable like this?"

She swallowed as she met his gaze. The sincerity in those brown depths unnerved her. How could she hate him when he looked at her like that? That didn't make her feel stable at all, but she nodded anyway. "Sure."

He stood and eyed her form. "Uh, right. This would be easier if I can position your arms. Do you mind?"

*He's asking permission to touch me?* She couldn't remember the last time someone had given her the choice. Her heart fluttered in response, and she gave him a nod. *All right.*

A woodsy scent assaulted her senses as he wrapped his arms around her from behind and took hold of her wrists. This was not at all how she expected a man to smell or feel after exercising without a shower. The earthy undertone was actually quite pleasant, if a little distracting.

"Gun in your right hand. Good. Now you're going to lock your right arm like this." He demonstrated by pulling it straight and locking her elbow. "Lower your head a little so your line of sight is focused on the target." He slid a hand to her bicep on the other side. "Left arm, not as tight; you want a slight bend in your elbow. Your right arm will control the recoil."

"Recoil?" she repeated as he pressed his body tight against her back. *Why does that feel so good?*

"You'll understand in a minute." He curled her finger around the trigger and swiveled her hips a bit to the right. "Do you see the target there? Down the center of the barrel?" His breath was hot against her ear, making her shiver.

It took more effort than it should to focus on the bullseye. "I see it." Hitting it would be another matter.

"Okay. Don't move." He let go and bent to retrieve something from his bag. "Rule three, ear protection."

A pair of earmuffs appeared in her peripheral as he slid them over her head. If he put on a pair himself, she didn't notice because he wrapped himself around her again. Those nimble fingers of his flicked off the safety before gliding over her hands to help her readjust her aim.

"Focus on the target," he said, voice softened by the earmuffs, "and forget everything else. When you're ready, take a deep breath in, hold it for a beat, and squeeze the trigger."

Amelia couldn't believe she was about to do this, and with Tom of all people. She tried not to think about how secure she felt in his arms. It wasn't appropriate or relevant. All that mattered was that bullseye and learning how to fire this weapon. Because one day soon it would be him at the other end of this barrel, and she'd need to know how to aim.

She took several deep breaths, preparing herself for the inevitable, and pulled the trigger.

# CHAPTER FOUR

## Unwanted Emotions

Amelia woke to an empty cabin. She didn't think much of it at first. Tom went on an early morning run before breakfast every day, so she didn't expect today to be any different. But when the clock switched to the afternoon hour, she grew uneasy and finally glanced outside. That's when she noticed the car was gone.

*Tom isn't here.* A chill skittered down her spine. When he went grocery shopping last week, he reminded her not to run because of the collar. But this time he didn't mention leaving. *Why?*

Had he left her here for good? Was the CRF finally moving into the next phase of this game? By her estimation, they'd been stuck in this cabin together for three weeks, and Jonathan loved his diversions. It would be just like him to change the rules after letting her get used to this new environment. That was part of the reason she slept on the floor every night instead of the bed. She refused to allow herself the comfort when it could so easily be ripped out from under her.

She searched for any cameras that might be observing her reactions. Nothing obvious. Perhaps the replacements were on their way? They knew she couldn't run because of the explosive around her neck. She traced the metal with the pad of her finger and frowned. The device that controlled it was somewhere in this cabin. She considered looking for it the last time Tom left her alone, but didn't want to risk him catching her in the act.

*What if he's not coming back this time?* If she found the device before his replacement arrived, she could escape.

*And go where?*

*Semantics.*

She hunted for anything that resembled a remote in the living area. Aside from the two that controlled the television, she found nothing. Other than a few knives, the kitchen was useless. She bypassed the bathroom and paused at Tom's door. Her tummy did a funny little somersault at the notion of entering his private quarters. Ignoring the fluttering, she turned the knob and paused on the threshold.

Bold, masculine colors decorated the bedroom, and the sweet cedar scent she associated with him dusted the air. The deep brown quilt was haphazardly strewn across the bed, almost as if Tom had left in a hurry. And one of his dresser drawers hung open. She peeked inside and frowned when she found it empty. She threw open the closet beside it and discovered several moving boxes. No clothes. Her heart skipped a beat. This confirmed her suspicions.

*Tom's gone.*

Fear-inducing panic settled across her shoulders, forcing her into action. She had to find that remote before the next phase of this madness began. The boxes were all taped shut, making them impossible to search, so she went through all the drawers instead and paused when she opened the nightstand. A gun.

She danced her fingers along the cool metal. It wasn't what she hoped to find, but it was better than nothing. She carried it with her to the kitchen to search for a knife. Those sealed boxes were about to become unsealed.

Her hand was on the drawer handle when the front door opened. The galley kitchen wall hid her from view, giving her just enough time to lean against the counter and hide the illegal item behind her back.

Tom entered the kitchen with two paper bags and gave her a lopsided grin. "Sorry, grocery shopping and laundry took a little longer than I expected. But we needed food."

"Uh, right." She tried to clear the cotton balls from her throat and failed. *He's back.* Why did that make her feel so light, and safe? "Yes, I was trying to find something for lunch." Complete farce, but it explained her presence in the kitchen. Now she just needed him to walk away so she could slip out and hide the weapon. *Did I remember to close his door?*

His dark chocolate gaze slid over her in a quick assessment, making her want to squirm. She held her breath when he paused on her hips and again on her breasts. "I need to get the other things from the car." Was it her imagination, or did his voice drop an octave? And what happened to the handsome grin?

"Okay."

He gave her another cursory glance and stepped backwards out of the kitchen. The second she heard the front door swing shut, she sprinted for the bedrooms. Closing all the drawers and the closet took priority, then his door. She was on her way to the kitchen when she remembered the pistol in her hand. Tom turned the corner with a laundry basket before she could fix the problem, forcing her to tuck the gun behind her back.

*I'm so dead.* The smile she forced felt like plastic against her lips.

"Uh, the clothes you ordered finally arrived." His sharp gaze went to her free hand, then to her opposite arm. When he met her gaze again, amusement danced in his dark depths. Maybe he thought she was a loon? She was certainly acting like one. "I went ahead and washed these with my clothes at the laundromat in town. Here." He held the basket out for her. "I hope they fit."

She considered the basket and then his cheeky grin. "Are you making fun of me?"

"Me?" The look on his face was overtly innocent. "Never."

"No, I think you're teasing me."

"Or I'm genuinely hoping these fit so we don't have to go through the online shopping experience again."

That made her scowl. "It's not my fault they make it so bloody difficult."

"You have to be the only woman I've ever met who finds shopping online difficult, especially when it's under someone else's credit card."

She folded her arms and glowered up at him. "I didn't ask for clothes or to be forced to order them online. That was all your idea, Sentinel."

"Yes, one I thought you might appreciate, *asset*, but I learned my lesson. So hopefully these fit so we don't have to do it again."

They spent several hours last week trying to order clothes. Technology and Amelia were not friends. Firing a handgun had been easier than shopping online. She frowned at the offending object in his hands. A basket full of shorts and tank tops. If Eli could see her now, he'd die of a heart attack. His precious little flower wearing street clothes? Never. Except when given the option to buy anything she wanted, these were the outfits she chose. The Amelia who loved dressing up died a long time ago.

"Fine." She gestured to her room in an *after you* manner

that had him raising his blond eyebrows.

"Is that your way of politely asking me to set this in your room?"

"If you're looking for a please and thank you, trust me when I say you'll be waiting for a very long time."

"Ouch. I probably deserve that, but ouch." He shook all that glorious hair and flashed her a dimpled smile. "After you, sweetheart."

"What?"

"Lead the way."

"Oh, er, okay." She started to turn and stopped. *The gun. Damn it.* She did an awkward skip to the side to keep the wall at her back and felt the metal slip in her clammy hand. *Okay, so no jumps or the evidence will fall to my feet.*

Tom cocked an eyebrow at her bizarre behavior, but didn't say anything as she moved down the hallway to her door. She kept her front to him while turning the knob with her free hand and stepped inside backwards. Heat caressed her cheeks when she bumped into the bed behind her. Tom set the basket on the ground beside the door and shocked her by kicking it closed.

"Easy way, or hard way? Ladies choice."

Her pulse leapt. She had to clear her throat twice to speak. "Excuse me?" *He couldn't mean...*

"Hard way it is." He stepped forward and caught her hip before she could scramble to the side.

"What—?" The words froze in her throat when his opposite hand snaked around her back to the illicit item in her palm.

He tsked. "Someone was in my room. Find anything else interesting while snooping?"

She bristled at that. "I was not snooping." *Liar.*

"No?" He removed the weapon and threw it on the bed. Instead of moving away, he turned his hand to her lower back and pulled her closer. Her palms flattened against his chest to maintain a slight gap between them. It did nothing to ease the flutter in her lower belly or dispel the heat at the back of her neck.

"So the gun from my nightstand magically appeared behind your back? That's a neat trick, sweetheart."

"Stop calling me that." She bloody hated the way his endearment made her heart race. It was hard enough having his body pressed up against hers. Did the man have to be so hard? Eli had a bulky muscular build, but Tom's athletic form felt sharper, more lethal.

"What else did you find, Amelia?"

"Nothing." *Because I wasted too much time this morning waiting for you to come back from your run.* A mistake she would not make again in the future.

All traces of amusement fled as he narrowed his gaze. "Did you go through the boxes?"

"Is that where you hid the remote?" She kicked herself for the hope in her voice. If it was where he hid the remote, it would be moved now.

His chuckle vibrated through her hands and went straight to her gut. Why was that sound so charming? "So, what was your plan? You shoot me, and then what? I wake up a pissed off immortal tomorrow, and you ask me nicely for the remote?"

She blinked. Shooting Tom hadn't been a part of her plan at all. Did she suspect it might come to that in the future? Yes. But not today. "I thought Jonathan was moving into phase two of this game and sending a replacement."

He stared down at her with intense brown eyes so much like his father's, and yet so very different. Jonathan's vapid gaze held no soul while Tom's were a richer brown and underlined in candor.

"So you intended to shoot my replacement?" he asked.

"I intended to defend myself."

"With my second favorite Smith & Wesson. Nice."

She had no idea who Smith was, but assumed he meant the item she found in his drawer.

"No, I intended to defend myself with the weapon I

found in your *empty* room," she corrected.

The hand on her back felt like a brand through her shirt. She wondered if he realized his thumb was tracing the top of her shorts or if he understood how close they were standing. The heat radiating from his muscular chest seemed to be melting into her veins, making all sorts of strange things happen throughout her body. Maybe it was time to revisit her earlier plan of seducing him? If she could get him to tell her where he hid the remote, she could use it to free herself.

*And how will you get away from him?*

*One step at a time.*

"My room is not empty," Tom countered. "There are boxes, a bed, a dresser, but you know all that since you snooped through my things."

"Your clothes were gone."

"Because I took them to the laundromat."

"Yes, well, I didn't know that."

"And then you stole the gun to shoot my replacement." He shook his head and tsked again. "We need to work on your planning skills, sweetheart."

"I swear you want me to hit you." It came out as a growl, which only seemed to amuse him if his responding smile was anything to go by. *There are those damn dimples again...*

"You tried that already and failed." He lowered his lips to her ear. "But feel free to give it another go," he whispered.

*Taunting arse.*

She shifted to meet his gaze and ended up way too close to his face, because he hadn't lifted his head yet. The retort died in her throat. His breath feathered over her parted lips, making her shiver. She flattened her palms against his chest again and slid them up to his strong shoulders. What would he do if she closed the gap between them? Could she do this? Seduce him into helping her escape, and then kill him? *Yes.* She would do anything to survive, even if it meant—

Tom took a step backwards, causing her hands to drop to her sides. The unexpected move left her feeling cold. It took her a moment to realize the temperature difference stemmed from him releasing his hold when he moved away. She preferred his natural heat over the cool air.

"Right." He cleared his throat and palmed the back of his neck. "I, uh, need to put the groceries away. You should try these on and make sure they fit." His tone lacked the humor from earlier when he gestured to the clothing basket. He definitely wasn't teasing this time.

Her tongue felt thick in her mouth, making a vocal response impossible. She gave a wobbly nod instead. *I almost kissed him.* Why did he move away?

"Okay." He turned to leave and paused at the door. That strong hand of his was still wrapped around the back of his neck, making her fingers twitch. She wanted to touch him again, to finish what she started. *Who am I?*

"If you try to use that on me, you'll regret it." There was nothing funny about his tone or the way his dark gaze pinned her to the spot. A threat lingered between them; a threat underlined with challenge.

"You're letting me keep the gun?" That was the only object in the room he could be talking about, and he'd left it lying on the bed behind her.

"For now." He walked out of her room, leaving her gaping at the doorway.

~*~

*What the hell is wrong with me?* Tom's father would kill him if he found out about this. He let the asset keep a thirty-eight caliber Smith & Wesson. It didn't matter the age of that particular piece, because it was loaded and could be used against him at any moment. But he couldn't bring himself to walk over to the bed to grab it, not with her standing so close.

Clearly, he had a death wish. Or maybe he wanted a challenge or something to do or a way to distract himself from this passion radiating between them. Either way, it was a stupid move. Especially considering how well her aim had improved over the last two weeks of training. It filled him with pride to watch her shoot, but also unnerved him.

*Her brother brutally murdered your mother.*

*True, but how is that* her *fault?*

*You're playing a dangerous game by teaching her how to shoot, encouraging her to exercise, and giving her a gun...*

"I've officially lost my damn mind," he muttered to himself in the kitchen. Not only had he given his charge a lethal toy, he'd almost kissed her. Both were entirely inappropriate. Amelia was his ward. She wouldn't have a choice but to respond, and no way would he take something that wasn't willingly given. John Fitzgerald may have raised him with unscrupulous morals, but he'd never force himself on a woman. Ever.

"Fuck." He gripped the counter beside the refrigerator and strove for control. This wasn't him. He didn't crave women he couldn't touch. But Amelia was far from the average female. Three weeks of eating right and regular activity had given her a healthy glow. Not to mention it was filling out all those natural curves of hers. He didn't follow the scientific nuances of immortal genetics, but he understood the high-level benefits of being a Hydraian or an Ichorian. Unnatural healing, immunity to disease, and body regeneration at fast speeds. Because Amelia no longer had that emaciated look, but was turning into a healthy woman with lethal curves.

Grocery shopping felt too much like playing house. He kept wondering what food she would prefer and debating what meals to prepare. She didn't appear to be picky when it came to eating, but he suspected that was a result of living in captivity for six years. He wanted to make something special for her, which was utterly fucked up considering their situation. They weren't dating. And Tom didn't woo women. His wealthy background and appearance afforded him an array of willing bed partners. The words *Special Forces* brought them to their knees, and he knew it. Somehow, he suspected those two words wouldn't work so effectively on Amelia.

*Enough. Not going to happen.*

He slammed the door on his wayward thoughts and focused on putting the groceries away before they went bad. When that task completed too soon, he grabbed a few items for sandwiches and slapped something together for lunch. Amelia walked in just as he finished, and his jaw almost hit the floor. She looked hot in his clothes, but this? *Holy shit.*

"Seems like the clothes fit," he managed through his dry mouth. How did the woman manage to look like a knock out in a tank top and shorts? Her dark hair was piled up into a haphazard ponytail that hung past her exposed shoulders. Not the sort of outfit that should draw the eye, but with her shapely legs and subtle curves? Oh, it definitely grabbed his attention. *I need to get laid.*

Amelia's brow creased as she glanced down at her new tennis shoes. "I suppose, but it feels strange being in real clothing."

The way she said it sent an arrow through his heart. *This is wrong.* He should have fought harder when he discovered her in the CRF basement, but even now, he knew there wasn't a damn thing he could do other than be decent to her. Because helping her escape equaled a death sentence. No one would help him, and everyone would hunt him. And his contingency plans weren't robust enough yet.

"I made you a sandwich." *Yes, that's a fantastic apology for ruining her life.*

"Thank you."

Her puzzled expression had him quirking an eyebrow. "Not a fan of turkey and cheese?" Most of their meals were quick due to his lack of skill in the kitchen, but this was the first time she eyed his offerings with confusion.

She blinked big blue eyes up at him. "No, I actually quite like your sandwiches. I was just thinking about how much I used to adore being in the kitchen, but I can't for the life of me remember why." Her fingers danced over the stove to the counter beside it. "I find I have no desire to cook. Is that odd?"

He snorted. "Not to me, but there's a reason our fridge is packed full of easy meals to prep." Minus the lasagna ingredients he bought. Why he decided that sounded like a good idea was beyond him. Part of the whole wanting to please her thing. As if that were possible in this situation.

Picking up the sandwich, she gave him a small smile. "Cheers."

He grinned at her adorable English accent. It seemed thicker at times than others, almost as if she had been around Americans too long. Perhaps it was an age thing? Based on her appearance, Tom guessed Amelia was in her mid-twenties when she became a Hydraian. Her actual birth date remained a mystery to him, but it had to be at least three centuries ago. Maybe closer to four. That type of thing would shock most humans, but having an immortal father born over a thousand years ago lessened the impact.

Amelia led the way to the living area and folded herself gracefully onto the couch. All those lean, elegant lines were far too tempting in those fitted clothes, so he settled himself a few feet away and focused on his sandwich.

It dawned on him when he finished that the television wasn't on and they'd eaten in companionable silence. Most women required constant conversation, but not Amelia. He wondered if she always preferred quiet or if her years with the CRF had something to do with it. His military academy upbringing and sniper experience altered him on a fundamental level. The boy his mother once loved became a man she would never recognize. Or maybe she would. He'd become an adult version of his father, but with a conscience.

"Tom?" Amelia turned to him with a determined gleam in her eyes that made him nervous. Nothing good ever happened as a result of that expression on a woman's face. He set his empty plate on the table and cocked an eyebrow in expectation. "Will you——?"

The ringing of his phone cut her off. He pulled it out of his pocket and fought a growl. Of course his father would call now. *Fucking GPS.* His next assignment better be overseas or he might kill the man who helped create him.

"Hi, Dad. Didn't we just chat last night?"—like they did every night—"I had no idea you missed me so much. Maybe we should grab dinner later this week?" Amelia frowned at his sugary tone. He'd played the role of obedient soldier for last two weeks, yet his father still monitored his every move. Tom was more than over this game, and his tone implied that.

"Why did you leave the asset unattended?"

"Because I needed food, and you specifically told me not to have Rosalie over. So I went out to get groceries, just like last week and the week before."

"And the detour to the post office?"

Tom didn't miss a beat. "I wanted to send you a postcard, but they didn't have any with the greeting I wanted. Apparently 'Fuck You' isn't a common card. Who knew?"

Silence answered his sarcasm. It should have unnerved him, but he had no patience for this shit anymore. What was his father going to do? Disown him for a little back talk? Not likely. The threats got old after a while. Would he die without his father's protection? Maybe, maybe not. All those years of training had paid off, and Tom had the means to take care of himself. At least for a little while.

"So look, are we done here?" he continued when his father said nothing. "I'm doing my job, just as I've been doing it for the last twenty-one, almost twenty-two, days. We don't need the daily briefings. If I have something important to report I will, but how about we not talk until that happens?"

"Am I being dismissed?"

"No, I'm suggesting you use your time more wisely. You don't need to babysit the babysitter. I know what I'm doing, and if you don't trust me to do it, send someone else." He didn't really mean it. The idea of another Sentinel watching Amelia made his skin crawl.

"I don't need you to advise me on how to use my time. I'll continue to monitor as I see fit."

"Sure. Then we'll chat again in five or so hours, unless there was something else?"

"I would like an update on the asset's condition."

He glanced at the woman in question. Her current condition? *Gorgeous.* "She's secure," he said instead.

"Good."

The phone line went dead, making Tom roll his eyes. "Bye to you, too, Dad." He pocketed the phone and turned back to Amelia. "Sorry, what were you asking me before?"

Her brow drew downward as she studied him. "Your relationship with Jonathan is curious. I thought you were close."

*We used to be.* "I don't want to talk about him. What did you want to know?"

"Oh." She wrung her hands in her lap and licked her lips. "I, er, I was wondering if you could show me how you did that gun trick. You know, the one where you took it from me after...?"

Her voice trailed off, but he knew what she meant to say. *After Anita's visit.* That was the only time he disarmed her, other than today, which didn't count.

"You want me to teach you how to disarm someone," he murmured. Because that wasn't walking a dangerous line at all. *Oh, like you haven't already leapt over that line.* His conscious was an ass.

She bit her lip and nodded. "I don't plan to use it on you. I'm just... curious."

The woman was a terrible liar. Guilt dilated her pupils and settled on her stiff shoulders. *What are you planning, little asset?* Why did evening the stakes between them sound fun? He almost wanted her to fight him, just to see how far she could get. Too bad her request couldn't be summed up in a single lesson.

"All right, give me your hand." She did as requested without hesitation. A sign of trust? He placed his fingers against a pressure point just above her thumb. "Okay, see what happens when I press down?"

"It forces my hand to move."

"Right. If I tug this way, you have to move." He demonstrated by pulling her closer. She went up on her knees beside him in response and stared at her hand in fascination. "I can control you with two fingers now."

"That's brilliant." Her excitement was palpable, making him grin.

"Sure. There are several pressure points all over the human body. Each one can be used to a disadvantage."

"And you use them to disarm someone?"

"You can, or you can use it for simple defense. Pressure points can bring a man twice your size to his knees, if you know how to do it right." He showed her several more points, each one making her smile wider. She tried a few on him, and each touch went straight to his gut. By the end, she was gazing at him with a reverence that discomforted him. Mostly because all the touching had excited his hormones. All he wanted to do was lay her out on the couch and introduce her to more pleasurable points.

"Okay, but none of that tells me how to take the gun away from someone," she murmured when they were done.

"No, because disarming a person depends on a variety

of factors. Their weight, height, angle, strength, type of firearm, the way it's being held, and several other things. I can't teach you that in a day,"—or even a month—"so we started with self-defense basics."

"Oh." Her hands dropped to her lap only scant inches from him. How had they managed to get so close? He swore he kept putting room between them, but their bodies seemed to gravitate to one another. She tugged her plump bottom lip between her teeth and nibbled. Amelia Wakefield was a gorgeous woman, but her innocent gestures made her all the more alluring.

*I've got to get out of here before I do something stupid.* Because kissing her would be wrong on so many levels.

Tom stood and took a step away from the hypnotic brunette. He could busy himself with cleaning their dishes, but what he really needed was some fresh air.

"I'm going to go for a run." *Again.* He went for one this morning before the sun rose. Maybe he would enjoy some target practice as well. And do some bodyweight exercises. That should keep him busy for a few hours and take his mind off of sex. Hopefully.

"Oh, so no more self-defense basics?" Those guileless blue eyes were going to get him killed.

"I can show you a few helpful things tomorrow." He'd already stepped way over the boundaries on this assignment, so why not push the envelope a little more? "Outside," he added. Because inside wasn't working, and her floral scent was intoxicating enough. At least outside he would have other sights and sounds to distract him. "Right. Be back in a bit."

He didn't bother to change into workout clothes. Jeans, boots, and a t-shirt would make for an uncomfortable run. But it couldn't be worse than having a hot, unattainable woman within arm's reach and not be able to touch her.

# CHAPTER FIVE

## Unwelcome Visitors

"Okay, straddle me again."

*This woman is trying to kill me,* Tom thought.

The first few days of training were a breeze because they kept the touching to a minimum. He taught Amelia the weak points on the shin, how to properly form a punch, and general self-defense basics. Today, they graduated to full body contact.

*Why am I doing this to myself?* he wondered—not for the first time—as he straddled Amelia's hips. This had gone beyond a death wish and firmly into torture territory. What had started as a fun way to pass the time had escalated to a risky activity that required too much skin-on-skin contact.

"Hold me down like you mean it," Amelia chided when he gently placed his hands on her shoulders. "No going easy on me."

*How about you go easy on me then?* "If I use all my strength, you won't be able to push me off."

Her brow puckered. "Then what's the point?"

*What's the point, indeed…?* "To teach you how to escape in a normal situation. I'm the opposite of a normal opponent."

"Then take this collar off so we can play fair."

*Nice try.* "Make your move, sweetheart." He purposely used the nickname she loathed to get her moving, and it worked. She slid her right arm between them, hooked her leg over his ankle, then rotated her body in an attempt to roll him off of her. The mediocre defense maneuver might shift an aggressor with the right angle and force, but he knew how to roll with it. Literally. He rotated with her and used the momentum to carry them in a full circle so her back hit the ground again.

Her resulting growl went straight to his groin. *All right, maybe that was a bad idea.* But it was oh-so-fun.

"Something wrong, sweetheart?" he asked, feigning innocence.

Blue fire glared up at him. "I would like to shoot you now."

The threat was so unexpected and said with such venom, he couldn't help but laugh. "I'd love to see you try."

"I'll more than try." She sounded so confident. Too bad she didn't stand a chance.

"Hmm." He settled more heavily on her by stretching his legs alongside hers and going to his elbows on either side of her head. Danger instincts flared through his brain while heat licked through his veins. "And then what?"

Her glare cooled as her gaze dropped to his lips. "I would run." Some of her earlier confidence seemed to have disappeared. *Smart woman.*

He toyed with the loose strand of her hair lying beside his hand. "Probably a good idea considering you'd miss and I'd be chasing you. Can you do me a favor, though?"

She blinked up at him. "What?"

"Try not to run in circles. It takes the fun out of things."

"Arse." The slap to his shoulder barely registered. He enjoyed having her beneath him too much to notice. A soft, pliant female with spirit was his favorite kind of woman. Too bad he couldn't have this one. Getting laid might cure the itch, but heading into town for a one night stand didn't appeal. So working out had taken priority, as had training Amelia. He secretly hoped she would use her new skills on his father someday. Not to kill the man, just to hurt him a little. Tom would pay good money to see the look on the old man's face after she hit him.

*I really do have a death wish.*

"Okay, teach me how to get out of this position." Amelia started to squirm beneath him, making his decision to lay over her a bad one. If she kept doing that, his cock would never forgive him. *Down, boy.*

"You have to gain the upper-hand," he managed. Not that he had any desire to help her do that. He rather liked being in charge and on top of her.

"And how do I do that?"

"What do I keep telling you about the element of surprise?"

"Right." Her plump bottom lip disappeared between her teeth. It made him want to close the gap between them and take a nibble himself, but that would be inappropriate.

*Right, because you haven't already run a mile over that line…*

Warm hands ran up his back to the nape of his neck, making him shiver. Her expression gave little away as her long fingers wove into his hair. A slight tug had him lowering his head towards hers, only to be yanked back violently by her fist.

*Fuck.* As far as defensive maneuvers went, it was effective, but pain was an old friend. He wrapped his hands around her wrists and pressed them to the ground beside her head. She started wiggling again as a result, which intrigued the lower half of his body. If this went much further, he would end up doing something they would both regret.

"Bloody hell. I have no arms, no legs, and your big body is impossible to move. Now what?"

"It's all about surprise, sweetheart. In this situation, you roll with whatever your aggressor is doing and look for an opening. The more comfortable they are with you, the more likely they are to lessen their guard. That's when you attack."

"But you'll never lessen your guard."

"Then I guess you're stuck with me." He gave her a grin he knew was cocky and pushed away from her. After getting to his feet, he held out a hand to help her up. She accepted it with a grimace.

"There are worse people to be stuck with," she muttered as she wiped the grass off her jean shorts and bare legs. He suspected that wasn't a compliment.

"I think that's enough for today." Because he couldn't handle any more. A long run, some bodyweight exercises, and a cold shower, were his afternoon agenda. He started towards the house and paused when something hard hit the center of his back. A look at the ground near his feet indicated the culprit. "Did you just throw a rock at me?"

"Surprised?" was her snarky reply.

He turned around and took in her empty hands and open stance. *Someone wants to play. Okay.* "Next time try a smaller stone you can actually throw."

Her brows shot up. "Excuse me? I nailed you in the back."

"And it felt like a raindrop." Not true, but it had his desired impact. Those blue eyes of hers lit up like liquid fire, and a faint pink tinted her pretty face. He leaned against the tree beside him and hooked one ankle over the other while keeping his arms loose at his sides. "Go ahead and try again."

"I'd rather use your head for target practice."

"Well, you do have my Smith & Wesson." *Against my better judgment.*

"Smith and...? Oh, right. You mean the gun. Well, it's not on me."

"That sounds like a *you* problem." He caressed the sidearm at his hip. "I always carry mine."

She rolled her eyes. "We both know you would just take it from me."

He smirked. "Oh, I'd more than take it from you, sweetheart."

"Arse."

"Asset."

The glower she shot him inspired all sorts of sordid thoughts. Oh, how he'd love to kiss that mouth of hers into submission. Bickering with Amelia had become his secret indulgence. Her quiet demeanor from the first week was long gone, and he didn't miss it. This feisty side was far more attractive and fun. He winked at her and resumed his trek towards the cabin.

~*~

"One of these days, you'll regret turning your back on me," Amelia muttered.

"Sounds fun," was all the arse said as he continued moving in those confident strides of his through the woods. The man was all lean, muscular lines, and it was bloody distracting. He felt far too tempting when straddling her, which was why Amelia demanded he do it again. If she stood any chance of taking him down, she needed to master this ridiculous attraction. Too bad he made it worse by sprawling over her like some big, lazy predatory cat.

She should have tried to seduce him while he had her pinned, but her oxygen-deprived brain refused to function. That's what happened when one forgot how to breathe, and it seemed to occur every time Tom touched her. It bothered her on a deep level because the last person to affect her that way was Eli, when they first met all those centuries ago. One glance from him, and her world stopped. She never expected to feel that way about anyone ever again. Especially not the son of her enemy.

*Maybe I'm on the verge of having a fit.* Wouldn't Jonathan love that? A hysterical laugh bubbled in her chest and died on an exhale as Tom shoved her up against a tree. He moved so fast she didn't realize he was there until his hands were on her shoulders and her back hit the uneven bark.

"Is this another lesson in surprise?" she asked on a harsh breath. Because that would not be fair. He said they were done training today and hadn't seemed at all phased by her attempt with the rock. She opened her mouth to say more, but stilled upon catching the panic in his dark eyes. This was not another lesson. "What's wrong?"

"There's someone in the driveway."

Ice crept through her veins, going straight to her heart. "Anita?" It felt like forever had passed since her last visit. Amelia was no doubt due for another round of experimentation. It bothered her more than it should; an indication that she'd grown too comfortable in this situation. Was that part of Jonathan's plan all along? For Tom to gain her trust, just to squash it?

The man in question gave her a concerned look, almost as if he could read her thoughts. But she knew mind reading did not run in his genes.

"No, it's Rosalie. My aunt."

*Pardon?* "Your aunt?" He mentioned a Rosalie before, but never indicated a familial relation.

"Yes. She's the one who maintains the cabin when I'm not here."

She processed his words. *Oh...* "You mean Anna's sister." Because Jonathan didn't have any siblings. None that were alive anyway. That made this woman an aunt on his mother's side of the family.

He frowned. "You knew my mother?"

"Not well, but yes. We met once a few decades ago." Tom had told Amelia the date last week. Six years in captivity had felt more like six centuries.

"You met my mom?" Tom seemed bothered by that. Well, too bad. She couldn't change her history any more than he could.

"She came over for a dinner party once with Jonathan before you were born." *Back when I trusted him and considered him a friend.* "She was a lovely woman." Or at least appeared that way on the surface. Issac knew her better than Amelia did, and only had pleasant things to say about her.

It seemed like Tom wanted to ask her something, but he changed the subject instead. "Okay, I know you don't owe me anything, and this is a lot to ask. But can you stay here while I get Rosalie away from the cabin?"

*What an odd request, almost as if...* "You don't want her to see me." Because Rosalie could help her escape? Maybe go to the authorities? Or maybe get a message to someone on her behalf?

"No, your thoughts are written all over your face. Please, I'll beg if I have to. I need you to stay here."

Oh, she liked this. What a conundrum for him indeed. "And if I decide not to?"

His heavy sigh settled over her shoulders in a wave of sadness. "If Rosalie discovers you, I'll have to kill her. My father will require it."

Okay, maybe this wasn't as fun as she originally thought. "What do you mean 'require it?'" What happened to free will?

"He'll consider it my punishment for fucking up."

"And if you refuse?"

"I can't." He made it sound so simple. Black and white. No gray.

"Everyone has a choice."

"Not me. I'm a fledgling with no allies and hundreds of enemies." He peered around the tree and grimaced. "Look, she's already gone in the cabin. I need you to stay here. I'll get her away by taking her to an early dinner in town, and then you can go inside. Please. I'm begging you, Amelia. Don't make me kill her."

She wanted to argue that last point about making him kill someone. Jonathan was the culprit here, but she understood the implication. If she created a scene, he wouldn't have a choice, at least from what he said. And from what she'd gathered, the freedom he afforded her wasn't standard. She overheard several of the conversations with his father where they discussed the *asset in the basement.* It could all still be part of a simulation to gain her trust, but it seemed too long of a game for Jonathan to play. He'd be bored by now. And why teach her about self-defense?

"Amelia." The urgency in Tom's voice snapped her back to the present. "She's back outside. Please, will you stay here?"

She met his pleading gaze and felt a little piece of her heart break at the hopelessness she found there. Maybe she wasn't the only prisoner here... An interesting twist to their situation.

"All right," she agreed. "I'll stay here until you leave."

Tom seemed to sense the sincerity in her tone because relief filled his handsome face, making her heart race. She'd done something to please him. Why did that realization warm her all over?

"Thank you," he whispered and pressed his forehead to hers. "I'll be back soon, I promise." A dangerous word that sent a shiver down her spine.

"All right," she whispered, unable to say anything else. The moment was over too quickly as he pushed away and jogged down the path towards the cabin. She peeked out from behind the tree and watched him embrace his aunt in a familial hug on the gravel driveway. Rosalie's back was to

Amelia—something Tom no doubt did on purpose - as they spoke. It didn't take him long to get his aunt in her car. Then he disappeared into the house and reappeared with what she guessed were keys, because he started his own car, and followed Rosalie down the driveway.

Amelia waited a few minutes before heading towards the cabin and considered Tom's comments. *I'm a fledgling with no allies and hundreds of enemies.* Why would he believe such a thing? Surely Lucian and the Elders would accept him into Hydria. Fledglings were so rare, thanks to the infamous Nizari who specialized in slaughtering Ichorian offspring. She couldn't remember the last time she met a fledgling. Maybe over a century ago? That was why her brother and the Elders had helped Jonathan keep Tom safe throughout his youth.

Why would he think the Elders wouldn't help him now? Because of his kinship? He couldn't be charged for the sins of his father. Lucian was a fair leader. He would understand Tom's innocence. Besides, it was Jonathan who deserved retribution for murdering Eli and taking her hostage, not Tom.

She muttered an expletive under her breath and laughed at how ridiculous it sounded. Her former self cringed somewhere deep inside at the vulgarity of it. Amelia never cursed. Not in her past life, anyway. But this new version of herself enjoyed the words very much. Hence her pet name for Tom. *Arse* had a lovely ring to it and fit the man to perfection.

"Because he has quite the backside as well," she said to herself with a smile as she entered her bedroom. Maybe she would take a hot shower and think more on her captor. The man was a puzzle she intended to solve, and she had nothing better to do.

*That's not true*, her conscious muttered. She could search for the device that controlled her collar. *By checking the boxes in Tom's room...*

That's what he questioned her about first the other day.

She frowned. Could she snoop again? It felt oddly wrong to invade his privacy, especially knowing he didn't want her to search his closet. But what if she found her freedom? *And where would you go?* An excellent question, one she would answer after she got away.

Her feet moved of their own volition, but she paused outside his door. Her stomach revolted at the idea of going farther. *Why?* This was what she wanted. To escape. Why did it suddenly feel so wrong to get away?

*Because you'll never see Tom again.* And why should that bother her? He was a means to an end. Surely he understood that as well as she did. He taught her a few defense moves, of which she was thankful, but she needed to go home.

*And where is that exactly?*

"I really am on the verge of a fit," she decided. Might as well make it worse.

She pushed open the door and enjoyed the subtle hint of pine floating in the air. Either Tom wore a woodsy cologne or all that running outside had given him a natural foresty scent. Her nose approved. She went straight for the closet and found it in the same state as the other day. Empty, except for a few sealed boxes.

"Seems an odd place for a device, but let's see." She picked up the first one and carried it over to the bed. It was lighter than she expected, but taped shut. After a quick wander to the kitchen, she retrieved a knife and sliced it opened. What lay inside was not what she expected to find.

"Oh." Little toy soldiers stared up at her. She grabbed another box. More childhood items. It wasn't until she pulled the final box that she found something more interesting. Photos, jewelry, and a set of delicate scarves. Her gaze caught on a photograph of a young Tom clinging to Anna's pant leg. It warmed her heart in a way it shouldn't have, but she couldn't help it. The love and adoration in the woman's face reminded Amelia of her own mother. She turned over the photo to look for a date and froze. The back was splattered with dark brown stains.

"No..." She recognized dried blood all too well. And it decorated all the items sitting beside the photographs. Nightmares lived in this box. She closed it on a whim and shoved it back in the closet. But it was already too late. Invisible spiders crawled up her legs, along her spine, and down her arms. Death lived here. In this cabin. Was this where his mother died? She couldn't remember. Issac mentioned it once, saying they didn't get there in time to save her. But she never pressed for details. Polite Amelia never involved herself in derogatory affairs. That was for the men in her life. But now she wanted to know. What happened to Anna Fitzgerald?

A sound outside had her freezing in the middle of Tom's room. Was that a car door? The dimming sun peeking through the curtains surprised her. Surely she hadn't been sorting through his personal effects for that long. But then time always seemed to elude her. She grabbed the boxes of toys from the bed and shoved them in the closet. Not that it would help. He'd clearly see the broken seals. She would have to try to sneak back in here later to fix it somehow, or deal with the consequences. Tom would not be pleased, but he wouldn't physically punish her. Not in the way Jonathan would anyway.

*You trust him.* Her conscious truly grated on her last nerves, but she did not have time to argue. There was definitely someone here, and the only person it could be was Tom. She tucked the kitchen knife into the back of her jean shorts as the front door of the cabin opened. Masking her expression into one of innocence, she moved towards the living area and froze.

Three people in lab coats. None of them were Tom.

"Well. It seems I'll have quite the report for John when I get back." Anita Patel's voice reminded Amelia of nails on a chalkboard, but it was the maniacal grin that made her want to crawl inside herself and die.

*Oh, this is going to hurt.*

Her blood ran cold at the bags in Anita Patel's hands. Amelia's initial thought was one of submission, but the cold blade at her back suggested an alternative. *Fight*, it whispered.

"I'd ask if you managed to escape, but your clean clothes and healthy state suggest otherwise." Anita's evil gaze slid over Amelia in a chilling manner, making her heart race. The doctor pursed her lips. "I had such high hopes for Tom, but it seems he's like most men and follows his dick instead of his head. His father is going to be so disappointed. Maybe he'll let me be your new warden?"

If Amelia had any inclination left that this was all one of Jonathan's games, it died with that threat. No way would he keep Anita in the dark. They enjoyed playing together too much to maintain such a charade. Which meant Tom taught her self-defense because he wanted to, not because of his role as good-cop. *But why?*

"Well, we can get to the reporting in a bit. I have a few samples I need. Then I'll talk to John about taking ownership here. It'll take away from some of my other research, but I'm sure we'll have fun together."

*Fun. Yes. That's exactly what you'll be having.*

A tiny fire brewed at the center of Amelia's chest, spreading warmth to her frozen limbs. The idea of spending any alone time with this sadistic woman, with no supervision or Stark to heal her, did not appeal. She wondered if the infamous healer stood outside, guarding.

"Shall we move to the bedroom?" Anita continued. "I would hate to ruin any of the furnishings out here." She motioned to her minions to get moving. Amelia moved backwards to keep the knife concealed and walked sideways towards the room. The doctor was too caught up in her internal scheming to notice. Amelia could see the plans running through those beady eyes as the petite woman considered her favorite torture methods.

*Not this time...* A small voice whispered. If she could

get to the gun tucked between her mattresses, she could end this. *Unless there's a Sentinel outside.* But would it matter? Dr. Patel would be dead before they reached her.

She backed up to the other side of the bed to allow room for the researchers. They unzipped their bags, and the one with frail shoulders and a balding head pulled out a plastic sheet. If he draped it over the bed before she got ahold of the weapon, it would ruin everything.

"Go ahead and undress," Anita said dismissively as she started assembling needles on the nightstand.

Amelia gave the woman an obedient glance and pretended to bend down to unlace her shoes. But instead of untying them, she slid her hand between the mattress at her side and wrapped her fingers around the cool metal handle of the gun. She checked the location daily, so she knew it would be there, because for whatever reason, her warden let her keep it. And it was loaded. Slipping it from the bed, she held it loosely at her side and considered her options.

*It's all about surprise.* Tom's deep tones rolled through her mind, making her shiver. *Make them comfortable. Lessen their guard. Attack.*

They seemed content at the moment, and preoccupied. Like they would never suspect her of retaliating. Because the old Amelia would never dare. She wouldn't know how. For years, she did whatever they told her to do and allowed unspeakable things to happen to her body due to hopelessness and a lack of a choice. But the metal in her hand afforded her an opportunity she didn't have before.

*It's now or never, sweetheart.* She swore his voice took on a taunting edge to force her into action. Not that it was real. The smooth tones in her head were of her own making. *Because I'm losing my mind.* And she had no doubt the mad doctor would officially break her psyche if she became Amelia's warden. She refused to sit by and let that happen.

Anita pulled out her torture toys as the researchers finished covering the bed with plastic. Seeing the bone saw churned Amelia's stomach. Her last encounter with that tool had not ended well. Anita had used it to saw open her chest, right through the center of her sternum. The pain had thrown her into a dark state, so close to death, that she'd wondered if her eyes would ever open again. Unfortunately, they did.

*I can't go through that again. Not here.*

*You can do this, Amelia.* Tom's warm tones flooded her body with a confidence she didn't know existed. *Now shoot before they notice you.*

She lifted the gun and aimed it at the head of the researcher closest to her, flicked the safety to off, and fired.

# CHAPTER SIX

## Sentinel Code

"I swear, you're just like your father," Rosalie said with a shake of her head.

Tom forced a smile. "Not sure that's a compliment," he responded with a light tone, but deep down, he meant it. Being told he was like John Fitzgerald used to please him. He idolized the man growing up and wanted to be him most of his life. But now all he did was cringe. *I don't want to be like him anymore.*

All those subtle threats about having nowhere to go hadn't fazed him much as a youth because the only place he wanted to be was by his father's side. All the training, military experience, and college education suddenly took on a new meaning when he started working as a Sentinel. His father had bred his own private soldier; a man he expected to carry out missions without any questions. A man who would remain loyal without fault. Tom was slowly proving not to be that man. Did that make him more or less like his father? He wasn't sure, but he hoped it made him better.

Rosalie's laugh stabbed him through the heart. She sounded so much like his mother. It hurt to be around her, which was why he avoided her. They saw each other once a year or so, if that. Her petite frame and near-black hair was a stark contrast to his mother's blonde bob and svelte figure, but her almond-shaped eyes were the same shade as his mother's. Every time he met his aunt's gaze, his stomach churned. There were too many memories lurking in those brown depths.

"You know it's a compliment," she chided, bringing him back to the present. "Your father is a successful man, powerful, too."

*Don't remind me.* "I'm sure he'd love to see you." A complete lie. His dad had no interest in his mother's side of the family. Hell, he hadn't shown much of an interest in the woman herself.

*She came over for a dinner party once with Jonathan before you were born.* Amelia's words from earlier didn't match his memories of his dad's relationship with his mother at all. The John he knew left his son with Anna in that cabin for a decade, visiting once in a blue moon to check on his future toy soldier. That didn't strike Tom as a man who cared enough about his wife to take her out for a dinner party. The only time they ever ate as a family was on his tenth birthday when his father had stopped by with a surprise announcement. Military school.

That was the last day he saw his mother alive.

Tom finished his beer and considered ordering another. If Amelia wasn't waiting for him back at the cabin, he probably would have, but as it was, he needed to drive home. Sober. Or he might end up doing something stupid when he got there. Not to mention, he wasn't the type to drive drunk.

"I've missed you," Rosalie said, her voice taking on a melancholy tone. "You realize you're the only family I have that I actually like, right?"

He chuckled, thinking of his mother's extended family. His grandparents were long dead on that side, but she had a few cousins who were still alive.

"I'll try to come around more." He refrained from making that a promise because he knew he wouldn't keep it. Shit, with the way he was going, he'd end up in hiding soon anyway. This might be the last time they ever saw each other. It bothered him a little that he wouldn't be around to keep her safe, but she was far from being on his father's radar. His aunt had no immortal ancestry. She was a nurse and very human.

"No, you won't." She sounded sad, but gave him a smile. "You forget I know you, Tom. You're too busy for an old lady like me."

"You're not old, Aunt Rosalie."

"Oh, don't let the hair fool you, kid. I have an excellent hairdresser who hides all the gray."

He rolled his eyes. "You're only forty-seven." His mother would have been fifty-two if she were still alive.

"Yeah, I'm half-dead."

"Bullshit. Don't talk like that."

"Just trying to put it into perspective that I'm getting old and you need to visit more."

"And I said I would."

"Uh huh. You said that two years ago, which was the last time I saw you. And the only reason I'm seeing you today is because I hunted you down at that cabin of yours. How many more weeks were you going to live there before reaching out?"

*Uh, a lot.* "I was busy."

Her gaze narrowed, making him distinctly uncomfortable. His mother used to give him that look just before scolding him as a boy. Sometimes, it unnerved him how much Rosalie resembled her, but they were sisters.

"I know what you're going to say," he started, only to be cut off by his phone vibrating on the bar table. A glance down had his insides turning cold.

*Oh, shit.*

"I've gotta go," he said, standing. The code scrawling across the display was a Sentinel distress signal, and the coordinates matched his cabin. *Fuck.*

~*~

Amelia stared at the dark blood coating her hands. *What have I done?* The ringing in her ears had yet to subside from using the gun. No wonder Tom insisted on hearing protection during training. She swore the entire world heard the shots fired in the small bedroom.

"He'll... kill... you." Anita's raspy threat floated up in a cloud from the floor. Amelia almost forgot about the woman beneath her. She'd been too consumed in the blood dripping from her fingers. The kitchen knife sat idle in her palm. After the shots went off, Anita had lunged at her and knocked the pistol from her hands. But not before Amelia had managed to send a bullet into the woman's stomach. It brought the doctor to her knees, while the other two researchers lay dead on the other side of the room.

Five shots in total, two of them misses. At least that's what Amelia remembered. It all happened so fast before her brain could process the repercussions of her actions. She had straddled Doctor Patel and pressed the blade to her slender throat—poised to kill—when she realized she needed the woman alive. For now.

"Deactivate my collar," Amelia demanded again. Being the torturer was a new experience for her. Years of being a victim had taught her a few things, but she didn't much care for this role. She thought killing her aggressors would help her feel some sort of justice or relief, but all she felt was empty as she stared down at the woman quivering beneath her.

Amelia pressed the sharp point to the tender place beneath Anita's eye and repeated her demand a third time. No Sentinels had arrived yet to investigate the thunderous gunshots, which told her the trio had arrived alone. But she knew a few of them were on the way thanks to the doctor. She mentioned backup with one of those evil grins, her black eyes smiling with triumph. Amelia didn't care because she planned to be long gone by the time they arrived, which required someone to deactivate the device around her neck.

"Do you remember that time you removed my eyes to see how long it took them to regenerate? I wonder what would happen if I did that to you. I bet I can remove them before the Sentinels arrive. Want to see?" Amelia loathed every word coming out of her mouth, but she needed her enemy to cooperate. And recalling one of the worst days of her existence in this cruel woman's custody helped ground her resolve. If anyone deserved this treatment, it was the monster beneath her.

"Remove this device from my neck, or say goodbye to your right eye." She pressed the blade hard enough to draw blood.

"Stop!" Anita cried, her head thrashing to the side. An idiotic move on her part considering her position. The blade sliced open her cheek and potentially something worse, causing the woman to shriek in pain. Amelia almost lost the knife to a cringe, but Tom's voice in her head held her steady. She had the upper-hand here; she just needed to finish the job.

A bloody hand flew up to cover the wounded eye. The woman didn't have much time before she bled out on the floor. That gunshot to her abdomen had hit something vital, if all the blood was something to go by. Amelia tried to feel remorse for it, but couldn't manage it. Anita Patel deserved her fate, and worse. She started to cut her again, but the doctor squealed.

"I can't! I fu-fucking can't!" Those words seemed to take everything out of her as she deflated on a shaky exhale.

"Then how do I deactivate the explosive?" she wondered, more to herself than to Anita. If she couldn't remove the collar, Amelia was a dead woman. Decapitation killed immortals, which explained why Jonathan installed the safety measure. She wasn't ready to give into death. Not when she was this close to freedom.

"Ex-explosive?" The doctor couldn't seem to decide which injury she wanted to guard more as her palm went from her eye to the wound at her stomach. Anita's opposite arm laid limp at her side. "Wha-what explosive?" Her shaky words unnerved Amelia.

*I did this to her. And I killed two people.*

How was that possible?

*Who am I?* The blade trembled in her hand. *I don't want to be this person.*

Torture didn't suit. She liked the confidence of knowing how to handle a gun, but didn't enjoy using it to hurt someone. It emboldened her and weakened her at the same time. She expected her revenge to be empowering, to be a sort of cathartic experience, but it didn't have that impact at all. If anything, she felt evil, like Anita and Jonathan.

*I can't do this.*

She set the knife on the bed and stood on shaky legs. It didn't matter how much this woman deserved a dose of her own medicine. Amelia wasn't the one to do it.

"D-Don't." Anita held up her only working hand for a split second before clasping her abdomen. "I-I can't. Ex-explosive?" The uptick in her voice was unexpected. Why did she sound so confused?

"Yes, the one in my collar." Amelia pointed to her neck for reference. "Tom said it's tied to a device in the house. Do you know what it looks like?"

Anita blinked one eye up at her and grimaced. Or maybe that was supposed to be a laugh? She couldn't tell through the haze of blood and gore. *Had I really been about to remove her eye?*

"Th-that's why," the doctor rasped. An odd choking sound came from her throat, followed by a violent cough. Blood seeped from the edge of her mouth. Amelia often suspected the woman might experiment on herself with immortal blood. If she did, it wasn't working in her favor. *She's going to die.*

"That's why, what?"

"Why... ha-aven't r-run... threat." Several words were cut off by a horrid hacking that had Amelia taking a step back.

"I don't understand."

Anita's chest rose and fell in quick succession, as her single eye drooped. "T-Tom," she whispered. "Li-lied. No ex..." The silence that followed was deafening. It seemed to stretch on, and on.

*Her chest isn't moving.*

*Because she's dead.*

*And I'm the one that killed her.*

Dizziness hit Amelia hard and fast, making her stumble backwards into the wall beside the bed. She finally did it.

"Anita's gone," she whispered to the quiet room. Why didn't she feel elated? Triumphant? Free?

*Tom lied about the explosive.*

She could run...

Or was that Anita's final form of torture? Making Amelia question everything and debate escaping over waiting for someone who could remove her collar?

What a terrible conundrum indeed. But there'd been shock in the woman's expression when Amelia mentioned the explosive then an odd form of respectful understanding, almost as if she were amused by the joke. Did Tom lie to keep her from running? From what she'd learned about the man, it seemed like something he would do. A way to keep her pliant without locking her up.

"Bloody hell." She couldn't believe she fell for it. The clever arse had duped her.

She couldn't wait to give him a piece of her mind later. Or maybe not. No way would he approve of the events in this room. Blood splatter, bullet holes, and three very dead CRF personnel. He wouldn't have a choice but to report it, and then he'd end up having to kill her, or worse. Just this afternoon he spoke about having to do whatever his father wanted, which meant he would carry out the orders dealt. And Jonathan's form of punishment would not be pleasant.

"I need to get out of here." She striped the soiled clothes from her body, scrubbed the filth from her body as best she could in a quick shower, and redressed in clean shorts and a tank top. Her shoes were speckled with blood, but there wasn't anything she could do about it now. They were her only option, and she'd need them to escape.

*Might need this, too,* she thought as she picked up the handgun. It felt heavier in her hands than it should.

*I killed three people with this little thing.*

*Don't think about that right now.* She could lose herself to the emotions racing through her mind later. Right now, she had Sentinels to worry about, and having a weapon made sense. The knife could stay on the bed.

Flicking on the safety, she tucked the cold metal into the back of her jean shorts and headed outside. That's when she noticed the car. As far as escape methods went, *that* would be the fastest.

*How hard could it be to drive a car?* Automobiles didn't exist in Hydria, and Eli did all the driving when they traveled. But surely she could figure this out. All she needed were keys.

Heading back to the massacre, she searched everyone and eventually found what she needed in Anita's lab coat. She pocketed the keys and started towards the living area again, but froze upon hearing the crunch of gravel beneath boots. It was a good thing she left the front door open, or she may not have heard them until it was too late. She darted into Tom's room and unlocked the back window. It was just the right size for her to squeeze out, and she didn't bother shutting it. No time.

Amelia snuck around the side of the cabin, hoping to steal the car while the new arrivals were inside, and nearly ran into a Sentinel.

# CHAPTER SEVEN

## A Sentinel's Betrayal

"Well, well." Sentinel Blake stood a good foot over her with shoulders twice the size of hers. If that wasn't bad enough, he had his pistol drawn and aimed at her head.

She gulped. "Erm, hello." What else could she say?

"You're not where you should be, asset seven."

She hated when they called her that. Like she was property, not a person. Although Tom seemed to use it as an endearment, sort of like when she called him an arse in jest. *Now isn't the time to think about him.* Right. Because there was a gun pointed in her direction.

"Where should I be?" she asked, feigning confusion. If she could get him to drop his guard, she might be able to shoot him like she did the researchers. He stood close enough that she wouldn't miss, but his training rivaled

Tom's, making it unlikely for her to take him down with one shot. And from what she had observed of Blake in her holding cell at the CRF, he didn't distract easily.

"How did you get out?" His silver-blue eyes danced over her in amusement, but his aim never wavered. "And where did you get these clothes?"

She fidgeted with the hem of her tank top. Should she answer truthfully or lie? "I found them." *Online*, she added to herself. *There. Not a lie.*

He snorted. "Right. Yo, Scott! I've got her!"

Ice slid down her spine at the familiar name. Sentinel Scott had a tendency to eye her with a little too much interest during his guard shifts. She didn't know Blake as well, but he kept their brief meetings professional. *Although that look in his eyes right now isn't very proper…*

A stout man jogged around the corner and came to a stop beside his much taller counterpart. It must have reassured Blake, because he holstered the sidearm and folded his thick arms over his wide chest.

*Good news, no more bullets pointed my way. Bad news, two pissed off Sentinels.*

"Anita's dead," was the stocky man's greeting. He stood half a head shorter than Blake, but had twice as much muscle.

"No shit?" Blake frowned. "Where the hell is Fitzgerald?"

"No sign of him. Did you check the asset?" Scott took in the other man's curious expression and snorted. "I'm going to take that as a no." His charcoal gaze landed squarely on her, making her take a step back into the side of the cabin. No way could she pull the handgun in time and hit them both. Not without suffering injury herself, or worse.

Blake aimed his firearm at her again as his bulky partner approached. Grubby hands patted her sides, down and up both legs, then settled on her hips to turn her around. His tsk made her cringe. She knew he'd find the weapon, but having him remove it left her feeling deflated. Escape had tasted so refreshing, if just for a moment. And now it was gone. She should have known better than to ever believe in hope.

Scott tucked the metal into the band of his jeans and continued his pat down. Bile rose in her throat as he spent a little too long examining her breasts. It worsened when those fingers went to the waist of her shorts and dipped inside for a feel along her underwear.

"I doubt she's hiding anything there," Blake said, voice bland.

"Can never be so sure after what I just saw."

The taller man whistled. "That bad?"

"All three of them are dead, and Anita had some weird cuts to her face," Scott explained as he continued his search on the outside of her jean shorts. Her stomach revolted when his palm slid between her thighs and pressed to her most private area. It was a good thing she hadn't eaten in a while, or she was sure the contents would be on the ground at her feet.

"See, man, I told you we should have stayed here instead of going to grab a bite to eat. It didn't feel right with Fitzgerald's car being gone."

"Anita told us to leave." Those thick fingers moved to her backside again, exploring every bit of her covered by the jeans, and again up her back over the tank top. Fire licked at her face, making her want to hide even more than she already did. Coupled with the nausea, she was surprised she could still stand.

"We should have ignored her, and, dude, I think you got the only weapon. It's not like she's wearing much."

"Oh, I know. I'm just enjoying these new curves she's put on." He gave her ass a slap, making Amelia yelp. Rough hands on her waist flipped her around so her back was to the cabin again.

"You're terrible." Blake holstered his sidearm again and cocked a brow. "What are we going to do with her?"

"I can think of a few things I'd like to do," was the licentious reply as his head dropped a little too close to her face. "How did you manage to kill them all, asset?"

The rumble of a car coming up the driveway saved her from having to answer. Scott's arm snaked around her waist as he moved her in front of him. A metal barrel appeared in her peripheral as he used her as a shield for whoever had just arrived. *How chivalrous.* A nod to his partner sent him out to investigate.

*Could this get any worse?* Her answer sauntered around the corner a minute later with a scowling Blake at his side. *Yes.*

"I leave for three hours and you two juggernauts fuck this up. How?" Tom sounded furious as he addressed the two Sentinels. He planted his feet in a wide stance, arms folded, and glowered at the man holding her. The metal disappeared from her peripheral as Scott holstered the firearm.

"Explain. Now." Tom's authoritative tone reminded her so much of his father.

*This* was the man groomed by Jonathan to take over the CRF. Had she been wrong about him? Did Tom take on the compassionate role just to put her at ease? Was all the training a trust-building exercise? If the ache in her heart was anything to go by, it worked like a charm. Because seeing him like this broke something inside of her. She'd felt hope for the first time in six years, and he'd snatched it away in an instant. Breathing became laborious as her insides crumbled into a pile of self-pity. She knew better than to trust him—she did—but somehow, he'd figured out a way under her skin.

"Someone better start talking." His smoldering gaze went to the taller Sentinel since the one at her back hadn't muttered a word.

Blake rubbed his bald head and scratched his jaw. "Well, see, Anita told us not to bother guarding since we're in the middle of nowhere, so we went to grab dinner…" He cleared his throat and cocked a blond brow at the man holding her.

"Right, well, Anita sent out the distress call, and we came back," Scott said, his meaty arm tight around her waist. He continued by outlining everything they'd done upon returning to the cabin and included a vague description of the murder scene inside. It was enough to make her skin crawl.

*I killed three people.* Getting caught by the Sentinels seemed a fitting punishment. No amount of cruelty warranted her actions. The research technicians only did as they were told. They didn't deserve to die. Anita could at least be somewhat justified, but the torture...

She shivered. No. No one deserved to be tortured.

*Those researchers tortured you,* her conscious reminded. *They got what they deserved.*

*At what cost?* she wondered. *Maybe I don't want to be that woman.*

*Maybe you already are.*

"Did you search the asset?" Tom asked, interrupting her thoughts.

"Yes," Scott replied and released her long enough to hand over the item he confiscated earlier. Then his tree trunk of an arm settled around her again. When he pulled her back more firmly against him, her butt met his groin, and he pressed back. She felt it then, his desire to do more than just fondle. Acid crept up the back of her throat, making her once again thank the heavens for skipping lunch.

Would this be her punishment? Jonathan forced her through countless forms of pain, but never rape. Everything else was fair game, but defilement remained out-of-bounds. She never understood why. He allowed all sorts of unspeakable things to be done to her, but never that. Had he reserved sexual torture for a moment such as this? She would prefer death over that fate.

"And where's Stark?" Tom asked as he slid the pistol into the waistband of his jeans. He scanned the woods as if he expected the blond Sentinel to appear out of thin air. It wouldn't surprise Amelia. She'd seen the inhuman healer pull that trick more than once in her cell.

"He's busy with Stas." Scott sounded annoyed by that. "Why did he get to train the hot Sentinel?"

Tom gave the man a droll look and changed the subject. "Have you reported in yet?"

Blake shook his head. "Not yet. We haven't finished assessing the scene, and we were in the process of securing the asset when you arrived."

Those dark brown eyes finally met hers, but only briefly. "Yes, I see that. Have you requested backup yet?"

"No need. Headquarters was notified when Anita hit the panic button on her watch." Blake's summary explained the doctor's comment regarding backup. Amelia hadn't doubted her, but wondered how she knew.

Tom gave a nod and focused those angry eyes on her. If there wasn't a solid wall of male behind her, she'd have taken a step back. "You checked her thoroughly?"

"Well, I didn't have her strip if that's what you mean." Scott's smug tones sent a tornado of unease through her stomach. "But I'd say I was pretty thorough." His hand splayed along the side of her abdomen as he spoke, and his thumb traced the underwire of her bra.

"I see. Mind if I check her again?" The smirk Tom paired with the request squeezed her heart. *This is it. The charade is done.* Why did she ever trust him? Amazing what a little kindness could do for a woman in her condition. She'd probably put faith in a goat at this point.

"I'd take that as an insult, but I don't blame you for wanting to check this one out yourself. She's a gorgeous little thing." The palm against her abdomen lifted to her breast as Scott spoke. He gave it a firm squeeze before releasing her into Tom's custody.

"Blake, why don't you call in an update? I'm sure Scott can cover me." Familiar hands grabbed her hips and pushed her up against the wall.

"Got it, boss," Blake said as he presumably pulled out his phone. Her vision was obscured by the fuming Sentinel in front of her.

"Keep your legs spread, arms above your head." Tom's commanding tone showered goosebumps down her limbs, and not the good kind. She met his cool gaze with one of her own and lifted her arms as requested. His betrayal hurt, but she wouldn't give him the satisfaction of knowing that.

Warmth spread up her side as his palms ran from her waist to the sides of her breasts. Unlike Scott, he didn't take any liberties, but kept it light and professional. His fingers trailed down the center of her sternum to her abdomen, before running over the front of her thighs. She shivered when he told her to face the house. The heat from his body confused her senses, as did the seductive hint of pine teasing her nostrils. *I cannot still be attracted to him. Not after everything.*

"Remember what I told you?" His words were a breath against her ear, so low, she barely heard him. "Element of surprise, sweetheart."

Her eyes widened. *He's helping me? Or is this another trick?*

His belt brushed her backside as he crowded her personal space. Strong fingers wrapped around her wrists as he placed her hands against the wall over her head then traced her arms down to her shoulders and lower. When he paused at her lower back, she trembled.

*What is he doing?*

Then she felt it.

The subtle sensation of metal glided against her spine as he returned her weapon. Of all the things she anticipated him doing to her, this was not it.

"Hard to let go, isn't it?" Scott's voice left a bad taste in her mouth.

Tom's tension radiated through her for a split moment, but was dispelled by a deep laugh of his own. It reminded her of fresh hot chocolate, dangerously tempting.

*Take a sip too soon, and you'll get burned.*

"Oh, you have no idea what I want to do right now." The dark humor in his tone made her pulse race. His actions probably appeared indecent to their Sentinel audience, but his hands never strayed out of bounds.

*He's making them comfortable.*

"I'm pretty sure I do," Scott replied.

Gripping her hips, Tom turned her around and slid a thigh between her legs. She clutched his shoulders and stared up into his molten chocolate eyes.

*If looks could kill...*

"Don't move" was the only warning he gave before spinning into action.

She thought the events in the bedroom moved quickly, but they were nothing compared to this.

One shot sent Scott to his knees in a howl of pain, and a second caused Blake to the drop the phone and pull a gun of his own. But the tall Sentinel wasn't fast enough.

Tom slammed his pistol into the side of Scott's skull before grabbing Blake's arm and twisting it at an awkward angle with one hand to confiscate the firearm. He threw it at Amelia's feet followed by a blade he pulled from the Sentinel's belt and a second flash of metal.

"What are you doing?" Blake gritted between his teeth.

Scott remained motionless on the ground. He was either dead or knocked out, Amelia couldn't tell.

"Not killing you," Tom replied while countering Blake's attempt at a struggle. "Look, I didn't hit anything vital, so you'll live. But keep fighting me, and you'll lose your only good arm."

Right. Because the other shoulder had a bullet put through it. Blood pooled from the wound, soiling the Sentinel's t-shirt.

Amelia gaped at them.

Blake's tall, muscular physique made him the obvious winner in this duel, but Tom controlled the bigger man with one hand around his wrist.

*Fascinating.*

"What the fuck man? What's wrong with you?"

~*~

"So many things," Tom replied. "Walk with me."

"Dude, she's in your head. Think about what you're doing."

He grunted. *Oh, trust me, thinking is all I'm doing right now.* "Let's go." Using the leverage he had on Blake's arm, Tom maneuvered his friend towards the front of the house.

He felt mildly better after putting a bullet through Scott's kneecap and pistol whipping him upside the head. Maybe it would knock some fucking sense into the bastard. It took all Tom's willpower not to shoot the asshole on the spot when he rounded the corner. Years of training held him in check until the time was right to make his move. And now that he'd pulled the trigger, he had no choice but to follow through.

"Seriously, I know you, man. This isn't you." Blake's deep voice had taken on the trained tone of a negotiator. Too bad Tom knew all the tricks.

"Maybe, maybe not." He stopped at the trunk of his sedan and used the remote in his pocket to pop it open. "Any idea why I wasn't notified of this surprise visit?" he wondered as he grabbed a handful of rope.

After receiving the page, Tom tried to call headquarters, but no one answered. He knew then that his father had played him. Why else would he send the cavalry in without warning? *A test.* One he undoubtedly failed. Who knew what Anita reported back after discovering Amelia walking freely about the cabin.

"I don't know, dude. I just did as I was told."

"Which is exactly why I'm not going to kill you for it." Tom nudged the big guy towards the other sedan in the driveway. "Where are your keys?"

"Fuck, man. What the fuck is wrong with you?"

Not an answer, and he had no desire to search the

man's pockets.

*All right, inside then.* Probably a safer place than the trunk, and if he tied the ropes right, Blake would be able to free himself. He forced the guy into the living area and bound him to the only chair in the room. All the while, Blake pleaded with Tom to *snap out of it*. He wished he could. This all felt like a nightmare come to life.

For twenty-seven years, Tom anticipated the day his father would take him under his wing and teach him more about the family legacy. Oh, he knew all along that the CRF humanitarian wing was a front for hunting and killing rogue immortals. And he approved of it because he knew firsthand the things those beings were capable of doing. But Amelia? She could hardly hurt a fly. Her captivity never felt right, but finding her beaten to a pulp had taken his distaste to a whole new level. What kind of a man could do that to a defenseless woman? Especially one as beautiful and charming as Amelia Wakefield?

John Fitzgerald wasn't a hero. He was a manipulative bastard with self-serving goals and principles that he expected Tom to follow blindly. And he did for a while because that's what he was raised to do. But then he started to question things, and the disagreements began. The most recent one regarding Stas had forced him to take action behind his father's back, which drove an even deeper wedge between them. And now, with everything he'd learned about Amelia? He had no respect left for his father.

Sending Anita to the cabin behind his back spoke of a level of distrust that could not be repaired. His father loved games, but he rarely played them with Tom. Not like this. He clearly wanted to give Anita privacy, which meant he authorized whatever she planned to do. And it couldn't have been good if it forced Amelia to kill three people.

Their father-son bond was officially severed. And any notion of repairing that bond shattered when Tom pulled the trigger on his own men. He had chosen Amelia and his freedom over the Sentinels.

There would be no coming back from this decision.

*So I'll make my own path.* He had the necessary resources to survive, at least for a little while.

"I need you to give my dad a message," Tom said as he tied the final knot around the man's ankles. The strategic combination should take the trained Sentinel twenty minutes to dismantle. Fifteen if he pushed through the pain in his right arm. The bullet had severed his tendon. A necessary move to weaken Blake's shot. The man had killer aim.

"That you've lost your motherfucking mind?" he guessed, voice flat.

Tom snorted. "Tell him I quit."

Blake shook his head. "You've fucking lost it, man."

He patted the big man's uninjured shoulder. "Just two words. I quit. Got it?"

Tom didn't wait for confirmation. No time. By his calculations, the back-up unit would arrive in thirty minutes, maybe sooner, and Scott would wake up any minute. The Sentinel wouldn't be able to do much with his shattered kneecap, unless he crawled. *Likely.* He probably should have disarmed him, but Blake was the bigger threat.

*Time to run.*

Tom grabbed his go-bag from his bedroom and paused outside the door of Amelia's room. The bloody scene unsettled his stomach. Dead bodies didn't bother him, but blood in that particular space did. An onslaught of gruesome memories threatened to overwhelm him, but he forced them away and focused on Anita Patel's corpse instead. A bullet to the stomach appeared to be the cause of death. Too easy. If what he suspected about the woman was true, then she deserved far worse. Her assistants suffered even easier fates, with one of them dying instantly from a bullet to the brain.

*Nice aim.* His chest warmed. Amelia defended herself because of the tools he gave her. It seemed those lessons were worthwhile after all.

Pulling the bag over one shoulder, he headed outside to find Amelia waiting for him with a perplexed expression near the driveway. Surely she'd figured this out by now.

"We need to get moving."

Amelia blinked those beautiful blue eyes at him. "Excuse me?"

"We have about thirty minutes at best before backup arrives, so we need to move." He demonstrated by walking towards to the car, and she followed.

"And go where?"

He put his bag in the trunk before replying, "Right, I just knocked out a Sentinel and tied another one up in the living room, and from what I understand, you killed my father's favorite researcher. We can't stand here chatting. I need you to either trust me right now or not. Up to you, but I can't wait forever. If you need anything from your room, I suggest you get it now."

Pulling a pocket knife from his jeans, he knelt to deal with the GPS locator. He knew his father used it to track him earlier. Once he saw Tom's location, he sent in the crew to assess Amelia. Which meant his dad suspected foul play. *Probably shouldn't have antagonized him so much over the phone.* Not like he could change that now.

"I don't understand," Amelia said as he located the tracker above the tire.

"Not sure how to make this any clearer," he muttered. The damn locator did not want to part ways with his car. "We're running."

"From who?"

"My father and the CRF."

"But why?"

Tom sighed and glanced up at her. "Look, this place is going to be swarming with Sentinels soon, and I don't have enough ammo or heart to take them all down. Just give me a second to remove this GPS tracker, and we'll go."

He went back to his task. *Almost there.*

"Oh, you arse!" She kicked his shoe as hard as she could, making him flinch. "Anita told me about your lie. There's no explosive."

He paused to cock an eyebrow. "Seriously? *That* is what you want to talk about right now? A white lie that kept me from having to lock you up?"

"I could have escaped weeks ago!"

"And gone where, Amelia? To the woods? Maybe for a swim in the lake?" He snorted and finished removing the device.

"That's not the point."

"It's entirely the point," he countered as he pushed off from the ground and wiped his hands on his jeans. "Look, you need to decide what you want to do. Come with me or stay. Up to you, but I'm getting the hell out of here with or without you. And honestly, without you would make it a hell of a lot easier to disappear." He added that last part to piss her off. If he got her riled up enough, maybe she'd stop thinking and do the logical thing, which would be to go with him.

Amelia gasped. "Oh! You... You... Arse!"

Tom smirked and set the GPS on the car in front of him. He turned just in time to catch her fist. "I'm trying to help you," he reminded as he lowered her arm.

She snorted. "And why should I believe you?"

*Why indeed?* "How about a gesture of good faith?"

Her fury dimmed a fraction as suspicion leaked into her gaze. "What do you mean?"

"Here." He showed her his palms before gently clasping her neck and pressing his right thumb to the side of her metal collar. Her pupils dilated as a pretty flush touched her cheeks. He wasn't sure how to interpret that. Arousal or fear? Likely the latter, so he explained why he had his hands on her. "It's genetically modified to unlock for certain biometrics at a very specific point."

Tom had researched the device after he found Amelia

in the basement. The technology intrigued him, and the cautious side of him wanted to know how it worked in case he ever found himself wearing one. None of the technicians batted an eye when he requested his credentials be added to the biometrics code. A perk to being Jonathan Fitzgerald's only son.

The metal separated with a gentle hiss that made Amelia stiffen. He carefully removed the collar from her neck and handed it to her. A faint red line marked her skin, the only indicator of the choker. He suspected it would disappear in minutes, given her immortal genes.

"You're free, Amelia. The decision is yours."

"Why?" Amelia whispered as she studied the item in her hands. He expected her to throw it or try to rip the thing apart, but she didn't. "Why are you helping me?"

"Maybe I'm helping myself." *Maybe you gave me the push I needed to finally break free.* He'd thought about it more and more over the last few months. A nagging idea in the back of his mind to run away from it all, but he didn't know where to go. *Well, I'm about to figure that out.*

"We both know I'm your best bet to get out of here." He tucked a piece of her silky hair behind her ear before cupping her cheek with one hand. "But I won't force you to come with me."

A river of emotion swam in those deep blue irises, each one pricking at his heart. He'd given up everything today for a woman he barely knew; a woman who despised his existence. Yet, despite knowing she would never trust him or care for him in any way, he didn't regret the decision. It was the right thing to do. She deserved his sacrifice, and so much more.

"If you're determined to part ways, then I suggest taking one of the cars, because you won't stand a chance on foot in these woods. When you can get to town, ditch the car and shift forms to blend in with the locals. That's the best advice I can give you." He gave her one last, searching look and sighed. "Good luck, Amelia."

He dropped his hand and got in the car.

"Wait." She grabbed the door before he could close it. Her bottom lip disappeared between her teeth, and she let it go with a huff and tossed her collar to the ground. "All right, I'll go with you," was all she said. No explanation as to why or ultimatum. But he could see in her eyes that she had a plan. Or at least the beginning of one. And he had a feeling it involved turning against him in some way.

*Oh, this should be fun.*

*Game on, sweetheart.*

# CHAPTER EIGHT

## Diversions

"What are you doing?" Amelia asked, confused. They were standing in the middle of a cinema car park after leaving their vehicle at a restaurant several blocks away.

Tom snorted. "What does it look like I'm doing?"

"Playing with wires?" she guessed.

"It's called hot-wiring, sweetheart."

Heat crept up her neck at the now-familiar endearment. *I like that far too much.* And if she was honest with herself, she'd always enjoyed it. Terms of affection were commonplace in her former life, but not this new one. Only Tom called her sweetheart, and the way he said it made her feel cherished and a teensy bit girlish. Something she never expected to experience again. It suggested that maybe not all of her personality had been erased during her six years of torment.

When he removed that collar from her neck...

No. She refused to think about how his touch had burned her in all the right ways. Completely inappropriate and never going to happen. Tom was a means to an end. She'd use him until the opportunity struck, and she'd escape. For good.

She cleared her throat and pinched her lips to the side. "This appears to be entirely too complicated. Why not use a key or go and get the car you left in the other car park?"

Molten chocolate peered up at her. "First, I don't have a key. Second, it's called a parking lot. And third, we're switching cars."

Her brow creased. "Why? Your car is in perfectly good condition."

"Yes, and owned by the CRF. Which means they'll have all electronic surveillance on this side of the continent searching..." His gaze narrowed on her breasts then widened. "Down!" he shouted as he leapt from the car and tackled her to the ground.

Pain shot up her spine, making her limbs tingle and her head spun. *What in the world just happened?* She blinked against Tom's shoulder. He held her tightly beneath him with his palm cradling the back of her skull. She couldn't see a damn thing from this angle, but her ears worked. Shattering glass and a sharp thud against the car beside them had followed his tackle. A low growl rumbled in Tom's chest as he moved above her. Those dark eyes searched her in a quick, efficient wave.

"Are you all right?" The concern in his voice made her heart flutter. She hadn't heard a tone like that directed at her in years.

She swallowed and gave a short nod. Her backside ached, but otherwise, she felt fine.

"Keep your head down," he advised as he lifted his arm. A soft crack sounded as he took out a nearby light with a bullet. Shadows fell over them as he shot out two more. She frowned as he holstered the weapon. The gunfire was nothing like the ones from earlier. These shots were nearly silent. Or were they really loud and she'd lost her hearing?

"Your white top is too bright." He went to his knees and removed his leather jacket. After shaking the glass from it, he handed it to her. "Put this on."

The command in his tone sent a shiver down her spine. She liked that voice. It oozed confidence and left her feeling safe. Which was insane considering someone had clearly been shooting at them.

Tom's position over her made shrugging into the coat difficult, but she managed. He dusted off the bag beside them and put it on his back. "I need you to do exactly what I say."

She didn't hesitate. "Okay."

He went into a crouch beside her and motioned for her to do the same. "The sniper no doubt has night vision, so we're going to need to do some clever maneuvering and hope there are no Sentinels on foot lurking around yet." He outlined the path, pointing to the cars she could see that created a route to the cinema doors. It seemed an odd plan, but he'd been right about most everything so far.

"I want you on my left, got it?" He paused, waited for her nod, then continued. "If they shoot me, keep moving. Ignore everything. Just get to that theater, shift, and blend in. Good?"

*Easier said than done.* But she didn't tell him that. He wouldn't understand. "Okay," she repeated.

He removed the pistol from his hip and gave her a nod. "On my count. Three, two, one." He moved.

She went with him, keeping low as he did, and matching his confident strides. Glass shattered in her wake, and something zipped too close to her shoulder, but she kept pace with Tom, trusting him to lead the way.

They reached the cinema as a group of people walked out, causing her to pause until Tom wrapped a sturdy arm around her lower back and pulled her into the middle of the throng. She took in his empty hand then the missing holster on his hip and frowned. Where did he hide the gun? He hadn't removed the bag from his back during their run, and his grey cotton shirt was practically glued to his muscular chest and abdomen. Did he specialize in invisibility?

He didn't give her time to ask, but maneuvered her up to the clerk and requested movie tickets. His charming grin made the blonde woman blush. Amelia's heart beat an erratic rhythm in her chest as she fought to catch her breath while he appeared unfazed and casual. How did he do that?

The red-faced attendant exchanged Tom's paper money for tickets without giving Amelia a second glance. *Probably a good thing since I feel like hell turned over.*

"Shh." Tom pressed his lips to her temple in a date-like gesture that sent butterflies dancing about in her lower belly. "Blend, Amelia. Just breathe." The words were a breath against her ear as he guided her to an unpopulated area in the cinema and through a door marked "staff only."

He turned on the light to what appeared to be a storage room and locked the door. Slipping the backpack from his shoulders, he shuffled through it and pulled out a slender electronic device.

"Frequency jammer," he explained as he flipped a switch and slipped it into his pocket. "It'll buy us some time while I figure out where they hid a tracker on you."

Her eyebrows shot up. "What? Like the one you removed from the car?"

"Exactly like that, only it'll be smaller." He pulled out a pocketknife and handed it to her. "It should be close to the surface and, if we're lucky, protruding just enough for me to feel. Take off the jacket."

She did as he requested and was surprised by how heavy the coat felt. Tom pulled the holster and gun from one of the pockets and reattached them to his hip before dropping the leather garment over his bag. Oh, well, that explained his arm around her waist. Clever man.

"Okay, so I didn't realize the CRF tagged their assets. Any idea where they put the tracker before I get started?" he wondered, eyeing her exposed arms and legs in a clinical manner.

She swallowed and shook her head. "It could be anywhere."

"Right." He kneeled and started with her left ankle. The pads of his fingers worked over her skin in tender, sure strokes, all the way up to her jean shorts. Goosebumps danced along her calves and thighs as heat pooled in her lower belly.

It'd been a long time since a man touched her with such care. His strong hands were so different from Eli's soft caresses. He was always afraid he might break her, a side effect of his inherent ability to kill through touch. Eli could never lose control around her, or he risked her life.

Tom didn't have that problem. He handled her with self-assurance and didn't seem at all fearful of hurting her. She wondered how that type of boldness would be applied in the bedroom. Would he allow her to explore him? To lick him? She always craved that with Eli, but his gift required ultimate control, and he never let her touch him as she wanted. Would it be like that with Tom, or would he control her in a different way?

Warmth crept up her neck and into her cheeks. How inappropriate could she be? Men outside were trying to kill her or, worse, capture her alive. And they were surrounded by bathroom essentials. Nothing about this situation could be defined as sexy or even remotely appealing, apart from the hands sliding up her side. Tom stayed on his knees before her as he lifted the hem of her shirt to explore the lower half of her stomach. He went to her hips on both sides then turned her around to repeat the action on her lower back.

Foreign sensations built between her thighs, making her want to squirm. His thorough touch did things to her she hadn't felt in a very long time; things she never expected to ever feel again. *I'm obviously on the verge of a fit.*

He stood behind her and slid her shirt upwards to examine her spine then lowered the fabric before moving onto her shoulder blades. Would he fondle her breasts next? Butterflies danced in her belly, making her flush hotter. Strong hands slid up her bare arms to her neck and paused at the base of her scalp. His thumb pressed something that tingled. "Should have gone from top to bottom." He held out his palm for the pocketknife, and she gave it to him. "This is going to sting."

Her subtle nod urged him to continue. A minor slice of the blade wouldn't compare to Anita's version. He wrapped his fingers around the front of her neck and puffed out a breath that tickled her exposed shoulders. The sharp point pierced her tender skin below her hairline and was gone quicker than she expected. Tom blew on the abrasion, as if would remove the pain.

"I'd give you a Band-Aid, but I know you'll heal in a minute." The palm against her throat tightened in a tender way before he let go. She turned as he shrugged on his jacket and a baseball cap from the bag. The tracker must have gone into the pocket of his jeans.

"Can you shift clothes or just, uh, skin?" he asked as he pulled on his backpack.

"Humanoid appearance," she corrected. "And no, clothes are not part of the process."

"Right." He rubbed the back of his neck, and stared at his shoes. "Okay, the sniper means a full unit hasn't arrived yet, but is close. My guess is Greg jumped the gun, because he's the only one I know incapable of handling a rifle. Which means we're about to be surrounded. So we put the tracker on someone else and wait it out. They might anticipate that, but they'll also expect us to run. Staying here is the worst idea, and therefore, the one thing they won't consider."

She gathered from his conversational tone that he was conversing with himself and not her, so she remained silent.

"Right. Let's find a movie to watch." He held out his hand, and she eyed it with curiosity. "We're on a date, sweetheart. Act the part."

~*~

Tom expected Amelia to shift forms at the earliest opportunity and leave him to handle the Sentinels alone. He wouldn't blame her. It's what he would do in her situation. But she stayed by his side, holding his hand, and went into the nearest theater without comment. He left her there with his bag and went into the busy lobby area to deal with the locator.

Weekend nights at the movie theater yielded large crowds, something he worked to his advantage as he identified the appropriate target. Someone with a similar build to Amelia, but surrounded by a lot of people. He didn't want to get the person hurt and knew the Sentinels wouldn't attack a crowd. Especially a large group of females.

There, a brunette with shapely legs and a tiny waist. She would do and seemed to be on a girl's night out. Their proximity to the bathroom near the exit indicated they were getting ready to leave as well. *Excellent.* He scanned the room for faces he recognized and, finding none, approached the target.

"Carol?" He tapped the woman on the shoulder and feigned an apologetic expression when she turned around. Her bag bumped his leg, giving him the opportunity to drop the tracker inside. "Oh, I'm so sorry. I thought you were this girl I used to date in college, which isn't awkward at all, is it?" He gave a little chuckle he knew women found endearing and shook his head. "Sorry to interrupt, ladies."

Giggles broke out at the smile he flashed them, and a few of them flushed. He gave them all a charming grin and turned before anyone could engage him in conversation. Once he reached the hallway, he flipped the frequency jammer off and searched for any lurking Sentinels. *Still alone.* It proved his suspicion that Greg operated without thinking through his actions. Tom never thought he'd be thankful for the idiot's career aspirations. His superiors would be pissed when they found out. *Poor bastard.*

Tom opened the door to the theater and found Amelia where he left her in the third row from the back. *Why hasn't she shifted yet?* It seemed the most reasonable defense mechanism and would help her hide. The CRF would never find her without the locator. He slid into the chair on her right side—a position where he could see the door best—and returned the jammer to his bag. The pack had all his favorite toys and remained ready at all times. A man in his position never knew when he'd have to run, like he did today. But it would only last them a few days, which was why they needed a car.

He slid an arm around Amelia's shoulders and pressed his lips to her ear. "Tracker is placed, and no sign of anyone yet. How's the movie?" It appeared to be a romantic comedy of sorts, but his pseudo date didn't seem very amused.

"I've been too busy wondering whether or not you'd be back to focus on it."

He grinned against her neck. "Aww, you were worried about me. That's sweet."

"Arse." She elbowed his side, but his leather jacket acted as a cushion and took the brunt of her move. Some of the tension tightening her limbs seemed to disappear with the playful jab, making her relax a little into the chair beside him. "What now?" she whispered.

"We wait and hope this movie lasts another sixty minutes or so." Otherwise, they would be hopping theaters, and that would appear suspicious on security feeds. Baseball caps weren't the best disguise—even if this one was for a team he would never be caught dead supporting. And his leather jacket looked out of place in the summer heat, but he needed it to conceal his firearm. At least Amelia could change physical appearance. He doubted they would think twice about her white tank top and jean shorts.

Light seeped in from the hall as someone opened the door and stepped inside. A lone male without a date in this particular theater stuck out like a sore thumb. That was why Tom chose it, so he would have ample warning.

"I need you to shift, Amelia. Right now." He should have told her to do that the second he sat down. Hell, he should have recommended it as soon as they entered the theater.

She blinked at him. "What?"

"Change your hair, or something. Now."

"I... I... Why?"

The Sentinel at the back of the theater started forward, eyes scanning. *Fuck.* Not enough time to explain why or push the point. Tom did the only thing he could think to do and kissed her. Hard.

She tried to pull back, but he tightened his hold on her shoulders and fisted his hand in her hair to keep her in place. Making a scene would get them both caught, and he had no intention of letting that happen. He wrapped his free hand around one of her wrists and placed it on his upper arm. When he moved to grab the other, she surprised him by pressing it to his stomach beneath his coat. If her goal was to find his firearm and shoot him with it, then she had the wrong side. But he'd let her figure that out for herself.

He angled her head to give him a better view of the walkway. The tall man—definitely a Sentinel—stood a few rows in front of them. *Excellent.* Public displays of affection made people uncomfortable. They never wanted to get caught staring, so their natural reaction to kissing couples was to turn away. In this case, it worked like a charm. Tom just had to maintain the charade. He kept his body relaxed and his eyes mostly closed, but remained alert. Then Amelia returned the kiss and blasted his plan to hell.

Her lips softened beneath his as a soft moan slipped from her mouth. And damn if that wasn't the sexiest sound he'd ever heard. Fuck. If this was her idea of playing along, she needed to tone it down a bit, because he couldn't focus with her reacting like that. She derailed his resolve by running her hand up his arm to the back of his neck. Exploring her body in the closet without misbehaving had been hard enough. Her caressing him while they kissed? He considered himself a good man, but even that would tempt a saint to sin.

The palm on his abdomen slid to his hip as Amelia shifted closer. He should have put the armrest down before putting his arm around her earlier. But no way could he have anticipated her doing this. Her breasts felt like heaven against his chest, and her hand was far too close to his groin. *Shit.* He needed to regain control of the situation, because if she got any closer, she'd be straddling him, and he couldn't be held liable for his response to that.

He grabbed her shoulder to force her back when her tongue slipped into his mouth. *So tentative and sweet...* He had half a brain to check the aisle again just as the Sentinel left the theater. *Thank fuck for that.* With what little remained of his restraint, he pulled a hairsbreadth away and swallowed his tongue. The bright arousal in her gaze slammed into his gut and pulled everything tight down below. It had to be a trick of the lighting in the theater. No way she desired him. Not after everything she'd be through.

"The, uh, Sentinel is gone," he managed in a whisper.

"Sentinel?" she repeated.

"Yeah, he's gone."

She blinked again. "Oh. That's why...?"

"Yeah, sorry. You wouldn't shift, so I, uh, yeah." He cleared his throat. Talk about awkward. "Sorry," he repeated, looking away.

"I don't understand."

Right. It seemed like a natural course of action to him, but wouldn't to a person without field training. He pressed his lips to her ear and kept his voice low to avoid any unwanted attention. "Most people avoid public displays of affection because they don't want to get caught staring. Kissing you kept him from studying us long enough to recognize us."

When she didn't say anything, he pulled back to examine her expression. A blank expression replaced the earlier arousal, which confirmed his thought that the light in here had tricked him. *Damn.*

"Then next time I'll shift."

"Good. That would be easier." *And far less enticing.*

She gave him a stiff nod and focused on the movie ahead. "Right. Let me know when we're allowed to leave."

Her flat tone prickled at his conscience. He'd hurt her somehow. Because he kissed her? He shouldn't have done that, but what choice did he have? At least he held his passion in check. Even now with his arm around her stiff shoulders, he felt a pull to take her. Fire licked through his veins as a deep-seated need settled in his lower abdomen. His attraction had gotten worse, not better, and he knew he didn't deserve her. Not after everything she'd been through.

He vowed to get her to safety, even if it killed him, because he owed her that much. Allowing his father to continue her captivity after discovering her was unacceptable. He should have put a stop to it, but he ignored his instincts. And now he'd kissed her. *I'm an asshole.* She wouldn't want him, not after everything, and he'd practically forced himself on her. An apology wouldn't cut it.

He ran a hand over his face and tried to focus on the

movie, but couldn't. Shooting something would help get his mind off of it. Maybe he should go out and play with some Sentinels. But no, those were his colleagues. Rather, his former friends. He couldn't shoot to kill any of them without due cause. The majority of them were just doing their jobs. Even Scott, though Tom would argue he more than deserved that pistol whip to the head.

*I'm a fucking mess.*

Understatement of the century. Whatever. He'd keep his shit together long enough to get Amelia to Hydria. Then he'd let fate take over.

The movie flashed by in a blur neither of them seemed to enjoy. A hazard of knowing what waited for them outside. By the time it ended, Tom had formulated a plan of action. He estimated a fifty percent success rate at that, and it hinged on the Sentinels having split up to follow the tracker.

"We're going to move with that group," he whispered, gesturing to a large crowd in the middle that had started walking up the aisle. "And if you can at least change your hair color, that would be great."

She glared at him. "It's not as easy as flipping a switch, you know."

*It's not?* His father's abilities triggered automatically. Amelia should be able to shift on demand as well, but maybe it took more energy? "Okay, can you put it in a bun or something?"

Her movements were stiff as she refashioned her ponytail into a messy array of brown curls. Somehow it was more alluring like this and not the least bit inconspicuous. "Blonde would be better." Or a duller color. Her dark, luscious waves were too memorable.

She narrowed her gaze. "I'm not going to change on command just because you prefer blonde hair."

*Stubborn woman.* He preferred her hair, but that was neither here nor there. The passing group meant they didn't have time to argue. He wrapped his arm around her shoulders to pull her forward without a word.

"Loosen up," he murmured against her temple. It felt like walking with a robot, and they needed to resemble a couple on a date. If anything his words caused her to stiffen more. This wasn't going to work. They'd stand out in a crowd moving like this, and her beauty already made her more noticeable than the average woman. At the next theater, he pulled her inside the door and thanked heaven above for the vacant room. The lights were low, but not off, and commercials scrolled silently over the large screen. Given the late hour, he doubted a new movie would be showing in this theater any time soon.

"Amelia, I need you to calm down, or we're never going to get out of here." As it was, he already needed to formulate a new plan because the crowd was long gone. Maybe they could wait until another theater released in a few minutes? The emergency exit door at the back would be their last resort. He had no idea if it would trip an alarm, not to mention the Sentinels waiting outside. That'd be the first place he'd put a man on a stakeout.

"Talk to me," he murmured when she said nothing. "What's wrong?"

"I can't shift." Big blue eyes met his, and what he saw nearly broke his heart. Terror mingled with something darker in those oceanic depths, causing his stomach to flip over with unease.

"What do you mean?"

"I... The last time... I couldn't." She nibbled her bottom lip and dropped her gaze. "Anita," she whispered. "She did something to keep me from shifting, and it worked."

His hands fisted at his sides as the urge to hit someone overwhelmed all reason. His father had allowed this type of experimentation? A way to block Hydraian and Ichorian genetics beyond the metal collar? What the fuck was he thinking? He had to know how that would bite everyone in the ass, himself included. *Did they ever do something to me without my knowledge?* There wasn't time to think about that. This was about Amelia.

"Is it permanent?" He kept his voice low to hide the fury boiling beneath the surface.

"I don't know, but I'm afraid to try." Her soft, defeated tones killed a part of him. How had he let this happen?

"How long?" he wondered. "How long did it go on?"

"What do you mean?" Confusion trickled in to replace the sadness in her gaze.

"The experiments. How long did they go on?"

She blinked. "The entire time."

"Why didn't you say anything?" The question tumbled out of him without thought. Even if she had said something to him, what could he have done? His father would have waved him off with a reminder about staying in line. It'd been a miracle Tom had been able to convince him to let Amelia go to the cabin, and even then, it'd been Stark's input his dad had listened to most.

"Say anything?" she repeated, her brow furrowed. "I wouldn't give Jonathan the satisfaction of a response of any kind. He'd only use it against me."

"What did Anita do to you at the cabin?" he wondered and regretted it the second he saw the horror trickle back into her expression. *Nothing good.* "Actually, don't answer that. We don't have time and need to get out of here. Can you relax a little and follow my lead?"

The fear melted as she studied him with an intensity that set his soul on fire. He liked this look so much more than the wounded one. The wheels ticked behind those sapphire eyes as she formulated some sort of plan. It intrigued him.

*What are you plotting now, sweetheart?* He liked a good challenge, and he had a feeling Amelia would provide him just that.

"All right," she murmured. "Tell me what to do."

*Gladly.*

# CHAPTER NINE

## Official Resignation

Amelia's heart raced. She couldn't believe she'd told Tom about her inability to shift. The last time she tried left her feeling empty inside, like a key part of her was missing. She couldn't go through that again without breaking. To be able to do something for centuries, and have that ripped away from her was like forgetting how to breathe.

His arm felt solid against her shoulders as he maneuvered into a hallway crowd. They'd waited for the theater beside them to open before blending into the throng. Tom's presence kept her moving. He seemed so self-assured that she couldn't help but trust him in this situation.

On her own, she wouldn't last a day. She had no phone, no identity, no money, and no way to contact anyone. In Hydria, she used supernatural resources to reach out to friends and family. If she wanted to see her brother or father, she asked Jacque to teleport her to them. Now she had no way of phoning anyone because she didn't know their numbers. And she couldn't tell Jacque where to find her because she didn't know her location.

Never had she felt so hopeless and idiotic in her life. She could finally escape, but didn't have the means or wherewithal to do so. How childlike could she be? Here she was centuries old and unable to fend for herself. Tom had taught her more about defense in the last few weeks than her family and friends did in a lifetime. Her prim and proper former self didn't need to learn such things. How the new Amelia longed to knock some sense into her previous version. *You dolt, how could you go through life so blind?*

"This way." Tom's lips against her ear sent a shiver down her spine. He'd kissed her with that mouth, and it had melted her down to her toes. Too bad it hadn't meant a damn thing to him. A simple diversion to keep them hidden. She wanted to thank him for that, but her palm itched to slap him.

That kiss had unraveled her. Eli never touched her like that. He treated her like a vase he might break; Tom ravaged her. He handled her with the confidence of a man who took what he wanted when he wanted it. And to know that it had all been for show both angered and intrigued her. If his controlled touch could do that to her, then what would it be like to truly kiss him?

She trembled at the thought. It was best she didn't find out, or she may never be able to carry out her plans. He had to remain a means to an end, or she might never return home. Because she had a feeling the woman she'd become wouldn't belong there. She belonged with him.

The crowd started to dissipate around them as they reached the car park. Tom veered them to the left with two other couples and kept an easy smile on his face that warmed her inside. If the grin met his chocolate eyes, then she'd be in trouble. They paused as one of the couples said good night. It seemed a strange place to lurk, but she liked the way Tom pulled her into a hug and kissed her temple. He massaged the back of her neck and slid his lips to her cheek then back to her ear.

"Don't scream," he whispered.

She had no idea what he had planned until his hand swung into the neck of the guy in front of them. Amelia's hand flew to her mouth as a tiny yelp of surprise darted out. Thankfully, it was too soft for his date to hear; she had already walked out of eyesight. The guy rocked backwards, and Tom caught him with his free arm to ease his fall to the ground.

"He'll wake up with a headache later, but he'll be fine," he whispered as he fished a set of keys from the guy's jeans. "Sorry, buddy." He clicked one of the remote buttons and smiled when the car beside them lit up. "Okay, I don't feel as bad since he didn't bother walking his date to her car. Bad form, kid."

Amelia gaped at him. "Seriously?"

"What? I can be chivalrous when I want to be."

She sputtered. "You're going to give an unconscious man dating advice whilst stealing his car?"

He shrugged those big shoulders and set his bag in the backseat. "Well, someone had to do it. Hop in, sweetheart. I'll even close the door for you."

She eyed the messy interior and scrunched her nose. The old Amelia would never agree to this. The new one, however, recognized they didn't have a lot of options. She brushed some stray crumbs off the seat and climbed in then watched in the rearview mirror as Tom carried the blond kid to the sidewalk near the building. He set him down with a tenderness Amelia hadn't expected from him and started to jog back towards her, but stopped at a car one aisle over. Had he forgotten where he left her?

She put her hand on the door, but froze when glass

shattered beside Tom. *Oh, God.* Her eyes darted left to where he stood a second ago.

He was gone.

~*~

Tom knew their exit had gone too smoothly. He felt eyes on him the second he hit the sidewalk. It didn't appear that they'd seen the car he dropped Amelia in, which was his only saving grace. Protecting her while trying not to kill his former colleagues would be nearly impossible. At least this way she remained safe while he dealt with three—make that four—Sentinels.

His instincts flared a second before the glass shattered beside him. The shot barely missed his shoulder when he ducked. He picked up the bullet shell and snorted. Apparently, it was shoot first, ask questions later. His father knew killing him wouldn't be permanent, but his teammates didn't know that. Tom had kept his fledgling status secret from the majority of the unit, but maybe his dad had let the cat out of the bag. Or his teammates wanted to assassinate him for betraying the cause. Either way, not good.

He rolled to his side to get between the row of cars and chose a new set farther away from Amelia to duck between. He hoped like hell she stayed in the car. If she got out, this would go south fast. With a pistol in one hand, he crept forward and ducked around the hood to put himself closer to the sidewalk again. The quad were no doubt trying to surround his last position, which meant he needed to get outside of the circle.

Subtle movement near the van at his right forced him to pause. Blake's hulking shoulders appeared as he zeroed in on Tom's original location. Whoever shot at him probably thought he'd made contact and sent the tall man to confirm. Or, knowing Blake, he volunteered for the job. The bastard should be in a hospital room recovering, not performing reconnaissance with a bum shoulder. *Stubborn ass.*

Tom slipped around the opposite side of the oversized vehicle and swept out his leg to take down the top heavy Sentinel. Blake went down with a surprised oomph, but came up fighting. Tom anticipated his moves and snagged the tall man in a chokehold from behind on the ground. He locked his legs around the Sentinel's waist to keep him still and bear hugged the shit out of him.

"Sorry, man," he murmured as Blake tried futilely to knock him off his back. Tom took a few elbows to the side, but his high pain tolerance kept him from flinching. His rib would be bruised later, which was the least he deserved for this. His friend tried a final jab, but the effect lacked passion. It was his final move before passing out. Tom checked the Sentinel's pulse, felt it slowing, and let go.

Snagging the handcuffs from his unconscious buddy's belt, he secured one end to the big guy's wrist and the other to his opposite ankle. That would keep him busy for a bit when he woke up. But just in case, Tom robbed the man of his guns and knife and added them to his personal collection. He might need them to take out the other three. His final move was to steal the man's earpiece and microphone.

"Gentleman," Tom greeted after assembling the communication unit. "Blake sends his regards. Who wants to dance next?" Knowing his words would reveal his location, he moved deeper into the parking lot on the other side, away from the sidewalk and farther from Amelia. He really hoped she'd been smart enough to hide in the car and not try to find him.

"Hello, son," his father replied. "You mind telling me what the fuck you're doing?"

John Fitzgerald using curse words brought a smile to Tom's face. He'd thoroughly pissed off the CRF's CEO enough that he had lost his cool over the communication channel. Nice. How far could he push him?

"Right now?" Tom asked, voice low. "I'm taking out your unit. Or did you mean in general?" A flash of metal grabbed his attention. Sentinel Charlie was in a crouch position thirty feet to his left and facing the wrong direction.

Tom shook his head. How many times had he told the man to watch his six? *Idiot*. He took a detour around a few cars to sneak up on his former teammate while John spoke.

"The asset is messing with your head, son. You need to come in so we can fix the issue."

Tom suppressed a snort at that plan. *Fixing the issue* no doubt equated to torture and eventual death by brainwashing techniques. Because Tom was built not to break, and his father knew that better than anyone.

He slammed his pistol into the back of Charlie's skull and sighed as the man went down. "Well, that wasn't even any fun," he said. "You really ought to send Charlie back to training, John. He still hasn't mastered surveillance."

He purposely used his father's first name instead of Dad or sir because he knew it would piss the man off. The pause on the other end told him it worked. He pictured his old man sitting behind his massive desk at headquarters, pinching the bridge of his nose while taking steadying breaths. All those years of creating the devoted father-son charade down the drain. *Too bad, so sad.*

"Think about what you're doing, Thomas."

"Oh, trust me, that's all I'm doing." He heard the shuffle behind him just in time to turn and block the fist coming at his head. "Seriously, Justin. Shoot me next time." Because he would have taken Tom down, but instead, the younger man had let his emotions drive him into a hand-to-hand fight he would never win.

The juvenile Sentinel went for a kick next. Tom caught the foot one-handed and twisted it hard to the left to expose his teammate's back. He slammed his palm into the center of the kid's spine and brought his knee up to connect with Justin's face when he keeled over. He had the guy in a headlock position a second later.

"Assss," Justin hissed as he clawed at the forearm around his throat.

"I love you, too, buddy," Tom murmured as the man lost consciousness. He handcuffed him in a similar fashion to Blake and sighed. "Did you leave all the trainees at the theater, John? Should I expect to see Stas next?" Because that would be rich. He had no idea what his father planned to tell the new female Sentinel about this.

*And Lizzie...*

*Oh, fuck.* He hadn't even thought about the girl he loved like a sister. Tom rubbed his chest on reflex. All of his decisions today were made in such haste that he hadn't considered the repercussions for his friends and family. What would John tell them? That Tom died overseas while on a humanitarian mission? Oh, he'd no doubt enjoy reaping the benefits and rewards that resulted in news like that. Scholarship funds and memorial services would be enacted in his son's honor, granting him unlimited access to money he did not need.

Tom shook his head and started hunting the fourth Sentinel. He knew at least four searched for him, because he'd seen them while leaving. They'd looked right over him, or so he thought. Obviously, someone had recognized him since the unit had relocated to the parking lot. Which told him there might be a fifth man out here. Had he seen Amelia? If yes, they would have snagged her from the car already, and knowing John, he'd have said something about it. So she must be safe. For now. Too bad telepathy wasn't one of her abilities.

A fresh surge of fury lit his blood on fire at the reminder of her immortal talents and how Anita had taken away her ability to shift. He bit his tongue to keep from saying something to the man who no doubt authorized that experiment. Did his father know the results? If yes, then he knew Amelia couldn't change her appearance. But he sent some of his men after the tracker, which indicated uncertainty. Maybe the research wasn't permanent?

The crack of a bullet several yards away had him ducking on instinct. Two more shots followed in quick succession as Greg's deep voice rumbled over the line. "Asset seven is down."

Tom's heart stopped. No. *No.* He left her in a safe place. Why the hell did she move? What was she thinking? The direction of the gunfire made no logical sense from their position. Running towards the crowds and the movie theater was a safer bet than going to the back of the lot near the road. She'd be an open target there, even with her trademark circle running.

He frowned. *Circles.* Several weeks together had taught him a few things about Amelia, specifically in regards to her movements. She wouldn't have gone that way. He knew in his gut that she would have crossed over to the opposite line of cars and headed North, not South. But the Sentinels wouldn't know that. They could only guess where Tom left her, and in this case, they'd guessed wrong. He'd purposely picked a car near her, knowing his former team would assume he'd run in the opposite direction of her to keep her safe. Hence, the location they chose for *shooting* her. Clever bastards.

"She better not be dead," he growled, pretending to play into his father's trap. If they thought he was heading towards the murder scene, that left his path to Amelia open. Assuming she still sat in the car.

"Don't tell me you care about her and that's what all this is about." His father sounded so disappointed. That voice used to eat at Tom's conscience. Now it only pissed him off. Why he ever admired this man was beyond him.

"Tell me, John. Are all your Sentinels aware of the experiments you're running on them to enhance their genetics? Or did they all volunteer for that?" He knew the answer, but wanted the old man to squirm a little.

"I don't know what you're talking about."

"No? Shall I refresh your memory then?" He approached the car he left Amelia in and felt a surge of relief when a pair of blue eyes gazed up from inside. She'd squeezed herself between the glovebox and the passenger seat. Smart girl. He pressed a finger to his lips as he slid into the driver's seat and motioned for her to stay put. If one of them caught sight of him driving off, he didn't want them to know Amelia was with him.

"All those vaccines you force everyone to get. Some of them are genetic enhancers, right? Things your little lab technicians developed from Hydraian and Ichorian DNA. I'm going to take your silence as recollection or, perhaps, shock that I know about it. You know, there are benefits to being John Fitzgerald's son. You'd be surprised what the technicians were willing to talk about in my presence."

Although they never answered his questions about what they did to Lizzie Watkins, something he had hoped to research more prior to tendering his resignation. But it seemed that wouldn't be happening. Helping his childhood friend would be his number one priority after he finished assisting Amelia. From what little he knew about Lizzie's involvement with the CRF, they considered her important and had no plans to harm her. Yet.

He pressed a button to mute his microphone. Let his father mull over that for a moment while he escaped. He threw his cap into the backseat with his leather jacket and dug around for anything that would act as a disguise. Sunglasses, no. What appeared to be a few day old leftovers, yuck. Then he spotted a beanie. It pained him to pull the thing over his head because God knew where it had been, but the hipster guise would help. He paired it with the fake blocky glasses he found in the door cupholder. If Amelia's expression was anything to go by, he looked like a fool. Good.

He un-muted the line long enough to ask, "Speechless, John?" and turned on the car.

"Is that why you're acting out? Because of something a technician told you? Because I'm disappointed. I thought we were closer than that."

Tom snorted. *Right.* He was a toy soldier in his father's game, one who had grown a brain of his own and started to misbehave. Their relationship was irreparable at this point.

"Come on, son. If you give yourself up now, we can talk about this and clear up whatever misunderstandings there are between us. I shouldn't have put you on this babysitting mission. That's clear to me now, and I apologize."

He pressed the button and asked, "Yeah, and what about Amelia? Why did you kill her?" The car idled quietly enough that they wouldn't be able to hear the engine while he spoke, but he had to keep it muted otherwise. Which he did.

Tom pulled out of the parking spot with a casual ease and headed toward the exit. There would no doubt be Sentinels in place, but the majority of them would be waiting near the trap. He deepened his voice when he mentioned Amelia to indicate his displeasure over her supposed murder. Let them think he was on his way to investigate and seek retribution.

"They used normal bullets, not the incendiary kind. She's fine, but your unnecessary concern for her is disconcerting, son. Have you forgotten our history with the Wakefields?"

*She's not her brother,* Tom wanted to say. But he needed to focus on getting out of the parking lot without notice. He pushed the glasses up the bridge of his nose and slouched in the bucket seat. Snagging a cigarette from the pack on the dash, he put it in his mouth unlit and drove the car single handed. Amelia's snort of disgust amused him. Good to know she approved of his disguise.

"I hope your silence means you're reconsidering whatever foolishness you have planned," his father continued. "We both know the CRF is your home. Where else would you go?"

He tightened his hand on the steering wheel. This line of bullshit had haunted him since childhood. As a kid, he believed every word and had nightmares about the bad men hunting him. But his father always saved him, because he loved Tom more than anything, and vowed to keep him safe from the evil in this world. No one else would ever want him because of his Ichorian genetics.

If anyone excelled at brainwashing, it was John Fitzgerald. And to an extent, his impact on Tom still held true today. Because he knew deep down that Hydria would turn him away and the Conclave would murder him on sight. He had nowhere to go, but that didn't make the CRF home, either.

Tom exited the parking lot without incident and kept an eye on his mirrors for anyone tailing him. *So far, so good.*

"If she told you Hydria would welcome you, she's lying," John added after a tense moment of silence. "Lucian will kill you on sight just for being a Sentinel, and if he doesn't get to you first, one of the Elders will do it for him. You won't be accepted there."

He pressed the button and murmured, "I'm not naive, John. Amelia didn't promise me anything."

"Then you agree we should have a conversation about this, and that what you've done is wrong."

"No, unfortunately, we don't agree, John. We don't agree at all. But you know, something's been bugging me, actually. Mind if we chat about that instead?"

"Sure." *Oh, one-word answers.* John Fitzgerald must be on the verge of a meltdown. Tom wondered if he was sitting in his office at corporate or in the car in route to the theater. Either way, he felt certain his father wasn't in the theater parking lot. There would have been a lot more Sentinels. And senior ones, like Stark.

"Greg, you mentioned the asset was down. Just curious, what did she look like? Because I put Amelia on a bus to the airport two hours ago, so I'm thinking you got the wrong girl. You might want to check that out." Let them stew on that for a bit. Of course, once they pulled the security feeds at the cinema, they would figure out the lie. But it would buy them a few hours head start, and by then, he'd be finished with this car.

"Oh, I'm sorry," he continued after a moment of silence. "You all probably thought I was on my way to investigate the scene for myself. My bad, truly. I just didn't feel like hanging around. This has all been enlightening, though, guys. I think I might miss this a little. Or maybe not." He rolled down the window to his left as he maneuvered onto the freeway and unsnapped the communication unit from his ear.

"Oh hey, *Dad*, one final thing," he said into the microphone. "Not sure whether or not Blake gave you my message, so I'll go ahead and repeat it now. Consider this my formal resignation." He tossed the equipment out the window and smiled. "I quit."

# CHAPTER TEN

## Waterworks

"We're sleeping here?" Amelia didn't mind the hotel room's crude furnishings or the questionable carpet, but she did mind the single bed. How would she explain her preference for the floor?

"I know it's a dump, but the good places require a credit card, and all mine are flagged at the moment," Tom replied.

He dropped his leather jacket and bag on an old chair and stretched his arms over his head. The grey t-shirt lifted to reveal a sliver of his toned abdomen. Amelia tried not to stare, but couldn't help herself. His body was a work of art. And she had to share a room with him. At least she knew the attraction wasn't mutual. He kissed her earlier as a diversion, not because he wanted to.

*Why am I even thinking about this?* There was no future between them. For six years, she craved her freedom, and to be reunited with her family. That was what she needed to worry about, not how Tom felt or what happened at the cinema.

*He's just a means to an end.*

*Keep telling yourself that.*

"Here." Tom pulled a shirt from his bag with a pair of boxer shorts and set them on the bed. "We'll get more clothes and supplies tomorrow. For now, we need to sleep."

The clock agreed with him. Was it just this morning that they were training outside by the lake? It felt like a lifetime ago.

*I killed three people less than twenty-four hours ago.* Ice trickled through her veins. She'd been so consumed with escaping that she'd pushed this afternoon's events from her mind. But now that they were settling down to rest, the emotions came back with a force that left her queasy.

She grabbed the clothes from the bed and headed to the washroom without a word. Her insides heaved as she closed the door. She had a split second thought to turn on the shower to mask the noise before emptying her stomach into the toilet. A deep ache settled in her gut as she slid down the wall behind her. Now that the adrenaline had worn off, everything hit her at once.

For years, she fantasized about killing Anita Patel. That woman had done unfathomable things to her. There was no question the doctor deserved her fate. But pulling the trigger today had changed Amelia on a fundamental level. She despised weapons in her former life and had chastised Eli about his fondness for them on multiple occasions. And today she used one to kill not one, but three people.

"Who am I?" she whispered. Maybe Jonathan had broken her after all, because the woman she used to be wouldn't recognize the person she'd become. A killer.

Her insides heaved again, but nothing was left in her

stomach. She leaned over the porcelain siding of the bath to turn the shower to a cooler setting and disrobed on the ground. Part of her acknowledged the filthy surroundings, but it was the fate she deserved. She crawled into the tub and curled into the ball while icy pellets rained over her. It did little to calm her heated skin, but helped dispel the nausea.

Not for the first time, she questioned her sanity. How did this become her life? Freedom tasted so sweet, yet so incredibly bitter. Home seemed a forbidden dream. Everyone would expect the old Amelia, not this new, hideous version of herself. What would Issac think? Lucian? Her heart ached at the thought of their disapproval. They would loathe her actions.

*Amelia, the murderer,* her subconscious whispered. That's what they would call her. Pity and disgust would color their expressions and destroy what little was left of her heart.

She hiccupped and shuddered. The tears wouldn't stop, and the ache deep inside consumed her very being. A black hole appeared above her, swallowed her whole, and refused to let go. She wasn't sure that she cared. It seemed a long time coming. Why not take her now?

Reality mingled with another plane of being. She'd found this place long ago during one of Anita's more infamous visits. It took her deep within her soul where no one and nothing could harm her and pain no longer existed. Darkness swirled around her here, but she embraced it. Loved it, even.

The nothingness made her feel numb.

Alone.

Fearless.

She curled deeper into the safe place, determined to hide forever. *Finally.*

A hot brand replaced the cold droplets on her shoulder, making her tremble in confusion. Warmth didn't exist here, or it shouldn't. Her frozen haven seemed to thaw around the edges as twinges of light threatened at the corners of her conscious.

*No.*

She clawed desperately at the dark space, begging it to let her stay.

*I'm not ready to leave yet.*

To not feel after years of excruciating pain...

*I can't go back to that.*

*Don't make me feel again.*

"Amelia." Her name drifted in and out of her thoughts. "You're okay," the deep voice told her. Oh, she liked that voice. It soothed her. She settled deeper into her safe place as he continued talking, telling her over and over again that everything would be all right.

*You're safe,* he repeated. *I'm here.*

*Eli?* she wondered. No. That didn't feel right.

*Tom...*

Heat enveloped her, as did a calming woodsy scent she rather enjoyed. Amelia nuzzled into the warmth and felt hard bands tighten around her. A sense of security washed over her, making her sigh. Another dream, no doubt. She had a lot of those and always woke to the horrors of her life. Except this time, she couldn't recall falling asleep. Her brow creased. She couldn't remember falling into bed, either, which explained the hard tile beneath her. But that didn't explain the water.

"Amelia," the deep voice murmured. "Come on, sweetheart. Talk to me."

Fingers combed through her hair, tracing a line down her bare spine and back up her arm. When the palm cupped her cheek, she leaned into the welcoming warmth. It'd been too long since someone had touched her in a gentle way that she wasn't sure how to respond other than to embrace it. Eli used to treat her like porcelain that might break, while the other men in her life held her on this invisible pedestal that she never quite understood. The male holding her in the tub gripped her with a foreign ferocity that made her feel secure and cherished.

She blinked at the absurdity of it all and found herself staring at a grey shirt. A warm palm held the back of her head to a hard chest, and a pair of wet jeans were beneath her. The water had gone from cold to hot and fell over them in a refreshing wave that thawed the chill from her limbs. She relaxed into the comfort of Tom's arms until understanding kickstarted her heart. *I'm naked.*

"Shh," Tom pressed his lips to her temple and tightened his hold when she tried to leap out of the tub. "I'm not trying to hurt you, sweetheart. But you scared the shit out of me."

Her limbs locked around her knees in an effort to keep everything hidden, but he had to have seen an eye full already. Not to mention, he wasn't the first Sentinel to see her nude.

*Supervised showers.*

She slammed a door shut on those memories and buried her head in Tom's neck. His hand resumed that caress up and down her back, his touch mysteriously peaceful. She melted against him, accepting his support.

*Don't let go...*

"Talk to me," he whispered.

She swallowed and winced. Had she screamed? Or was the ache in her throat a result of being sick? She couldn't remember, which sent a terrifying chill down her spine. That happened a few times before, usually when Anita's psychological trauma became too hard to contain. But no one had hurt her this time, so what sent her to the dark place?

"I..." She paused to allow some water from above to fall into her mouth and soothe her raw throat. Tom curled his hand around the back of her neck and massaged the tender area beneath her ear with his thumb. All the tension fled her body as she relaxed into his magical touch.

Exhaustion took over, making her eyes droop and her limbs heavy. She didn't want to ever move, but Tom seemed to have other ideas as he reached over to turn off the shower and wrapped her in a towel. It all happened in a daze. She barely registered him carrying her to the bed, but recognized his familiar warmth when he returned. His wet clothes were gone and replaced by a dry shirt and boxers. She rolled towards him on instinct and sighed when his arms settled around her.

"I'm so going to hell," he muttered.

"I'll welcome the company," she replied with a yawn. Hell was her reality for the last six or so years. If he wanted to join her, she wouldn't turn him away.

He snorted. "Get some sleep, Amelia."

For the first time in a very long time, sleep sounded pleasant. Maybe she would do that for a while and escape the tortures of her mind. With Tom's comforting strength surrounding her, she closed her eyes and allowed the exhaustion to takeover.

~*~

Waking up next to a naked woman in his bed had never been so uncomfortable. Amelia had one shapely leg draped over Tom's thigh, and her exposed breasts were pressed firmly into his side. But that wasn't the worst part. Her palm felt like an invitation against his lower abdomen. If she shifted those fingertips another half-inch, she'd be caressing the head of his cock. And then all hell would break loose.

Tom had firmly earned his saint badge last night by cuddling a gorgeous woman in the shower, and again in bed, without any inappropriate touching. But if she shifted downwards, his lower-half would take over and ruin everything.

Sex had to be the last thing on her mind, especially after whatever the fuck happened in that bathroom. He'd heard her throw-up through the too-thin walls and debated whether or not to intervene. But once the hysteria started, she'd left him no choice. The agony in her cries pierced his heart and sent him running into the other room. What he saw made his blood run cold. Her skin had turned blue from the icy water pouring over her. He didn't hesitate to reheat her, but then she went catatonic in his arms, which scared the ever-living shit out of him.

If he needed proof that she'd undergone trauma in his father's care, he more than had it. She had post-traumatic stress syndrome written all over her, and he'd done the only thing he knew how to do. He'd offered comfort and warmth, and given her current relaxed state, he'd say it worked. For now.

But something had set her off last night, and he was determined to figure out what. It could be her inability to shift. Ichorians and Hydraians operated their gifts with a natural ease, similar to the way a mortal might wave a hand or blink. To have something like that taken away… Well, he couldn't imagine how that felt, but devastated came to mind.

Amelia stirred beside him then relaxed with a moan that went straight to his balls. *Jesus.* Talk about mind over matter. His brain knew better, but his body sensed the warm, pliant woman beside him and reacted on instinct. And he swore that hand of hers just went a centimeter south. God, if she woke up and found his hard dick in her hands, she'd lose it. And that would be the end of any semblance of trust he had established between them.

If he shifted a little, he could reach the towel she'd lost overnight and re-cover her. That would shield his view, but of course, her fantastic curves would forever be engraved in his memory. Something to consider while alone in the shower later. Though he doubted any amount of jerking-off would help in this situation. His attraction to her had reached lethal levels over the last twenty-four hours, and not just physically.

Hysterical women terrified him, and usually sent him in the opposite direction. But when he heard Amelia's cries, he ran to her side without a second thought. He couldn't recall a single moment in his life where that had ever happened to him. Even Lizzie's tears caused him to scurry away like a frightened animal, and he loved that girl like his own flesh and blood.

Amelia's pain called out to him on a fundamental level, and he'd reacted without thought. Holding her felt right, too right. This bond forming between them wasn't healthy. He couldn't keep her. She belonged in Hydria, and he belonged in hell. Not the ideal match by a long shot. Tom served as a constant reminder of what the CRF had done to her. No amount of helping Amelia or saving her would erase that history between them. He may not have been the one to hurt her, but his presence would forever remind her of the man who did. *My father.*

A buzz on his wrist had him cringing. He forgot all about the alarm he'd set, and of course, it was the arm wrapped around Amelia. She jolted awake and flew upwards in a panic. Great. He thought having her breasts pressed against him was bad. This was worse—much worse. Because now they were on full display for his viewing pleasure. No amount of recited baseball stats could compete with that.

Perfection. That sole word described Amelia to a tee. The woman had the body of a goddess, and she deserved to be worshiped. *But not by me.* He cleared his throat and used what remained of his self-control to roll off the bed.

"Morning. I'm going to take a shower." *With cold fucking water.*

He didn't wait for a reply—he couldn't or he'd end up back on that bed with Amelia beneath him. His hands shook with a deep-seated need as he peeled off his shirt and boxers and climbed into the shower. The cold water pellets from the shower head did nothing to dispel the steam rolling off his body as he recalled the feel of Amelia's breasts against his side. He leaned back against the tile wall and fought the urge to stroke his shaft. Kissing her yesterday—platonic as it was—had stoked the fire in his veins to an overwhelming fury. He wanted her more than he wanted to breathe, and knowing it was forbidden only made matters worse.

*This is so wrong.* The last time he stood here, she was naked and catatonic in his arms. But the images in his head were of a vivacious woman with lips meant for sin, and oh, how he wanted to feel her mouth wrapped around his cock.

"Fuck," he muttered and turned to bang his head against the wall. His common sense had disappeared down the drain with what was left of his dignity. What harm could a little fantasy cause? She'd never know, and he'd feel a hell of a lot better afterwards. His guilty conscious would be worth the sweet relief.

Amelia's deep blue eyes flashed through his mind, and he recalled their vacant look from the night before. That woman had gone through enough. She didn't deserve to have his sordid thoughts on top of it. He fisted a hand at his side and bit off a curse. The sooner he got her back to Hydria, the better. Then he would take care of the ache in his balls. Until then, he'd behave. Even if it killed him.

His jeans were still damp from the night before, but he put them on anyway. It was that or boxers, and he needed pants. He used the shirt he slept in, and towel dried his hair. He'd need another shower later when he had proper soap and shampoo, but this would do for now. Amelia sat waiting for him on the bed, her dark hair tousled with sleep and a sheet pulled over her chest. The image almost sent him back into the bathroom to take care of business. He had to get rid of her, and soon.

"Bathroom's free if you want to use it." He cleared his throat. "We'll, uh, do some shopping for clothes this afternoon." They had to make a pit stop first and dispose of the stolen car at a nearby restaurant. Or maybe they would leave the car here and walk. His escape plan wasn't far, hence the reason he chose this motel.

Tom walked over to the window to check the lot. Nothing out of the ordinary. It appeared his evasion techniques had worked to fool the CRF. They wouldn't work forever, and he had no doubt the Sentinels would be crawling all over this small town by nightfall, if not sooner.

The bathroom door closed with a snick, indicating Amelia had left the bed. He hoped she held it together this time because his heart could not handle another breakdown, not when he didn't know for certain what caused the first one. As much as he wanted to know what happened, he wouldn't push her to talk to him. If she confided in him, it would be because she wanted to, not because he demanded it.

Her hair was pulled back into a damp ponytail when she stepped out of the bathroom in her shorts and tank top from yesterday. Those full lips of hers were curled down at the edges, making his heart hurt. He preferred curious Amelia over this sad version, but he wasn't sure how to fix it. Pulling on his jacket and backpack, he stepped over to the door and opened it for her. She hurried under his arm and paused on the sidewalk.

Yeah, this wasn't going to work today. He needed a confident partner to pull all this off, and this meek version wouldn't cut it.

"I hope you're up for a jog, because we're leaving the car here." Nothing like a little competition to get her blood pumping.

Her gaze darted up to his. "What?"

"You heard me. Let's go for a run."

Some of the uncertainty was replaced by incredulity. "Now?"

"Yeah, why not?" His body could certainly use the exercise. Maybe it would redirect the blood flow away from his groin.

She took in their surroundings with a frown. "We're in the middle of nowhere."

Not exactly true. The cabin they stayed in was more

remote than this place, but the population of this town topped out around a thousand. A good place to buy a small storage unit under a false name and hide some things no one would ever think to look twice at for his escape plan. The National Park nearby attracted a lot of tourists, especially those from the city, which meant the locals were used to new faces, which was why he selected this area three months ago.

He zipped up his jacket. The run would hurt in this heat, but he'd take the painful distraction over the ache down below. "Ready?"

The last bits of her wariness fled as she gaped at him. "You're serious."

"Always."

"And apparently, you've lost your bloody mind."

After everything that happened yesterday? "A possibility, sure." At a minimum, he had a death wish. "Shall we?"

"Do I have a choice?"

Technically, she did, but a pissed off Amelia trumped a depressed one. So... "No. Let's go." He rolled back onto the balls of his feet and took off at a pace he knew she could hold.

"Arse," she growled as she fought to catch up to him.

"Asset," he returned with a grin he knew she would find cocky. She'd probably kill him after this three-mile stint, but if it kept her grounded in reality, he'd consider it a win.

They arrived at the storage locker forty minutes later, which had to be a record for him in terms of slowness. But he didn't tell Amelia that. He spent half the run jogging backwards to taunt her into keeping up. The blue fire in her eyes served as an amusement and a turn-on. She threatened to shoot him several times, but he had all the guns. A good thing, too, because he suspected she was serious this time. She bent over, arms on her knees, outside the garage door, sputtering colorful phrases. As she kept repeating *arse*, he knew they were all directed at him.

"And…" She gulped in a lungful of air and blew a strand of hair from her eyes. "You're not… even… sweating."

True. The jog had felt more like a light walk to him. A good thing considering the heavy leather jacket and bag. Not to mention the damp jeans.

"I live for this shit," he told her as he pulled off his pack. The key he needed peered up from the outside pocket. Snagging it, he headed towards the unit under his alias with a panting Amelia trailing behind him. He wondered how exhausted she would be after a night in his bed. With how fiercely he wanted her, he'd leave her breathless and replete, over and over again.

"What is this place?" Amelia asked as he unfastened the padlock. Her pink cheeks and parted lips taunted his devious side. She looked freshly fucked, but not in the way he preferred. So much for that run helping to dissuade his arousal. If anything, it had gotten worse. *I need to get her away from me as soon as possible.* Which meant he'd need to expedite his plans. Not a problem.

He pulled the garage door upwards to reveal a ten by twelve room. Seeing Amelia's expression, he realized he never replied to her inquiry. His brain had been temporarily distracted by the member in his pants.

"I've suspected for a few months now that this choice might be inevitable," he explained, turning on the light overhead. "Of course, I didn't expect my exile to happen this soon, so I don't have everything in place yet, but I have enough to get started."

Various weapons littered the walls, and boxes cluttered the floor. But it was the safe in the corner he went to first. His fingers rotated the dial using the appropriate code, and it sprung open.

Two passports sat inside, one American, the second Canadian. Both were aliases the CRF knew nothing about.

Beneath them was a wallet filled with credit cards tied to bank accounts in each name, and large bills from various countries. All those humanitarian trips around the world made collecting foreign currency easy. It also aided in his ability to transfer his inheritance around without his father noticing. By the time John's analysts tracked the money, Tom would be long gone and using another identity on the opposite side of the world. Or that was the idea anyway.

He set the passports and money on top of the safe then bent to pull a set of dry clothes from a box near his feet. He knew these would come in handy one day. Dropping his bag and coat, he tugged off the dirty shirt and threw it to the ground. A tiny gasp from the other side of the unit reminded him that he wasn't alone. Right. Wide eyes were glued to his chest as he turned.

"I need to change out of these wet jeans." They were chafing his groin, which ached enough already. His hand went to the button of his jeans, as did her gaze. "You might want to turn around because I'm swapping the boxers, too."

Amelia licked her lips and gave him a strange look, like she wanted to say something. She must have thought better of it because she turned around to stare at his favorite sniper rifle instead. Too bad it wouldn't be going with them. He'd have to return for it later.

Losing his shoes, jeans, and damp boxers, he pulled on the dry clothes and re-laced his boots. He put the passports in one pocket and the wallet in another before closing the safe. A burner phone sat in a box on one of his shelves. He slipped that into his jacket pocket and started swapping items from his bag. Certain weapons would be required for where they were headed, not the standard ones in his pack. Amelia, realizing he was clothed, turned to observe with a curious expression.

When he finished, he walked out of the garage to the unit across from them and used the same key to open it. Inside sat his favorite toy. He bought it two months ago and drove it once. Here. Now he could have some fun with it.

"Are you going to do that wire thing again?"

He chuckled at the irritation in Amelia's tone. Apparently, she didn't enjoy their last hot-wiring experience. "Don't worry. This one has keys inside."

Tom opened the door to the beautiful machine and popped the trunk. His bag went in first, followed by a few additional firearms from the other unit and, lastly, a box of clothes. He'd need to procure a suitcase today for their stuff so the hotel didn't question them later. Minor detail.

After locking the other unit, he walked over to open the passenger side door. "Ladies first."

"How gentlemanly of you." She didn't sound all that impressed with him.

"You'd prefer to stay here?"

Those gorgeous eyes narrowed. "Are you going to force me to run again?"

"Probably."

She snorted. "Arse."

"Asset."

All the teasing today was worth it to see her responding grin. He could tell she didn't want to be amused, but couldn't help it. And he loved that. He'd made her happy, in a backwards, fucked up way.

"Tell me where we're going first."

"I could just leave you here," he replied, smiling. Not that he would. She didn't know it, but he'd promised her something last night after she fell asleep. And he intended to see it through, even if it killed him.

"Yes, or you could be a *gentleman* and tell me."

Oh, he liked that. Using his words against him. "Okay, sweetheart." He folded his arms on top of the open door and leaned over as if to let her in on a secret. She moved closer, expression curious. He loved that look on her and couldn't wait for it to mold to shock. "We're going back to New York City."

She didn't disappoint. Those luscious lips parted on a gasp, and her eyebrows shot up to her hairline. "What? Why the bloody hell would we do that?"

"Because it's the last place they'd ever expect us to go."

# CHAPTER ELEVEN

## A Moment of Hesitation

Amelia couldn't believe it. Of all the hotels in New York City, Tom chose *The Pierre* for the night. The Treaty of 1747 kept her from ever staying here, or anywhere in the city limits for that matter, but she knew of this place through her brother. He loved this hotel.

She wondered how far it was from Wakefield Pharmaceuticals. Jonathan had told her Issac had taken a more active role in his company after her supposed death. He used it as proof that her brother had moved on and would never come for her. She didn't let it break her spirit, not entirely anyway. Because she knew deep down her brother might believe she was dead, but he'd never forget her.

"Shall we, darlin'?" Tom drawled. He looked ridiculous in a pale pink polo shirt, khaki slacks, glasses, and a flat cap. Not that she appeared any better in her floppy hat and sundress. They were dressed for a croquet match, not a classy New York City hotel, but he insisted on the disguise.

She wrapped her gloved arm around his offered one and followed along. Her English accent couldn't be molded into a southern drawl, so she played the part of silent type at his side while he chatted with the bellman in the elevator.

Their room on the thirty-eighth floor boasted a splendid night view of Manhattan. Amelia almost felt bad that she wouldn't be sticking around to enjoy it. Being this close to freedom and her brother left her little choice but to flee, but she needed a few things from Tom first. *Money and a weapon.*

It sickened her stomach to think about touching a gun again, but she knew the necessary evil would come in handy. Hydraians like herself were not welcome in this city, and Ichorians lurked at every corner. Her father being one of the eldest of his kind made her recognizable to most immortal beings, especially the more dangerous ones. She'd be shot on sight if anyone recognized her. Thankfully the immortal world presumed her to be dead already.

"Amelia?" Tom called from the living area. She had wandered into the suite bedroom while he finished his discussion with the bellman. His lack of a drawl told her the hotel employee had left.

She turned away from the window to join him. He stood beside the couch with a book in his hand. "What do you want to eat?" he asked while reading.

Food was the last thing on her mind, but her stomach rumbled at the question. A quick meal before she ran away might be a good thing. It would help keep her energy levels high, something she suspected would be needed. She peered over his shoulder to review the room service menu and pointed to a random salad with chicken.

He snorted and faced her. "We haven't eaten since that crappy meal at the mall, and not a whole hell of a lot before that. You need more than a salad."

She folded her arms and raised an eyebrow at him. "Well, if you know what I should be eating, then why don't you order for me?"

"You know, I think I will." He picked up the phone while holding her gaze. "Evenin', darlin'. My fiancée and I are starving. Uh huh, yup. Okay, well, we'd like the shrimp starter and two bowls of lobster bisque. And for the main course, we'll take two filet mignons with some baked potatoes and string beans." He grinned at whatever the lady said to him. "Yes, ma'am, green beans are just fine. And yes, em', medium rare. As for dessert, the sundae bar with all the sides and some warm chocolate chip cookies oughta do. Thank ya much, darlin'. You, too."

"I hope you're hungry because that's a lot of food, *darlin'*," she said with a horrible accent. While he sounded sexy as sin, she came off as ridiculous. At least she wasn't wearing that stupid flat cap. *Though even I have to admit the arse pulls it off nicely.* The man could wear a trash bin and still be handsome.

Her attraction to him had worsened over the last twenty-four hours. Falling asleep in his arms after he pulled her away from the darkness had been refreshing. She couldn't think of a better word for it. After overcoming the shock of waking up naked beside him, she'd realized it'd been the best night of sleep for as long as she could remember. Part of her wanted to blame the bed, a luxury she hadn't experienced in over six years, but that would be a lie. She'd felt safe, and that terrified her. Any deeper and she'd be in trouble.

Which was why she needed to leave. She considered asking Tom to release her, but she didn't know how he would react. Escaping seemed easier.

*A coward's approach*, her conscience chided.

*Maybe.*

But if she didn't run tonight, she risked losing her heart to this man. She refused to rely on another person to take care of her, to save her. Not after what happened last time she fell into that trap. Amelia owed it to herself to follow through with her original plans of running away and finding her brother. She'd steal some money and a gun and ask the hotel concierge to send her to Wakefield Pharmaceuticals. Issac wouldn't be working at this late hour, but she'd find someone there who could help her contact him.

"What are you thinking so hard about, Amelia?" Tom asked, eyes narrowed in suspicion.

*Oops.* She tried to recall what they'd just been discussing and came up blank. "I don't remember." Not a lie because she couldn't recall their conversation.

"Uh huh." He folded his arms and cocked his head to the side. "Well, dinner will be here in thirty minutes. Why don't you go freshen up and take off that hideous hat? Your new clothes are in that suitcase."

She ignored his gesture to the bags by the bedroom door. "You're calling my hat hideous? Have you tried looking in a mirror?"

He flashed her a cocky grin. "Lose the hat, sweetheart."

"You're an arse."

"Yes, we've established that, little asset," he murmured with a wink. "I'm going to catch up on the news while you change." He plopped down on the couch beside them, kicked up his feet, and turned on the TV.

She wanted to stomp her foot at him for assuming she would do as he requested, but truthfully, she couldn't wait to get out of this hat and dress. Her former self lived for this brand of fashion, but the new Amelia preferred denim and tank tops. And maybe pajamas pants. She'd bought a pair on a whim and decided those might do for dinner tonight. *With the food he ordered for you.* That's what they'd been going on about before her mind took a detour.

"What if I don't fancy a steak?" she asked, arms still folded.

He smirked. "Then I guess I get two filet mignons, and yes, I know. I'm an arse. Go change."

She wanted to smack him. Or worse. Kiss him. A light flutter stirred in her lower belly at the thought. What would he do if she sat on his lap, wrapped her arms around his neck, and pressed her mouth against his? *He'd push you away*, her conscious grated. Just like he did this morning when she woke up naked beside him. He moved so fast it was as if her skin burned him. Not the sign of a man who wanted her attentions. So slapping him would be the better option of the two, then. Too bad he'd catch her hand before it reached his cheek.

With a huff, she grabbed the suitcase and rolled it into the bedroom. If he wanted her to change, then she would do just that, and take a shower. Might as well refresh before her escape later tonight.

The marble washroom came equipped with a bath and shower. After spending far too long beneath the hot spray, she pulled on her knickers, a pair of soft gray flannels, and a creamy tank top. She went braless beneath, because, why not? Tom had already seen her naked, and from his reaction, he clearly wasn't impressed. Might as well be comfortable then. She ran a comb through her clean hair and left it down to dry before returning to the living area.

Her nose twitched at the savory aroma filling the room. Tom sat at a small dining table of two chairs, waiting for her to join him. The stupid cap sat on the floor, as did his polo and khakis. In their place were a pair of sweatpants and a white shirt that clung to his biceps. She swallowed her tongue and forgot whatever witty comment she'd been planning to say.

His eyes went to her breasts and darkened, making her wonder if she'd been wrong about his feelings towards her. Then his gaze dropped to the table, and the moment passed. Of course he wouldn't want her. And she shouldn't want him.

He cleared his throat and gestured to the chair across from him. "Let's eat."

Her growling stomach agreed, so she sat and devoured her meal. Filet mignon had never tasted so good, and the bisque was a treat to her tastebuds. She felt positively spoiled when they were done, which caused her chest to ache. Despite their situation, Tom had been good to her, but she had no choice except to betray him. If she learned anything over the last decade, it was to watch out for herself first and foremost. And staying with him for any longer not only endangered her sanity, but her emotional wellbeing. She couldn't risk falling any deeper down the rabbit hole.

"Uh, you can take the bed," Tom said after cleaning up their dishes and placing them in the hallway. "I'll stay on the couch."

"I can sleep on the couch," she replied without thinking. At his speculative expression, she backtracked to better explain. "I mean, you should get the bed since you paid for the room." *And I want to be closer to the door.*

Tom shook his head. "I'm on the couch; you're on the bed. It's not up for debate."

She bristled at his dismissive tone. "And why not? What if I fancy sleeping on the couch?"

"We're in the middle of Ichorian and Sentinel territory, Amelia. I think we fooled the cameras, but one wrong glance is all it takes for facial recognition software to find us. And you better believe my dad is using every resource in his power to track us down. So if you don't mind, I'd like to sleep on the couch to keep guard while you sleep in the bedroom."

She blinked. Right. No way to argue with that logic. "I'll sleep in the other room then."

"Good." He blew out a breath. "You can take the bathroom first. Just let me know when you're done."

Which implied he would require the washroom next,

but for how long? If he took a shower, she would have plenty of time to steal a weapon from his bag and some money. But she doubted he planned to do that. Still, it could work if she moved quickly.

*I can escape.* Her heart kicked up a beat then sank to her stomach when she realized it also meant she would never see Tom again. *He's a means to an end.* But was she ready to end it now?

"You all right?" he asked, frowning. "You look a little pale."

She swallowed. Hard. "Yes, I just—I need some sleep." A lie. Thanks to last night, she'd never felt so well rested. Why did that make her feel like a horrible person?

"Right." He palmed the back of his neck as concern furrowed his brow. "I'm here if you need me."

A spike went through the center of her chest. He mistook her fretting for thoughts of last night, which she had been able to avoid all day thanks to his cheekiness and commanding attitude. Running had been the last thing she wanted to do this morning, but even she had to admit it distracted her from the darkness.

"You're a good man," she blurted out. Her version of goodbye, and thank you?

He snorted. "Yeah, I don't know about that."

"You are, though. You're nothing like Jonathan." Despite looking like a young version of him.

Tom's eyes darkened to a luscious brown. She liked when they smoldered like that. It made things low in her belly tighten in a way she hadn't experienced in a very long time.

"Thank you," he murmured and cleared his throat. "I'm, uh, going to get the couch ready."

"All right." She gave a nod and wandered to the washroom to freshen up. Escaping while he readied himself for bed meant she wouldn't have time to change, so she pulled on a bra beneath her tank top and stuffed a pair of socks in her pocket. She'd grab her shoes on the way out and put them on in the elevator. Her hair went up in a ponytail, she brushed her teeth, and gave herself a stern look in the mirror.

*You can do this*, she repeated to herself as she walked back to the living area. But what she found there had her freezing in the doorway.

"What the bloody hell did you do?" she asked, shocked.

Tom glanced up from his makeshift bed on the floor. His muscular arms were tucked behind his head, and his bare feet were crossed at the ankles. "As mentioned earlier, we're in renowned Sentinel and Ichorian territory."

"So you put the couch in front of the door?"

"Yes." A simple answer. No explanation.

"And you moved the cushions to the floor because...?"

"Because if someone comes for us and they try the door, they'll shoot there first." He pointed to the seating area of the couch. "And I'd prefer to avoid that."

"Right." Hysteria bubbled deep inside. How did she keep coming this close to fleeing only to have it yanked out from beneath her every bloody time? Someone up there found her misery humorous.

Tom popped up to his feet in that agile way of his and gave her a nod. "Be right back."

"Right," she repeated, her gaze on the obstacle. No way could she move that without making a ton of noise and attracting his attention. Not to mention, she didn't have time.

*Plan B.*

*Which would be?*

"Oh, I almost forgot." Tom stood in the doorway holding a gun. The sight of it made her stomach turn over. "I'm putting this in the nightstand, just in case. Try not to shoot me with it, okay?"

He didn't wait for her reply, which was good because she didn't have one. Her limbs went numb as her insides crumpled.

*What the bloody hell am I going to do?* She had a weapon, which meant little to her now that she couldn't leave.

*Unless I use it to disable him…*

No. No way could she consider hurting him in that way. Killing Anita had been one thing, but Tom? That would break her on a different level.

*But he'll wake up just fine in the morning.* A mortal death would trigger his immortal genetics, and he'd become a full blooded Hydraian in the morning. Just like her.

*No.*

The idea was unacceptable.

*But logical.*

She covered her ears with her palms in an attempt to shut up the devil in her mind, but it wouldn't stop.

*He's a fledgling. Being reborn a Hydraian is his destiny. You'll just be helping him along.*

*What if he isn't a fledgling, though?*

*Don't be daft. You know he is. He's the spitting image of his father, who is one hundred percent Ichorian.*

She couldn't believe the debate happening in her head. Was she really considering this? Shooting Tom to temporarily disable him long enough to run away?

"My God," she whispered, appalled. He saved her life, and this was how she intended to repay him?

"All done," he said from behind her. She'd been staring at the couch the entire time, debating his fate.

*I'm going to hell.*

*No, you're escaping it.*

"I'm going to bed," she announced, moving past him without looking up. He didn't try to stop her or say anything when she closed the door to the bedroom. Thank goodness for that because she didn't trust her mouth.

Flopping on the bed, she pulled a pillow over her head and willed the voices to stop. She'd never felt so conflicted in her entire life. Her goal only a few weeks ago had been to take him down, but now everything had changed.

She liked him. At some point, the arse had gotten inside of her heart and made her care. He taught her things no one else had ever considered teaching her and treated her as an equal. The men in her life told her she didn't need to know this or that because it would never be an issue. No. That wasn't entirely fair. Issac tried to show her a few things, but Eli always brushed him off with an "I've got it." Well, he didn't have it. He had died.

Amelia rubbed her chest. Not for the first time, she blamed her former love for putting her in this situation. Oh, he never meant to, and she knew it, but had he just showed her a few tricks, maybe things would have been different in the end. Or maybe not. They both trusted Jonathan, and neither saw his betrayal coming until it was too late.

*Sort of like how Tom won't predict you using the firearm . . .*

She groaned. The logical part of her agreed shooting him was a sound plan. He'd wake up tomorrow pissed off, but alive, and she'd be one step closer to her brother. Really, she'd be doing Tom a favor by removing herself from his life. He obviously had the means and knowledge to take care of himself, while she functioned as unwieldy baggage. He said so himself at the cabin that going on without her would be the easier route. She could help him out with that and assist herself in the process. A win-win.

Her head hurt by the time she decided what to do, and a glance at the clock said it had taken her long enough. No light trickled from under the door, indicating Tom had gone to bed.

It was now or never.

She retrieved the gun from the nightstand as quietly as she could and crept over to the threshold. Pausing with her hand on the knob, she listened and heard nothing from the other side. With a deep, calming breath, she twisted and pulled and gazed into the near-black room. Tom had drawn the curtains, but a soft glow between the cracks illuminated her path to him on the floor. He slept on his back, with one arm tucked behind his head, and the other sprawled at his side.

*He really is a beautiful man.* High cheekbones, long lashes, a solid jaw, and slightly bent nose. She'd miss his face. She'd miss him.

Her hand trembled as she aimed at his chest.

*Pull the trigger,* the sensible part of her urged. *Before he wakes up.*

Amelia hesitated, her stomach rolling in turmoil. She thought her mind was made up in the bedroom, but seeing him lying there so innocently had her backtracking. How could she do this to him after everything they'd been through? Captor or not, he never harmed her. And it seemed he never wanted to hold her hostage to begin with; it was all his father. Punishing him for Jonathan's sins felt wrong.

She fell to her knees beside him as her legs gave out. Her aim never wavered, though, as the gun remained pointed at his heart.

"Do it," Tom whispered, startling her. She met his wary gaze and felt a piece of her heart break. Witnessing the resignation in his gaze was too much. When he grabbed her shoulder to draw her closer, she went because she couldn't fight him. Not like this. His opposite hand wrapped around her wrist, but instead of disarming her, he guided the barrel to his ribcage.

"Shoot me," he urged. "If it's what you need to do, then do it."

A tear found its way to the corner of her eye and rolled down her cheek. She couldn't remember the last time she cried; she thought Jonathan had beaten it out of her.

The palm on her shoulder slid to the back of her neck as Tom pulled her down the rest of the way and rolled her beneath him. His grip on her wrist never faltered as he kept the gun aimed at his chest. She shuddered as his hips settled between her legs and closed her eyes when his lips brushed hers.

"I'll understand, Amelia. I know it's what I deserve."

But he didn't. Not at all. And she knew that deep down. It's why she couldn't kill him.

He balanced on his elbow beside her head, but kept his mouth a hairsbreadth away from hers. The quiver in her belly went lower and evolved into something hotter. Another tear slipped from her eye, a direct conflict to the sensations building deep inside. Darkness returned, but it held a different allure this time. A passionate one that tempted her to do things she never dreamed of doing with a man other than Eli.

Her fingers tried to slip from the weapon between them, but his grasp remained firm.

"Don't," he whispered. "Or I'll do something I shouldn't."

She shivered. "Like what?"

"This." His mouth captured hers in an unforgiving kiss that left her breathless beneath him. Their embrace in the theater had been a preview to what he did to her now. All his focus and confidence flowed from his lips to hers, as he provoked her deepest desires. She couldn't move, couldn't think, couldn't breathe...

He consumed her very being, leaving her in a puddle on the floor. All she wanted was him. Her tongue yearned for his, but he demanded control, and she gave it to him. The fingers around her wrist tightened as his hips pressed intimately into hers. His arousal was thick and hot between her thighs.

*My God...*

"Tell me to stop," he whispered against her lips. "Make me stop."

*No.* She closed the gap between them and tried again to move her hand away from the weapon. If she accidentally shot him, she'd never forgive herself. But his grip remained as he possessed her mouth.

When his tongue parted her lips, she moaned and lost all semblance of control. No man had ever kissed her this way. Tom treated her like a woman, not a girl, and he didn't hold back. His hips met hers again, and all hell broke loose. The gun disappeared as he set it on the floor away from them, and his palm went to her breast. She grabbed the back of his neck and arched into him with a force she didn't realize she possessed.

*What is he doing to me?* Everything felt so foreign, so good.

"Amelia," he breathed. "Fuck, I want you."

His hand slid to her neck, holding her in place as he devoured her once more. She wrapped both arms around his shoulders and threaded her fingers through his hair. Approval vibrated deep in his chest, making her squirm. She liked that low growl. The nerves in her lower belly tingled in anticipation at the sound, and it sent a fresh surge of desire to the apex between her thighs.

*I'm turned on,* she realized with a start. *Well and truly turned on.*

Did she ever expect to experience this again? With a man other than Eli? Thinking of her former lover should have ruined the moment, but all it did was reinforce it. The emotions Tom inspired in her were unlike anything she'd ever experienced. She was a new woman in his arms, cherished and protected, yet revered and respected. The way he dominated her with his body was just what she needed. An escape from reality, similar to the darkness, but so much better. Here she could feel and be and enjoy.

The palm on her neck went to her breast and down to the hem of her tank top. Heat met her bare skin as he ran his hand up her side. She quivered beneath him and luxuriated in the feel of pleasurable contact. It'd been so long...

"Tell me you want this," he breathed. "I need to know you want this, sweetheart." Her heart fluttered in response to the endearment. She loved the way it rolled off his lips onto hers.

Amelia tried to capture his mouth again, only to be

held down by the palm between her breasts. His eyes smoldered with an intensity that caused her pulse to race. Arousal never looked so good on a man. And she thought he didn't want her. *What was I thinking?*

"Kiss me," she pleaded. "I need you to kiss me."

"I want to do a lot more than kiss you, Amelia." The warning in his voice made her shiver.

She swallowed. "Then do it."

"One word, and I stop. Say no, and it all stops."

*Never.* "Kiss me," she repeated. "Please."

"I want to taste every inch of you," he whispered against her lips. He led with his tongue, taking her mouth with a possessiveness that left her breathless. A fire blossomed in her lower belly and spread heat to all her nerve endings. Her clothes were suffocating. She needed them off and moved to lift her tank top higher, but Tom caught both hands in one of his and stretched them over her head. His lips trailed down the column of her neck to her collarbone, where he nibbled her delicate skin.

She squirmed beneath him, desperate for more, but he prolonged the sensual torture by licking the swell of her breasts. When he dipped down to her bra and back up, she thought she might die with want. Too long had she gone without these sensations brewing in her abdomen. And the way he touched her was unlike anything she'd ever felt. No fear or hesitation, and all confidence. This man understood how to handle a woman, and knew what he wanted and how he wanted it.

Bunching her top in his free hand, he lifted it over her head and let it rest against her elbows while he flicked open her bra.

"Perfection," he murmured, making her hotter. One nipple disappeared between his lips as he sucked deep, and her body bowed off the makeshift bed beneath her. The heavy thickness of his arousal hit her right where she wanted it as his hips pushed her back down. Spasms shot down her legs, making her shake with need. He switched breasts to take her opposite peak deep into his mouth. Pain mingled with pleasure, sending a sharp sensation to her lower abdomen.

"Tom…" Her hoarse voice barely registered to her own ears, but he seemed to hear her. He shifted downwards, kissing and nipping her abdomen, before hooking his thumbs in the soft cotton of her panties beneath her pajama bottoms. His gaze held hers as he pulled the fabric, pants and all, over her thighs, knees, and ankles, leaving her completely naked before him.

His gaze drifted over her in lazy sweeps as he admired every inch of her exposed body. Hunger dilated his pupils, making her thighs clench.

"Your blush is very pretty, sweetheart. I wonder how red I can make you," he mused as he crawled over her, fully clothed, and stopped at the juncture between her legs. She opened her mouth to reply, but he nuzzled her core, and all coherent thought spiraled to a puddle at her feet. His hands ran up her thighs to spread her wider as his mouth settled over her clit. No warning or teasing, but direct, straightforward, and amazing.

She whimpered at the onslaught of sensation, and goosebumps rained down her arms. Pleasure overwhelmed her being, shutting down all thought of anything other than Tom's tongue against her damp flesh. He gave her a deep lick that made her toes curl and pulled her sensitive bud between his teeth. Time stopped as an incredible surge of ecstasy swept through her, starting at her center and bursting to every cell in her body. A scream ripped through her throat as her body convulsed beneath him. Tom's hand against her abdomen kept her grounded as he drew out the sensations with his tongue.

Lights flashed behind her eyes, making her dizzy, as he climbed over her. His grin was all satisfied male when she finally focused on him.

"This is a good look on you," he murmured against her lips. "Red, dazed, and thoroughly pleasured. I want to see it again with my cock deep inside of you." A fresh surge of arousal hit her lower belly at the taste of her own pleasure on his tongue. He kissed her hard, leaving his mark on her soul.

"Do you want me to stop, Amelia?" It was a breath against her ear. "Or do you want more?"

Her mouth went dry. "More," she whispered. "So much more."

# CHAPTER TWELVE

## Killing Isn't Easy

Those three words went straight to Tom's groin. His balls tightened to a painful degree as his cock twitched. Control resided in his blood, but even he had a limit. Amelia's irises deepened to an oceanic blue as desire enflamed her pupils. He knew that expression well, had seen it on countless women throughout the years, but on her, it felt brand new. A gift meant for only him to unwrap, and he had every intention of finding the prize inside.

He pulled his shirt over his head and grinned when she tried to lift her hands to touch him. Her tank top looked so pretty around her forearms. She didn't realize he'd hooked it to the button of the cushion beneath her. A spur of the moment twist of his fingers that kept her bound prettily for his viewing pleasure. Of course, he kept it loose enough for her to wiggle out if she wanted. A hard yank would set her free as well, but she appeared too mesmerized by his abdomen to try.

Her hot gaze went to his sweatpants as he pulled the tie loose. Stripping for her had its merits. To see a gorgeous woman sprawled out before him flushed with desire as he revealed his body never got old. But Amelia amplified it tenfold. Her eyes glinted as he set his cock free and shed the rest of his clothes, and her hands twitched. He leaned over to yank the top off her arms to see what she would do. Feather light fingertips flitted over his arms and pectorals then down his stomach to stop above the place he wanted her most.

"Touch me." The request sounded more like a demand due to the desire deepening his tone. He wanted her more than he could remember wanting any woman, but it would always be on her terms. "Please," he managed.

"Where?"

The innocent word gave him pause. It should be obvious, but he wouldn't push. "Anywhere you want."

Her eyebrows rose, and excitement touched her lips. "Anywhere?" she repeated. "Truly?"

Amelia couldn't possibly be a virgin. She and Eli had been lovers for centuries, and no way the former Elder hadn't taken her to bed. Unless his lethal touch prevented him from loving her properly. An image formed behind his eyes, making him growl low in his throat. The thought of anyone else worshipping this woman painted Tom's vision red. *No.* He would erase all those who came before him and make it impossible for her to forget him.

"Wherever you want, Amelia," he whispered and shifted to lie beside her on the bed of couch pillows and blankets.

She went to her elbow and licked her lips. "I can taste you?"

*Fuck.* Those words alone nearly pushed him over the edge. He was known for his restraint, yet this woman

153

could undo it with a few innocent phrases.

"Yes." It came out rough, and her expression suggested she liked it.

That mouth of hers was designed for sin, but that smile? Oh, he loved that smile. It made his dick throb in anticipation and his balls pull tight. Her nails traced the ridges of his abdomen, hesitant. When she reached his happy trail, his eyes fell shut on a groan he couldn't contain, and her hand disappeared.

"If you're trying to kill me, sweetheart, it's working."

"You like it?"

He peeked at her. "I'd like you to do a hell of a lot more." Preferably before he came apart at the seams, pinned her down, and fucked her. If her comfort didn't mean so much to him, he'd do exactly that.

"More?" She pressed her palm to the area above his groin. "I like the idea of more." Her silky strands danced against his chest as she lowered her mouth to his sternum. He laced his fingers through her hair in encouragement as she licked a path down the center of his torso to where her hand rested, and lower. His breath caught when she took his cock between her lips without warning.

*Shit.* The wet heat proved almost too much to bear, but he couldn't pull her away. Especially not as she took him deeper, her lips caressing every inch as a soft hum of approval sounded in the back of her throat. Her fingers wrapped around the base of his shaft as she swirled her tongue around the tip. His hips flexed on reflex as he hissed a curse. She paused, as if startled by the sound, and he glanced down to find her watching him.

"Fuck," he growled. *So fucking hot.*

Arousal shone bright in her eyes, making it impossible to look away as she took more of him between her lips and sucked. Hard. Another move like that would send him over the edge, and he wasn't ready to come in her mouth. Not tonight. Not after the weeks of tension and abstaining. He needed to be inside of her. With his fist in her hair, he pulled her off of him and rolled her beneath him. His hard length settled against her wet heat, sending electricity through his veins.

"I wasn't done." Her admonishment lacked fervor.

"You can taste me thoroughly later," he whispered and captured her lips in a punishing kiss. Her responding moan set his blood on fire. "I need you, Amelia. I need you now."

"Take me." The two words against his mouth sent him over the edge, pushing his hips forward. Her tight sheath fit him like a glove and made everything tighten down below, but he didn't like the way she stiffened. In his eagerness to be inside her, he'd moved too fast, and her body wasn't ready for a man his size. Rookie mistake.

Tom dropped his mouth to her neck as she acclimated to his intrusion. He placed soft, soothing kisses along the column of her throat, her chin, and up to her ear. "Sorry, sweetheart."

"I'm all right." She relaxed and eventually started to move against him. When her nails dug into his shoulders, he tried a shallow thrust, and she groaned his name. Her grip on him tightened when he shifted again, and her legs wrapped around his waist to allow for deeper access.

Tom let his control slip a notch, and pushed harder. She rewarded him with a guttural sound that went straight to his balls. He explored and learned her body and cravings through varying degrees of penetration and found that hard and rough seemed to be a pace she enjoyed most. Her nails scoured his skin as he pushed himself to the hilt, and her legs trembled around him.

His mouth found hers, and he ravaged her with his tongue. She felt perfect beneath him, as if destined to be there, and he worshiped her with each thrust. When he felt her slick walls tighten around him, he slid his thumb down to the center of her pleasure and jolted as she came around him. He moved with her, prolonging her orgasm, and bit off a curse as he followed her over the edge.

Ecstasy shot from his groin to every nerve ending as he emptied himself inside of her. All that bullshit about delayed gratification had merit, because this was unlike anything he'd ever experienced. His limbs shook from the impact, but he remained hard and ready inside her for another round. The earth-shattering explosion wasn't enough. He needed more. So much more.

Her legs loosened from his waist, but her arms remained around his neck as he kissed her with a ferocity he couldn't control. His tongue memorized every inch of her mouth before pulling back. She gazed up at him through hooded eyes and flashed an impish grin that excited his cock.

He brushed his lips against hers and moved lazily against her, luxuriating in the feel of their intimate connection. She surprised him by mimicking his thrust with one of her own.

"Careful, sweetheart, or I'll take that as an invitation."

"Maybe you should," she whispered. But the way her body strained beneath him confirmed she needed a break. He pushed deep one final time and gently pulled away before desire overrode reason.

"I want to hold you for a while first." He rolled to his side and wrapped an arm around her waist to cuddle her against him. It placed her curvy ass against his groin, but it was her giggle that pleased him most. She'd laughed around him a few times, but never quite like that. He smiled against her hair and kissed the top of her head. What a pair they made on the floor, beside the couch, sprawled out over cushions and blankets. He'd carry her to the bed once his arousal died. If he carried her now, he'd end up taking her again, and she wasn't ready for what he had in mind.

Her body stiffened, putting him on alert. Then he followed her gaze to the gun a few feet away and relaxed. He'd heard her creep into the living area and hadn't been shocked by the weapon in her hands. His reaction to it, however, surprised him.

Rather than find amusement in the situation, he had felt resigned. If she had needed to kill him in retribution, he wouldn't have stopped her. As Jonathan's son, he was the perfect person for her to punish for the sins leveled against her. He understood that better than anyone, even if it broke his heart to see that weapon in her hands and pointed at him. But now that he knew the truth about her feelings, he wouldn't let her go without a fight, and he certainly wouldn't offer up his life again. She deserved better than that.

Tightening his arm around her, he pressed his lips to the pulse at her neck. "If you're thinking about shooting me now, think again, little asset. I might be aroused as hell, but my reflexes work just as well while I'm naked as they do when I'm clothed."

Her responding tremble took the teasing right out of him. He eased her onto her back to stare down into her wide, wet eyes. Sorrow replaced the beautiful arousal deep in their depths. He wanted to destroy whatever caused her such grief.

"Talk to me, Amelia." He brushed the hair from her face and tucked it behind her ear before cupping her cheek. "What's wrong?"

She shuddered and whispered, "I don't know who I am anymore."

He frowned. "Why?"

"I... I shot people, threatened you with a gun, wear jeans and tank tops, and hate silk. And I don't know what any of that means. I don't know if anyone will recognize me." Tears were streaming down her cheeks by the end, which was not at all how he intended their evening to end. Then the first thing she said kicked him in the gut.

*Of course.*

"Yesterday was your first time killing someone." That explained her breakdown. He hadn't even considered it as a cause, because his first time happened so long ago. But of course that impacted her. It was never easy to pull the trigger, especially for a civilian.

"I didn't even think," she whispered. "I just reacted."

"Anita got what she deserved, Amelia." He brushed away her tears with his thumbs and kissed her. "I don't know what happened in the labs, but I've gathered it was bad. And if she showed up behind my back, I have no doubt she had a horrible session planned. You acted in self-defense."

"She threatened to call Jonathan and become my new guard."

"Because she found you roaming about freely?"

Amelia nodded and buried her head against his chest. He folded his arms around her and kissed the top of her head. This emotional breakdown seemed less intense than last night, which relieved him to an extent. Maybe talking it through would help her feel better.

"Why do you hate silk?" he wondered, starting off on a lighter topic.

She didn't reply right away, as if startled by his change in subject. "It's too soft," she finally said. "But I used to love it."

"And you don't anymore?"

She shook her head. "I also used to love skirts and dresses and never wore jeans. But softer fabrics don't feel right to me anymore. I prefer rougher, durable cloth."

"Well, jeans are more practical, but maybe you'll come around when you see your old clothes again." His words caused her to stiffen. "You do still want to go home, right?"

~*~

*Do I?* Amelia wasn't sure. "I'm worried they won't recognize me or want me anymore."

Tom's arms tightened around her in a protective gesture that melted her heart. Seeing the gun on the floor brought back her earlier plans, and guilt washed over her. She'd been about to shoot him. *Who have I become?*

"Of course they'll want you, Amelia. They'd be crazy not to."

"But I'm not who I used to be." He couldn't possibly understand. The old her thrived in Hydria, acting as a party planner and social butterfly. Throwing a dinner party with friends no longer held the same appeal.

"Maybe, maybe not." He pressed his cheek to the top of her head and sighed. "You're a gorgeous, strong, intelligent woman who has survived unspeakable things. If they can't love this version of you, then they're not worthy of you."

"Strong?" she repeated. No one had ever called her that before. "You think I'm strong?"

"I do." He pulled back to stare down at her. "You amaze me more every day."

Despite the fresh tears gathering in her eyes, she smiled. "Thank you."

"See? You're gorgeous." His lips touched hers, sending a flutter of excitement to her lower belly. Making love to him had been unlike anything she'd ever experienced with Eli. Tom's authority more than translated to the bedroom, and his domineering control set her blood on fire. She loved the way he handled her, never fearing for a minute that she might break. It was refreshing and hot and oh-so good.

"Mmm," he murmured. "Not yet. We're not done talking. You're afraid they won't recognize you, but haven't mentioned the elephant in the room."

She frowned. "Elephant?" What the bloody hell did an animal have to do with anything?

"Your ability to shift, Amelia."

Her blood ran cold. "I don't want to talk about that."

"What about your secondary gift? It has something to do with intelligence, right?"

She frowned. All Hydraians inherited a gift from each

parent, and she was no different. Her father, Aidan, passed on an intellectual ability, but no one ever asked her about it because her talent paled in comparison to what he could do. Being an Ichorian with several millennia of life, most considered him omniscient. Her half-brother Luc inherited the same talent, making them the perfect father-son duo for strategy. It left her feeling inadequate since all she could do was impart wisdom while they functioned as all-knowing Gods.

"What about it?" she wondered.

"You gift knowledge through touch, right?"

"Sort of. If it's something I know, like a language, I can gift it to someone. But I have to know it first, which makes it a useless talent. If I had Luc and Aidan's brain power? Now that would be worth discussing."

He went onto his elbow beside her, and she fell to her back to stare up at him.

"What languages do you speak?"

Not the question she expected. "English, French, and Greek. Some Spanish and German, too, but not well. Why?"

"Hmm." His palm felt hot against her hip as he slid one leg between hers. "Greek, I learned for obvious reasons, but never French."

"Did Jonathan teach you Greek?"

"No, it was one of the many curriculums assigned to me as a child. I didn't exactly have a standard upbringing." He spoke with a nonchalance that didn't match the turmoil in his gaze.

"Tell me about it."

"I'd rather you teach me French."

His deflection made her smile. "Truly? French?" Eli found it useless, but few things fascinated him. Being several millennia old did that to a man. He'd experienced so much, while she experienced so little. Perhaps that was why he never taught her practical things, like how to defend herself.

"Why not?" Tom replied. "I speak half a dozen other languages and only a little bit of French. Let's add it to my knowledge base."

"If I teach you French, then you have to tell me more about your upbringing." Because she wanted to know everything about him, to better understand why he chose to help her instead of stay by his father's side.

His gaze darkened and dropped to her lips. "You teach me French, and I'll tell you how I learned Greek."

"No, you already told me it was a curriculum. I want something more substantial."

"Hmm." He brushed his mouth over hers in a lingering kiss and grinned. "There isn't much to tell. My dad sent me to a military school when I turned ten,"—another kiss—"and paid someone to act as my guardian while he busied himself with the CRF. I didn't see him much, and when I did, it was usually during one of my exams."

"Jonathan monitored your examinations?" That sounded like the man she knew. He monitored more than a few of her own exams.

"Teach me French, and I'll tell you more."

"Tease," she accused. But she had to smile. His sly negotiation tactics matched the man she'd come to enjoy. "Okay, fine."

Amelia palmed his cheek and closed her eyes to concentrate. Transferring knowledge took minimal effort on the psychic plane, but she hadn't engaged this part of herself in a very long time. Sort of like riding a bicycle after a decade of sitting down. She murmured a few key phrases in French to herself and smiled as the tendril of knowledge flowed to the forefront of her mind.

"This might tingle," she warned as she strung the mental threads together.

"Tingle away, sweetheart."

With a smile, she released the psychic thread from her fingertips and guided it into his essence. It took less than a minute for the transfer to hold. *Like fitting a piece into a complicated puzzle.* Her heart fluttered at the awe in Tom's expression as she pulled her hand away.

"*C'est génial,*" he murmured. *That's amazing.* "*Ça dure combien de temps?*" *How long does it last?*

"Forever, if I will it." Which she did in this case. What would be the point in making a foreign language temporary?

"So you can gift someone knowledge temporarily?"

"Yes, but I've only done it once or twice. On the off-chance someone asks for something, it's usually long term."

"I take it you don't use it often then?"

"Well no, it's not like I have the knowledge base of Luc and Aidan. I can only gift things I know, which isn't very much when surrounded by Hydraians two or three times my age." Plus, she spent most of her time with the Elders, who had several millennia on her three centuries. Learning something as simple as French didn't compare to ancient Greek or Coptic.

Tom nuzzled her chin and placed a kiss against her neck. "I don't think you realize how powerful of a gift this is, Amelia. Knowledge isn't power. Personal experience is, and you have a lot of it."

She frowned. Why would she ever pass her history onto someone else? Her most recent experiences at the CRF, especially. No one would be interested in understanding those memories.

"But more importantly…" He pulled back to meet her gaze. "You just used one of your Hydraian talents, which suggests you can use them both as they are genetically related."

She blinked, not understanding. Then it hit her squarely in the chest. He tricked her into using her ability to test whether or not it worked. Heat washed over her, and not the good kind.

"You bastard." What if it hadn't worked? Did he realize what that would have done to her?

"Yes, but now you know—"

"No! You don't get to decide that for me!" She tried to push him off her, but he didn't budge. His leg between her thighs kept her from squirming out from beneath him.

"Amelia—"

"You don't get it!" Tears gathered in her eyes as she fought futilely to get away from him. "You bast—"

Firm lips sealed over hers, stealing the breath from her lungs. She bit his lower lip, hard, and dug her nails into his shoulders, all in an attempt to avoid the arousal thickening her blood. But that only turned his kiss more demanding. Damn the attractive man and his skilled tongue. He cupped her cheeks and angled her head to better take her mouth. She shuddered beneath him, defeated. This sensation felt so much better than climbing into her black hole of nothingness. He helped her forget everything with a few seductive caresses.

"I was trying to help," he breathed against her lips. "I'm sorry."

He kissed her again before she could reply, wooing her into submission. His hips settled between hers as his elbows caged her in above, and she couldn't help but wrap her arms around his back and pull him closer. She'd gone so long without physical comfort, and Tom's touch set her veins on fire. He was an arse for tricking her, even if he meant well. She needed him to understand why it hurt, why she hated that he tricked her, so he would never do it again.

"My powers are part of who I am. Imagine for a minute that someone cut off your legs and forced you to walk." The words clawed at her throat, but she forced them out. "Not once, not twice, but over and over again. And no matter how hard you tried, you couldn't do it anymore. That part of you was gone and all you had left was a constant reminder that you're less than what you were. Would you ever want to stand again?"

"Jesus, Amelia." Darkness swirled in his gaze as he

stared down at her. "Why didn't you ever say anything to me?"

"What would I have said?" He worked for the monster in charge of her captivity. Why would she ever expect him to help her?

"I didn't know, but I suspected. That's why I kept checking on you."

All the bottles of water. She didn't trust them at first, but dehydration proved a powerful motivator, and one day she caved. When it didn't affect her negatively, she accepted the others, but always wondered why he visited. He never said much, except on his last visit. "You were so angry that last time in my cell. Why?"

"Why?" Both his eyebrows lifted. "Are you seriously asking me that?"

She frowned. "Well, yes. All your other visits were cordial, but you were positively incensed that last time."

"Because I found you lying on the floor, vomiting blood."

"Right. Jonathan hated that, too." He used to make her lick it up afterwards. A punishment for daring to bleed in his presence. The blood of a Hydraian was toxic to an Ichorian, something she knew very well and fantasized about daily. If only she could get him to ingest it...

"I was furious because my father beat you for no fucking reason, not that there is ever a reason to hurt a woman." His lips flattened. "Why do you think we ended up in a cabin upstate? My dad was livid with me already and decided babysitting you was the perfect punishment, especially since moving you was my suggestion."

Her brow furrowed. "I thought Stark suggested it." He implied as much during their last healing session, didn't he?

"No, he agreed with my idea, which is why... Wait, how did you know that?"

"He told me."

"Stark told you moving to the cabin was his idea?"

"In a way, yes. He mentioned things not being black and white." Her memory was a bit fuzzy due to the drugs he administered, but she thought that's what he said. "He's a strange man." *With strange powers.*

"Well, it was my idea, but my father only agreed because Stark approved of it. And it gave my dad a way to punish me. Bet he's regretting that right about now." Amusement danced in his eyes, making her curious.

"Tell me more about the examinations." That was part of their deal before he distracted her with hot kisses and infuriating tricks.

Some of the amusement died at her request. "I suppose that's only fair." He blew out a long breath and shook his head. "My dad used to administer certain exams. Not the academic kind, but the practical kind."

"I'm not quite sure I understand. What is a practical test?"

"When I was thirteen, he dropped me off a block away from The Arcadia on the night of a Conclave, handed me a gun with eight incendiary bullets, and told me to fight my way home."

Amelia's lips parted. She'd never attended a Conclave, but knew of them. And placing a fledgling so close to all those Ichorians? Especially one as infamous as Tom? That was a death sentence. "That's horrid."

"I survived, barely, and he rewarded me by sending me back to school the same night. My private martial arts training took on a brutal twist the following week because my father wasn't impressed with my time." He shrugged. "As I said, my upbringing wasn't exactly normal, but if it taught me one thing, it's that sometimes you have to pull the trigger to survive."

"I had no idea." Jonathan always brimmed with pride when he talked about Tom. Another act or something else entirely?

"Well, that makes two of us then, because I didn't realize how bad it was for you until, well, recently." His

165

expression darkened. "What you did to Anita was a mercy compared to what I would have done to her, Amelia. Killing someone is never easy, and having a conscience about it is what keeps us humane." The intensity in his stare almost undid her. "You aren't a bad person for pulling the trigger, sweetheart. It's when you start enjoying the kill that you have something to be concerned about."

She swallowed, unnerved by the veracity of his words. "I don't want to think about this anymore."

His gaze dropped to her lips. "I can assist with that."

"Make me forget, Tom." Her fingers wove through his hair, pulling him closer. "Help me forget everything."

He nibbled on her lower lip and shifted his hips to align with hers. Despite the troubling conversation and frustration boiling through her, she remained ready for him. Something that became all the more obvious as he slid his erection through her damp folds. This man did something to her. Whether healthy or not, she wasn't quite sure, but she liked it. His ability to take her away from reality to a land of pleasure where only they existed was a place she could get used to going.

"Kiss me," she whispered.

His mouth captured hers in an addicting kiss. So much control, passion, and heat radiated from him, making her melt beneath him. A moan escaped her as he palmed her breast and tweaked her nipple. She loved how he handled her, so confident and commanding, yet gentle and attentive. With every stroke and caress, reality fled and pleasure overtook her being until all she could think about was him.

*Yes, this is what I want. Always.*

When he slid inside her again, she sighed. His slow, loving pace was what she craved. It created a fire deep inside and kindled the flames with each deep thrust until the fierce sensations rolled through her limbs, making her shake with uncontrollable lust. His hand slipped between them, going straight to where she needed him most, and sent her over the edge with one flick to her clit. She cried out as she came around him, her nails scouring his back, and his name a benediction on her tongue. He didn't come with her, but kept his lazy pace and kissed her like a man who had all the time in the world.

"Again," she begged, needing more.

Dark brown eyes held hers as amusement flirted across his luscious lips. "I can do this all night, sweetheart."

*Arrogant arse.* "Prove it."

His grin was all self-assured male. "A dangerous request, but as you wish."

# CHAPTER THIRTEEN

## Incendiary Bullets

"Isn't it a bit hot for that?" Amelia wondered, eyeing Tom's leather jacket.

"I lived in the desert for three years. Trust me, I can endure a New York City summer dressed like this. Besides, it hides my guns." He flashed her the weapons at his sides, making her grimace.

"Are all those necessary?" They were going to her brother's office, not the Arcadia.

"Yes." Flat, no room for negotiation.

"Issac isn't going to hurt you." She wouldn't let him. Not after everything Tom had done for her.

"It's not your brother I'm worried about."

Right. They were in a city filled with Ichorians and

Sentinels, and Tom wasn't wearing a disguise. Nor did he ask her to shift, something she thanked him for silently. It appeared their discussion last night had the desired effect. She might be able to shift, but she wasn't ready to try yet.

Amelia winced as she pulled on her jeans. The man wasn't kidding about going all night. When she woke up this afternoon with his head between her thighs, she didn't think it possible to come again, but he proved her wrong before taking her hard and fast in the shower. Impressive didn't begin to cover it. She could still feel him between her legs. The satisfaction in his gaze when she buttoned her jeans suggested he knew. *Cocky arse.*

"Keep staring at me like that, and I'll postpone our plans another day or two." His deep voice sent a shiver down her spine.

She batted her eyes in an innocent gesture that belied the heat blooming below. "I'm sure I don't know what you're talking about."

"No?"

*Oh, that look can only mean...* She scrambled backwards as he came after her, but hit the wall with her back. Pressing her palms to his chest, she said, "Okay, but—"

He silenced her with a scorching kiss that left her shaking. "Did that clarify things for you?" he whispered darkly against her lips.

She had to clear her throat to speak. "Maybe a little."

"Good. Are we staying or leaving, sweetheart?"

Tom had asked her what she wanted to do today after their lovemaking in the shower. Finding Issac had been at the top of her list and still was, but Tom provided an alluring alternative.

He licked her lower lip. "Mmm, I'd prefer to stay here another week or so, order room service, and lose myself in you for hours at a time." His words showered goosebumps down her arms. The good kind. "But that would be selfish of me and goes against all my training. We need to keep moving, and your brother is the one best positioned to help you survive."

"You mean us," she corrected. Issac would help them both.

"Sure."

The sarcasm in his tone wasn't lost on her, but she didn't argue. Her brother would prove Tom wrong, and then she'd say *I told you so.*

He let her go with a tender kiss and went to fuss over his bag while she put on a shirt and shoes. Her hair went up into a ponytail that she strung through the back of the ball cap he gave her to wear. He wore a matching one and sunglasses.

"I wish I had a camera," he murmured. "You're cute in Yankees garb."

She rolled her eyes. "If this is your idea of payback, I'm not amused."

"It's the heart of baseball season, and we're in New York City. Just trying to help you blend in."

"Yes, I'm sure that's what this is."

She followed Tom's lead as they left the hotel, averting her gaze when he did and avoiding the cameras in the elevator and reception area. Once outside, he linked his fingers with hers and kept her close. He commented on the sights and weather as they walked, acting as if they were on a date. But despite his casual demeanor and relaxed posture, she knew he was hyperaware of his surroundings and taking in every detail. When they entered the subway, he handed her a ticket and reminded her to keep her head down.

"There are cameras all over the place," he murmured. "And the CRF has access to everything in this city."

By the time they exited the subway, her stomach was in knots. Their destination stood a few blocks away. Her feet felt like lead with every step as she wondered what to say to Issac. Would he be able to accept the new her, or would he expect her to revert to her old self?

"How do you feel about a quick lunch?" Tom asked,

surprising her. They had room service shortly before leaving the hotel. How could he be hungry already? "Maybe here?" He picked a pizza place on their left and opened the door. "Ladies first."

"All right." Has he lost his mind?

"Let's sit and peruse the menu." He grabbed a stack of menus from the ordering counter, chose a table at the back, and gestured for her to scoot into the corner. His bag went between them as he settled beside her.

"Why are we…?" Her voice trailed off as the bell over the door announced the arrival of two broad-shouldered men wearing curious expressions. Tom gave them a little wave from the booth and wrapped his arm around Amelia's shoulders.

"You know them?" she whispered, frowning. They weren't Sentinels she recognized.

"Gentlemen." He greeted the pair with a grin. "Care for a bite to eat?"

"A Sentinel loose in the city during broad daylight? Never thought I'd see the day," the one with darker hair said.

Amelia's blood chilled. *Ichorians.* The hungry gleam in their eyes was a dead giveaway, especially when they focused on her. Rumor had it Hydraian blood acted as an aphrodisiac to their kind. A natural seduction to lure them to their deaths. Issac never seemed bothered by it, but her brother wasn't one to succumb to weakness easily.

"Now, boys, you wouldn't be looking to cause any trouble in a public place, would you?" Tom tsked. "Bad form."

"How about you walk outside quietly, and we let the pretty brunette live." This came from the shorter of the two. His blond waves were lush and tousled and didn't at all match the mean expression on his round face.

"You know, I think I'll pass. I promised her the full New York City experience, and that includes pizza. But hey, if you want to wait a bit, I might be able to accommodate, in oh, say, never? Does that work for you?"

"You're just as cocky as they say, but I don't see what has everyone so scared." The bulkier one folded his arms. "Maybe we should take them back for our Mistress to play with. Alive."

"Who do you think she'd set on fire first?"

"The girl, definitely. And force him to watch."

"That would be fun."

Tom's expression turned bored as they continued to discuss their fate. How long would it take the Ichorians to recognize her? Most immortals did immediately, but perhaps, her new fashion sense kept her incognito. Also the fact that they thought she was dead would help.

"I'm thinking pepperoni," Tom murmured to her. "Extra sauce?"

*Have you gone mad?* she asked with a look.

He shrugged. "Okay, okay. We'll go half-cheese." He drummed his fingers over the menu. "Boys, would you like anything before we get started?"

"I'm one hundred and eighteen," Mister Bulky replied. "Hardly a boy."

"Congratulations," Tom drawled. "I'm twenty-seven, but my birthday isn't for another few months. Want an invite to the party?"

"Can you believe this guy?" Bulky asked.

The blond shook his head in disbelief. "Unbelievable."

Tom pushed off the booth to come face-to-face with both men. "Now, just remember, I did offer to buy you lunch first."

"Are you—?"

Tom slammed his fist into the bulky one's jaw, cutting off whatever he'd been about to say, and nailed the other Ichorian with a knee to the groin. A flash of metal appeared as one of them drew a blade, but Tom snagged it in a move too fast for her eyes to catch.

Amelia worried one of the restaurant patrons might call the cops or try to break up the fight, but the employee only looked on with a concerned expression while the couple by the windows watched with mild curiosity.

She jumped as the bulky one crashed into her table. His eyes rolled into the back of his head as he lost consciousness, and the blond fell beside him to the floor a few seconds later.

"Bag," Tom asked without breaking his stride and held out his hand. "We've gotta go. Now."

She pushed the heavy pack towards the edge of the booth, and he snagged it. "Are they dead?" she asked as she stood on shaky legs.

"No, just unconscious." He pulled the straps over his shoulders and stepped over their hulking forms.

"Hey, y-you're not g-going anywhere," the employee stuttered, blocking their path with a phone in his hand. His scrawny build and curly hair suggested he was no older than twenty.

Tom sighed. "Look, kid, those two dickheads followed us for the last two blocks and said some not so pleasant things to my girl here. I'm sorry for the mess, but they had it coming."

The young man frowned then considered Amelia. "Is that true?"

She nodded. *Technically, yes.* The couple in the corner nodded along with her. She suspected they only did that because they wanted to be on Tom's side. Who wouldn't after a performance like that?

"I dunno man. I should probably call the cops," the employee murmured, scratching his head.

"You should," Tom agreed. "And while you're at it, have these two asshats arrested. Meanwhile, I'm getting her out of here." His tone brooked no argument, and as he stepped forward, the clerk jumped out of his way. "For the mess and trouble," her Sentinel added as he slapped a few bills on the counter. She ducked under his arm out the door and accepted his hand.

"We need to move quickly," he said as he tugged her

173

down the sidewalk. "Dumb and Dumber called for backup before entering the restaurant."

"How do you know that?" she wondered, baffled. He hadn't even hinted at them being followed until pulling her into the pizza place.

"Because I saw them."

"Where?"

"On the subway. It's why I chose this stop instead of the one closer to your brother's office."

She hadn't even noticed. New York City geography was foreign to her.

"We're moving on to plan B," Tom said as he took a left down an alley. "It won't take long for word to get back to the CRF that I'm in the city, so we need get the hell out and don't have time to go back to *The Pierre.*"

"Okay." She kept his brisk pace and came to an abrupt stop as a short woman with brown spikes stepped in front of them. A sharp blade played through her fingers as she twirled it with a casual ease and looked them over.

"Ya know, I never liked Bobby. Always thought he was an idiot and didn't understand why Lucinda kept him around, but Justin is a friend." The stranger's expression darkened on that final word. "And you just knocked him out."

*Another Ichorian.* There was a reason the treaty stated Hydraians entered New York City at their own risk. Hydria posed the same threat, just the other way around. What Amelia wouldn't give to be home on the island right about now.

"With a blow to the head," a voice from behind rumbled. Amelia jumped while Tom didn't react, probably because he already sensed the second party. The man behind them stood well over six feet, broad shouldered with a belly that suggested one too many American treats, and a beard. Oh, and he was glowering menacingly at them. Good. Just what they needed. Why had Tom suggested New York City again? Because no one would expect them to come here? She was beginning to understand why; only those who courted death would visit this city.

"She smells sweet. Too sweet," the girl murmured.

"Hydraian sweet," the male replied.

The brunette cocked her head in a birdlike manner and blinked. "Yes. I think you might be right, Steve."

A chill skittered down Amelia's spine. Once they recognized her, all hell would break loose. Aidan's progeny were infamous. As one of the oldest Ichorians in existence, he held a certain reverence over his kind, which meant they would have to take her to the Conclave, alive. Then Osiris would likely kill her for sport because he was a sadistic bastard who enjoyed torture, but it would be even worse for her family. Aidan and Issac would be forced to watch.

One rule: Stay out of New York City.

*Oops.*

~*~

Being discovered on the subway by two of Lucinda's favorite pets had not been part of the plan. They'd no doubt been drawn to Amelia's looks and maybe even her scent, but had settled their challenging gaze on Tom not a second later. And then the game of chess began with Tom moving his queen to safety and the pawns falling into the king's trap. Except he hadn't counted on two more knights showing up so quickly. Good thing he packed more than one gun for this mission.

The petite woman displayed a quiet confidence that identified her as the leader of this ambush. Two or three more were likely on their way, and perhaps Lucinda herself. If she showed up, he was a dead man. No amount of reflexes and guns would help him out of that predicament, which meant he needed to get this dance over with as soon as possible. He had no desire to become that sadistic bitch's new play thing. She had an affinity for fire and blood, and not necessarily in that order.

He took a step sideways towards Amelia, which forced her to back up into the wall beside them, and put his back to her chest so he could see both players.

"I have this thing about hurting women," he explained to the brunette, "so if you want to walk away, I'll wait."

Her hazel eyes lit with a fire, suggesting he'd struck a nerve. *Just trying to do the chivalrous thing here.* Okay, nope, he took that back. She threw her blade with a precision he would have admired had it not been aimed at his chest. Reflexes were all that saved his heart. He swiveled to the side and barely had enough time to take Amelia with him. She fell to the ground with an "Oomph." He dropped a gun in her lap before engaging the tiny girl in hand-to-hand combat. Size could be deceiving, because the chick had a powerful punch that hit him square in the jaw and made him see stars.

*Fuck, this woman is fast.* He wondered if that was her gift as he ducked to sweep her legs out from under her. She jumped and attempted a kick to his face, which had him backing up a step with hands raised.

"Low blow," he admonished. Facial injuries crossed the line, but Ichorians weren't known to play fair. Killing a woman didn't sit well with him, but as he said to Amelia last night, either he pulled the trigger or risked harm to himself and maybe even her. The coldness in the woman's gaze helped his decision, as did her connection to Lucinda. Anyone who worked with or for that bitch deserved a lethal fate.

He blocked another blow and twisted out of reach as she went for his family jewels. *Oh, hell no.* On her next kick, he whipped out the gun from beneath his jacket and fired a round between her dead eyes. The standard bullet was enough to knock her out, but not kill her. Something he might regret later, but for now, mission accomplished.

The fight felt like it had gone on for minutes, when in

reality, it was more like fifteen seconds. Amelia was rocking back and forth on the ground as the bearded dude stared down at her. Whatever psychic gift he'd engaged to hold her there couldn't be that strong if he had to focus that hard. Tom gave the Ichorian a solid kick to the back to snap his concentration and went to fire his weapon when Amelia beat him to the punch. She let lose a round into the man's chest and screamed as she did it. His brow rose at the colorful display of words leaving her lips. He had no idea she could curse like that.

"That bloody hurt!" She punctuated the statement with another bullet to the man's brain, making Tom cringe. Those incendiary bullets were not cheap, nor could he find them at any regular store, and she'd just used five or six of them on one very dead Ichorian.

He held out a hand to still her when she took aim again. "He's dead, sweetheart. Very, very dead."

She growled and stomped her foot. "He did something with wind that bloody hurt my ears."

"An elemental," Tom mused. "But a shitty one if all he could do was mess with your hearing." Her glower told him that was the wrong thing to say. "You showed him, though. Nicely done, sweetheart."

She eyed the man on the ground, frowned down at the pistol in her hand, and looked back at Tom. "He's dead?"

"Yeah, and we're going to be too if we don't get moving. There's more coming." He suspected this was the B-team, and he didn't want to wait around for the A-team.

"But only fire and Hydraian blood can kill an Ichorian, other than a beheading I mean."

"Yes. That's not your average gun." The CRF engineered it to hold bullets that ignited on contact. Hence the sizzle and smoke coming from the bearded dude. One of those babies to the heart set the bloodstream on fire and killed Ichorians instantly.

"This is the gun you gave me last night."

"Right, in case we were attacked by Ichorians. Can we

get moving?"

Blue fire swirled in her irises as she stalked towards him. That look froze him in his tracks. She resembled a pissed off Goddess.

"I almost shot you with this gun." She shook it in his face.

*Fuck.* "Are we going to do this now?" Because they really didn't have time for it.

"I almost *shot* you. I thought you'd wake up, but with these bullets? You would have *died.* For good!"

"True, but—" Her palm connected with his cheek so hard he couldn't speak. His face was not having a good day. "Amelia—"

"No! I almost killed you! Like really, truly killed you!" Tears gathered in her eyes, making his chest ache.

"I didn't..." He cleared his throat and tried again. "I wasn't going to stand in your way if you wanted to leave, Amelia."

When he saw that gun in her hands, all the excitement of a challenge fled, and grief settled in its place. Maybe it was exhaustion, but it felt a whole hell of a lot more like resignation. Death had knocked at his door more times than he could count. It caused him to be cavalier with his life and perhaps a tiny bit suicidal.

"You're a bloody arse for doing that to me. I couldn't. I wouldn't..." She slapped his shoulder, but it lacked heat. When she hit his sternum, he wrapped his arms around her, and she buried her head into his chest. Standing in this alley made them the perfect Ichorian bait, but she was useless to him like this. He needed her to calm down and fight with him later.

"I hate you," she whispered.

The words vibrated through his heart, leaving a stroke of pain he didn't expect. She wasn't the first woman to say those words to him, but she was the first to leave an imprint. He kissed her hair and held her close. "Why would you do that to me, Tom? Why?"

"I thought it was what you needed," he admitted. "For retribution against my father. A way of seeking punishment for the sins leveled against you. Who better to kill than the son of the man who tortured you?" It sounded ridiculous now after everything he'd learned, but a part of it still rang true. Tom *was* her best option for revenge, if she wanted it. She had the power to destroy him because he would never fight her. Ever.

Amelia remained quiet for too long. "I considered it once. In the beginning, I mean. But I could never..." She trembled and clung to him tighter.

"Shh, it's okay. I expected you to hate me, Amelia. I mean, I'm John's son, and all the things the CRF did to you..." He paused to breathe deep through his nose. *Not going there right now.* "I never would have put you in that situation last night had I known. I'm sorry. I thought it would help."

"Never." She implored him with her eyes. "That would *never* help."

"I know that now."

"Do you? Because if you do that to me again, I will shoot you. Just with a normal gun and a lot of normal bullets."

He couldn't help his grin. "Is that a promise?"

"No, don't you smile at me like that. I'm not done being mad at you."

"I know. But can you be mad at me later?" he asked softly. "After we get out of the city alive?"

"You wouldn't be alive if I had shot you," she grumbled. "But you're right, I don't want to die."

"Neither do I." He brushed his lips against hers and felt a smidgen of relief when she returned the kiss. "Can we go?"

She nodded against him and pulled away. He took the gun she offered and returned it to his holster then linked his fingers with hers to start a brisk walk down the alley. One perk of his job? He knew the city inside and out and had an escape plan ready. He took a left onto a busier street, then a right, and found his target.

"What are we doing?" she asked as they entered a parking garage.

"I'm going to need you to do me a favor," he replied. "See that guy over there?" He gestured to the valet station where a man sat behind the desk. "I'm going to need you to distract him."

"Distract him?" she repeated. "By what, shooting him?"

He chuckled as they walked. "Well, that would certainly be a distraction, but no. I was thinking you saunter over there and be your charming self while I snag a pair of keys. Unless you prefer to watch me hot wire a car again?"

She blinked. "You wish for me to flirt with them?"

"Yes." He stopped a few yards away and ducked behind a pillar. "Act like you're lost and trying to figure out how to retrieve your car from the valet. When they ask for your ticket, pretend you lost it and stall."

She gaped at him. "You can't be serious."

"You prefer the hot wiring?"

Her frown was cute. "Oh, all right, but you better be quick."

"On my honor," he murmured with a smile.

She shook her head. "Right. I'm still mad at you."

"Good. Now go distract him."

"Yes, sir." Sarcasm be damned, he liked the way that sounded on her lips. *Something to consider later.*

He watched as she strolled up to the valet and engaged the grinning man in conversation. The dude folded his arms on the counter and leaned towards Amelia while she pretended to search her pockets. *Worked like a charm.*

Tom crept towards the cabinet of keys behind them and selected a few for shopping purposes. Ducking into the staircase, he headed to the parking decks below ground and clicked the various buttons to find an appropriate ride. He stopped when a sleek motorcycle caught his eye.

"Well, hello, beautiful." He swapped his baseball cap for the helmet hanging from the handle and grabbed another from a nearby bike for Amelia. Then he settled over the sporty seat, tested the key, and gave the bike a good rev. "Oh, yeah. You'll do."

The garage had a self-park level in addition to the valet, making it easy to drive out without notice. Just needed to pick up his woman and go. He maneuvered the new ride to the valet desk where he left her and stopped by the curb. Amelia's gaze widened when she caught sight of him, and her lips parted.

"You cannot possibly expect me to get on that thing," she blurted out as the man behind the desk watched with a wrinkly brow.

*Just stealing a bike, kid. Nothing to see here.*

"I do," Tom replied. "Hop on."

Her head swung back and forth. "Absolutely not."

"Seriously? After everything we've gone through, a bike is what you take issue with?" Didn't they just agree not to bicker until they were safe?

"It's a death trap."

"And standing here arguing while a hoard of Ichorians are searching for us isn't?" he asked, baffled.

She bit her lip and shook her head again.

*Stubborn woman.* "Here." Tom held out the helmet, and she cocked a challenging brow in response. They didn't have time for this. "Put this on, and get on the bike. We've gotta go. Now."

"I'd prefer a car," was her succinct reply.

"And I'd prefer to get the hell out of here. Put on the damn helmet, Amelia."

"You know this guy?" The lanky valet guy went for the hero card and failed. One glance put the kid back in his place and allowed Tom to refocus on his rebellious asset.

"I'm not asking again, sweetheart."

Amelia shot him a glare and yanked the helmet from his hand. She seemed to take great pleasure in throwing her Yankees cap to the ground. *Vixen.*

"We're so having a talk about this later." The growl in her voice made him smile.

"I look forward to it."

"Arse," she muttered as she threw a leg over the bike.

"Hold on, asset." He waited for her arms to settle around his waist before maneuvering out of the garage. The valet would realize Tom had stolen the bike whenever they found all the missing keys, which he suspected would take them a few hours tops. By then he'd be well out of the city and on his way to plan B: The Hamptons.

* * *

Tom's last visit to Wakefield Manor had been one of desperation. Heading down the long driveway after pressing the call button felt much the same, if not worse.

Coming here was a risk for multiple reasons. The CRF would consider it a potential escape option, but his father's pride would come into play. John Fitzgerald would expect Tom to exhaust all his options before seeking help from their biggest enemy. In this case, his dad would fail to consider just how far Tom would go to protect Amelia. It turned out he would risk his life because it was very likely Issac Wakefield would kill him on sight.

*Like mother, like son.*

Amelia's tension behind him broke his heart. He understood her hesitation all too well, because he felt the same way every time he returned to the cabin.

*Death roams here.*

Tom's father betrayed Amelia in the darkest of ways on these grounds. He murdered her lover Eli before taking her hostage. The two unforgivable sins no doubt weighed on her thoughts now.

"This was the best alternative to your brother's office," he said, feeling like an asshole. She couldn't possibly want to be here anymore than he did, let alone with a Fitzgerald.

Didn't matter that he played no part in the crime; his blood made him guilty by association.

She nodded against his back and laid her head against his shoulder. He placed his hand over hers and squeezed as he came to a stop by the guest house. A round man with a curious glint in his kind eyes walked out with an elderly woman by his side.

"How can we help you?" He sounded so cordial, yet he had to recognize the name Tom gave him at the security gate. No way did he work for the Wakefields this long and not have a clue as to Issac's immortality.

"Not me." He removed the helmet from his head and shook out his hair. "Her."

Amelia's arms were cement around his waist, so he gave her hand another gentle squeeze. "You can do this, sweetheart," he murmured it low for her ears alone. "I'm here if you need me."

Another nod against his back, and her grasp loosened a fraction. He hung the helmet over the bars and ran his fingers over her hands and forearms, willing her to relax. The couple watched with concerned expressions, and he noted the phone in the older man's hand. Someone with immortal genes would be along shortly because no way did he call the cops. If not her brother, one of the Hydraians. They had a notorious teleporter with unimaginable skills. *Talk about a fun talent.*

"I can do this," she whispered.

"Yes."

"Okay." Her palms slid along his abdomen to his sides as she used him to climb off the bike. She unlatched the helmet and pulled it off slowly before handing it to him. The sunglasses went next, and the couple gasped loudly.

"Amelia?" the man asked with a hand at his mouth.

"Hi, Robert. Cherie."

"Oh, my God…"

# CHAPTER FOURTEEN

# A Sleepy Homecoming

Amelia refused to go in the main house. It held too many memories, good and bad, and her heart couldn't handle it. She sat by the swimming pool, nibbling on a sandwich Cherie had brought her, while Tom paced a few feet away. Roger said Issac would be here soon, something that should have pleased her, but this manor made happiness impossible.

The low hanging moon reminded her of that night—a dinner that started between friends and ended between enemies. Inviting Jonathan over for an evening of food and drinks had been second nature. She'd known him her entire life, likened him to an uncle due to his relationship with her father, and never expected his treachery. His familial charade burned to the ground when he pulled out that gun and shot Eli in the chest without blinking an eye.

She shivered despite the sultry summer heat. Tom's hands on her shoulders had her meeting his dark gaze. Kindness and concern with a touch of comfort stared down at her. Just what she needed at precisely the right moment. She stood and wrapped her arms around his neck as he folded his around her back. He pressed a kiss to her hair then rested his cheek on her head.

"It's going to be okay, sweetheart."

"I know," she whispered. "But this place... I can't stay here tonight."

"The history haunts you."

She pressed her chin to his chest and gazed up at him. "Did he tell you...?" She trailed off, unable to finish. Of course Jonathan told his son about that night. He considered it one of his biggest victories, taking down Eli the Elder, one of the strongest Hydraians in existence, with a bullet to the chest.

"I know enough of it, but that's not what I meant. That weight in your chest lessens over time, but I don't know if it ever goes away. Mine hasn't. Not completely anyway."

She considered his meaning, wondering what memory he could be referring to, when realization washed over her. The way he reacted in the room after Anita's first visit to the cabin, how he cursed and fled from the room as if he'd seen a ghost, and the blood on the photos in his closet. Of course. Anna's murder. It happened at the cabin. She had a vague memory of Issac calling to tell her about helping Jonathan, and being too late.

"Why do you keep the cabin?" she wondered.

"My mother left it in my name, and my father insisted on keeping it. I want nothing to do with it, so my aunt essentially maintains it in my absence."

"And sending you there with me?"

"Served as a punishment of sorts."

Tom mentioned that last night, but never explained

himself. "Punishment for what?"

He blew out a breath. "That's a long story, but in a nutshell, I went behind my dad's back to show a friend the truth about Ichorians, and she nearly died. Of course, he's reaping the benefits now because he's turning her into a fucking Sentinel."

"A female Sentinel?"

"Yeah, and about that. She's also sort of your brother's girlfriend, which is why—"

"Hold on." Her hands fell to her sides as she peered up at him. "My brother has a girlfriend?" No bloody way. Issac didn't go beyond a first date. Ever.

"Apparently."

"My brother, as in Issac?" The man who refused every woman she ever introduced him to? Who had no interest in relationships that lasted more than one night? *Monogamy might work for you and Eli, love, but it does not suit me.* How many times did he say that to her? "Are you certain we're talking about the same man?"

"Unfortunately, yeah. Definitely the same guy."

She didn't know how to process that. How many decades did she spend playing matchmaker with him and failing?

Tom went rigid against her, his hands fisting at her back as he squeezed his eyes shut. She studied him in alarm as his cheeks went white.

"Are you all right?"

"Your brother." He spoke through clenched teeth and grimaced. "He's here."

She spun around as his arms fell and took in the empty patio. Strands of soft lights illuminated the area without moonlight, while a soft glow emanated from the pool. "I don't see him."

"Trust me," he growled, posture stiff. "He's nearby."

Her brow furrowed then lifted as she caught on. "He's in your head." Issac could manipulate vision on a psychic level, similar and yet so different from Amelia's ability to shift humanoid appearance. They inherited their imagery skills from their mother. If her brother could tap into Tom, then he could also tap into her thoughts. She searched for a memory of their mum from childhood and painted a vivid picture of the woman lecturing them about how to properly treat guests. A blue butterfly fluttered through the image mid-lecture, making her heart race.

"He's here," she whispered. Tears filled her eyes, and for once, they weren't the sad kind. She pressed her hands to her mouth and spun to face Tom. "My brother is really, truly here."

"Yeah, and he's a dick." Tom muttered, glowering at the patio. He didn't appear to be in pain anymore, but he did look ready to commit murder.

"What did he do?"

He shook his head. "Let's just say it wasn't a thank you."

"My apologies, Thomas. Do I owe you a thank you?" Her brother's voice floated over the night air and showered goosebumps down her arms. She would recognize those cool tones anywhere.

*He's here.* Amelia turned and watched him saunter around the side of the manor with Tristan at his side. They resembled dark-haired angels in suits and wore matching warrior-like expressions. She pinched her side, a habit formed from nights of dreaming about this moment only to wake to an empty room. When Issac didn't disappear, her knees wobbled.

*Could it be?*

"You're here," she whispered. "I can't believe you're here." A sob caught in her throat as the fantasy she never thought would become a reality came to life before her eyes.

Issac's strong arms went around her as he pulled her into an unforgiving hug. *Is this real?* She inhaled the fresh linen of his crisp dress shirt and sighed at its familiarity. *My brother.* Tears rolled down her cheeks as his love and devotion washed over her in heady waves. She didn't need an emotive ability to feel it; his warmth and strength was enough.

"You're alive," he breathed, holding her impossibly tighter. "I'm so sorry, Amelia. I'm so fucking sorry."

She held him with the same ferocity and sobbed into his sturdy chest. God, how she missed him. The last two or three years had dulled her to the emptiness inside, but being near him again rekindled all those old feelings of dashed hope and resignation. At some point, she stopped believing in him, and that moment hurt the most.

*But he's here. He's real.* She clung to him for support as her legs threatened to buckle beneath her.

*I'm finally free.*

"I thought you were gone." His voice cracked on the words as he buried his face in her hair. "I would have come for you, Amelia. I'm so fucking sorry I didn't." The pain in his words broke her heart. Of course he would blame himself. Her brother had a knight complex, always wanting to protect her from the evils of the world. If she learned one thing during her captivity, it was that villains existed in all forms. *And so do heroes,* her heart whispered, thinking of Tom. He stood silent behind her, a wall of protection and warmth that soothed her soul.

"Finding your ashes was the worst day of my life," her brother continued. "God, Amelia, I missed you so fucking much." His agony trembled through her and ripped her chest wide open. Her brother, who rarely showed emotion, was falling apart in her arms. And he blamed himself for something he had no control over.

"I forgive you," she whispered, knowing he needed to hear it. *I don't blame you, dear brother. I could never blame you.* "Jonathan fooled us all."

Issac stiffened as his trademark armor snapped in place, and resolve straightened his spine. *There's the brother I know and adore.* Further proof that this was indeed not a hallucination. How many days and nights had she dreamed of this moment? Perhaps not with Tom as a witness, but his presence felt right here. *I'm home.*

"I'll execute him for this." A promise underlined with a conviction only her brother could convey. Ichorians were notorious for their grotesque murder scenes, and Issac had participated in more than a few of them. There was a reason his kind held him in a high regard. They feared him.

"If anyone has earned the right to seek vengeance against my father, it's Amelia. Not you." Challenge replaced the usual playfulness in Tom's tone, making her wonder what history she had missed between him and her brother. Or was he still sour over the vision game?

"Shall I silence him, Issac?" Tristan asked.

"That won't be necessary. Not yet, anyway." Issac kept his arm around her shoulders, tucking her into his side as he turned to face Tom with a bland expression. Her brother always could turn off his emotions in the blink of an eye. "Tell me why I shouldn't kill you, Thomas."

Amelia gasped. "Issac!"

"You probably should," Tom replied with a shrug.

"Okay, no, not this again." Amelia threw her brother's arm off of her shoulders and moved to stand in front of her suicidal lover. "If you hurt him, I'll never forgive you, Issac."

Her brother's brow hit his hairline. He glanced at Tristan, who appeared just as shocked. The old Amelia would never talk back in this manner unless they'd committed a social faux pas. Which, really, she could argue threatening to murder a houseguest was a major infraction, but that belied the point.

"Amelia, I'm…" Issac's voice trailed off as his phone started to ring. He put the device to his ear. "Yes, Mateo?" He nodded. "Very good. Yes, please." He pocketed the mobile and trained his gaze on the man behind her. "Sentinel chatter indicates they're on their way here for a scouting mission. Care to elaborate?"

"Sure. Knowing my father, he's covering his bases.

Wakefield Manor is the last place he would expect me to go, but it's not like I've let that stop me before, so he's sending men to watch your property. My guess is, he's more worried about you discovering Amelia's alive than he is with catching me."

"Because it would ruin the illusion," Issac murmured with a nod. His sapphire gaze softened as it lowered to her. "Jacque is on his way. Do you wish to change before we go?"

She fingered the Yankee's shirt. "Are my clothes still here?"

"Yes." No elaboration. Typical Issac.

"You didn't refashion the suite for yourself?"

"This is my second time to the estate since your, er, departure."

Her eyes widened. "You've only been here two times since...?"

His intense look unsettled her stomach almost as much as her unfinished question. She knew before he spoke that his words were going to hurt. "Jonathan left Eli in the ballroom with a vase holding your ashes. To say this place gives me nightmares is an understatement."

His blatant depiction weakened her knees. She fell back into Tom, and his arms came around her automatically. If he was intimidated by the death glare her brother flashed him, he didn't show it. He held her while she trembled and offered the support she so desperately needed. That night flashed through her mind as if it were yesterday. Jonathan had pointed the gun at her after shooting Eli and gave her a choice. *Comply or die.* She chose to comply at the time, but hadn't realized what that would mean in the end. Oh, how she selected the wrong option that night.

"I'll destroy him." Issac bit off, obviously seeing the scenes tumbling through her thoughts. She tried to stop them, but couldn't. This place overwhelmed her. All the memories of her life with Eli were tainted by that single night and what happened next. She turned in Tom's arms and buried her head against his chest to breathe in his masculine scent. Darkness loomed, threatening to consume her being, but his strength cocooned her, protecting her when she needed it most.

"We need to get her away from here," she heard him say. "It's too much."

"So now you're the expert when it comes to my sister?"

"Yes." Flat, no room for argument.

"We'll see about that." Issac's cool tones floated over her in a dreamy wave.

*Oh, no.* She recognized this sensation, the one of drowsiness right before falling asleep. Except there was nothing natural about it, not right now. She didn't want to leave Tom's warmth, but Issac gave her no choice. His gift for vision manipulation extended to the dream world, something he activated and flowed over her. He meant well, he always did, but the Amelia who accepted his comfort in the past wasn't here now. She craved a different type of escape, one that involved a certain blond Sentinel.

Her lips parted in protest, but no sound escaped. Heaviness settled over her shoulders and back and ventured downwards. Tom's hold was all that kept her from falling as her legs gave out. His responding curse sounded so far away.

*We'll be chatting about this later, dear brother.*

* * *

Silky sheets twined through Amelia's thighs as she rolled over the too-soft bed. She woke with a start, blinking into the fading sun outside her windows. The ocean lay beyond it with waves rolling over black sand.

*Oh my God.* Her hand flew to her mouth. *I'm trapped in a dream.*

This happened so often lately, especially after one of Jonathan's beatings. Memories tortured her every time she closed her eyes. Usually, she woke up just as she started to believe they were real, and then the crushing pain of reality fell on her, making it difficult to breathe.

*No. Never again.*

She tore off her flimsy tank top and shorts, refusing to let something so delicate ever touch her skin again, and was in the process of ripping the silk sheets from the bed when a male cleared his throat. Standing in nothing but a thong, she met a pair of chocolate eyes that only existed in her distant memories.

*It's about time Balthazar visited me in a dream.*

"You mean to tell me I don't visit them often?" he asked with a devilish grin. "I'm wounded, truly."

*Oh good, his mind reading ability works here, too.* Of course, it was her dream, so she could take it away. But what would be the fun in that?

Amelia sat on the pillow-top mattress and studied him. No one would blame her. Balthazar was a God among men, and he knew it. Square jaw, perfect nose, high cheekbones, dark eyelashes women would kill for, and a chiseled body made for sin. She'd seen him shirtless countless times, yet he wore jeans and a t-shirt. Too bad he couldn't show up in her head dressed to seduce. She could use a little escape.

A frown creased her brow. No. Pleasure wasn't what she desired right now. Not with him anyway. She craved a certain blond Sentinel, one who chased away the darkness...

"Oh, bollocks." Heat swam up her neck. "I'm not dreaming."

"No, you're very much awake and also very naked."

She grabbed the sheet and pulled it around her like a dress as memories overwhelmed her. They ended with Issac putting her to sleep for what felt like days.

*I'm finally really, truly home.* So why did it feel so foreign and wrong? She sat down on the mattress and flinched. *Too soft.*

Balthazar pushed off the doorframe and placed a mug on the nightstand before settling his big body on the bed beside her. The man could seduce a woman with a single look, but concern deepened his eyes and tugged at the edges of his full lips. "Come here, love."

She went willingly into his arms and rested her head against his chest. As an Elder, and one of her oldest friends, he knew her well. At least in her former life.

"God, it feels so good to hold you," he whispered. "When Issac told us you were alive, it was hard to believe."

"I missed you too, B." His nickname rolled off her tongue, but didn't feel quite right. None of this did. The bed was too comforting, the home too warm, and the setting sun was too bright.

He combed his fingers through her hair and sighed. "I can help."

She knew exactly what he meant, but couldn't bear it. "Don't."

"I'd never force it."

"And that's why I love you." She meant it. He might come off as arrogant and brazen, but deep down, he cared. His ability to control emotion and read minds made him a master manipulator. He could drown out all her concerns and cocoon her in a sea of bliss, but it wouldn't be real. She needed to feel, to remember, or she'd become a shell of nothingness. The darkness would be a better alternative. When it became too much, she knew who to turn to, unless...

Panic settled in her chest, forcing her to pull away from her old friend. "Where's Tom?" She fell asleep in his arms, but Jacque had obviously teleported her here. What about Tom? Did he leave without saying goodbye? Was he still in New York? And where was her brother? They needed to have a discussion about his actions.

Balthazar's mouth curled down into an uncharacteristic scowl. "The Sentinel's here."

"In Hydria?"

"Yes."

Her shoulders sagged in relief as her heart gave a little flutter. He hadn't left her. "Is he here now?" She suspected he wasn't or he would be in the room, not Balthazar. Unless the Elders had him occupied. They were a bit chatty on occasion, especially with visitors. And Tom's fledgling status would have Luc wanting to learn all about him.

"No."

She frowned at Balthazar's one word response. The man's notorious wit seemed to have disappeared behind a fog of frustration. "What aren't you telling me?" she wondered.

"He's indisposed at the moment."

"What the bloody hell does that mean, *indisposed?* Tell me what's going on."

He looked her up and down and smirked. "I'm liking this new feisty side of you, Amelia. It's kind of hot."

"Don't change the subject or distract me with sex. Where's Tom?"

All teasing fled his features, and the Elder in him peeked out from beneath the surface. "I'm not going to pretend I haven't figured out what happened between the two of you, but trust me when I say it's done."

She bristled. All the Elders, except Eli, treated her like their kid sister, and she could see that hadn't changed in her absence. Usually she felt special, but not today. "Excuse me, but that's not your decision to make."

"You're right, it's Luc's, and his word is law." He stood up and ran his fingers through his dark hair. "I know you think this is harsh, and I'm sorry for that, but we're doing what's best for you. That man is in your head, and not in a healthy way."

"Unbelievable." She stood to be on his level and didn't care for a second how ridiculous she looked dressed in a silky sheet. "You have no idea what he's done for me or what I've been through or why you couldn't be more wrong."

Tom never mistreated her or caused her to feel inferior. If anything, he treated her as an equal, taught her how to defend herself, and centered her when she needed it. Like the other night in the bathtub and again when she couldn't pull the trigger.

She thought back to his first visit in her cell, the surprise in his gaze she mistook as a game when he asked if she was okay. At the time, she called him the good cop, but he meant it. He genuinely cared. All those water bottles and sporadic visits were his way of checking up on her, which she understood now. And the grief in his eyes when he realized Anita's visit to the cabin hadn't been pleasant, that was real, too. What they had was unique and new and not something anyone would stop her from pursuing, because she needed him. And from what little she'd gathered over the last few days, he needed her, too. Because the man clearly had a death wish.

Curiosity colored Balthazar's expression, indicating he'd eavesdropped on her thoughts. He might not control emotion on a whim, but he always listened. Even when he shouldn't.

"He's locked up, but alive. That's all I can give you."

"Locked up?" she repeated, incredulous. "Why on earth would Luc lock him up? He's a fledging, one of us."

"That Sentinel is *not* one of us, Amelia. He's spent his short existence slaughtering immortals, and that includes Hydraians. He's about as welcome here as his father."

Amelia's mouth fell open. "You cannot compare him to Jonathan."

"Oh yes, I can. You don't know him like we do."

"And likewise!" She hadn't meant to shout at him, but locking Tom up after everything he had done for her was madness. They should be welcoming him with open arms. Fledglings weren't common, and a man with his skills could be exceptionally useful. "You know nothing about him," she added in a normal tone.

"If that's true, we're about to know a hell of a lot more."

Her blood ran cold. "What are you doing to him?"

He blew out a breath and palmed the back of his neck. "Nothing. Yet."

Her brow crinkled at the irritation in his reply. It didn't appear to be directed towards her, but someone else. "Tell me what's going on, B."

"No." All playing left his stance and expression, telling her he wouldn't budge. The Elder stared at her now, not her big brother or friend. Her lips trembled at the feeling of being an outsider, but she expected this. She wasn't the woman they once adored, and Balthazar would see that better than anyone.

"I'll always love you, Amelia," he murmured, his veneer cracking. "Don't ever think otherwise." She knew he meant that literally since he could read her thoughts.

"Why won't you tell me what's happening to him?"

"Give us some time to figure this out, okay?"

She nibbled her lip, considering. If Balthazar wouldn't talk to her, no one would, except maybe Issac. And she doubted even he would say anything in this situation after the way he treated Tom last night. They meant well and wanted to keep her safe, but ignorance wasn't always bliss. Her friends and family remembered the Amelia who would bow down and do nothing. She'd introduce them to the new her soon, but not yet. "Fine."

Balthazar narrowed his eyes, obviously having heard that last thought, but didn't press her. Knowing him, he'd prefer to find out by observing. He looked her up and down and folded his arms. "I'll have you know those are not cheap sheets you tried to destroy, and last I knew, you loved silk. That's why I put them on the bed for you."

His words had her glancing around. She hadn't thought much of the warm tones, masculine furniture, or the colossal bed until he pointed it out. "Why am I at your house?"

"Because your home was repurposed after the incident and turned into a guest house for fledglings. Luc thought it the best way to honor your memory."

She shivered. *Honoring my memory.* Because they all thought she was dead. Such a surreal feeling, though she agreed that refashioning her home for fledglings was a fitting tribute. Amelia served as a mother hen to several future Hydraians, teaching them about immortal life on the island and serving as a social coordinator. Would she ever be that woman again? Just thinking about it made her sick to her stomach. How could she serve as a role model in her current mental state?

"Hey," Balthazar murmured, his hand settling on her bare shoulder. "Don't worry yourself about the future. Just focus on the now. And remember, you're not alone. We're going to love you no matter what, Amelia. There are no expectations. Do you understand?"

She bit her lip. He meant well, but he couldn't understand just how different she'd become, how her experience shaped her. Six years to an immortal his age meant little to nothing, but to her, it redefined her existence. Jonathan stole her innocence, destroyed her faith, and removed all aspect of hope. How did she even begin to describe that?

*He did the same thing to Tom,* her conscious whispered. Which explained her bond with him. Of all the people she knew, Tom was the only one who understood how it felt to be manipulated and destroyed by a loved one. Neither of them had a choice; they were just held in different cages. And now he was in a cell somewhere on the island. She intended to do something about that.

"I need clothes," she told Balthazar. "And preferably not a dress." Who would have thought she'd rather wear Tom's boxers and shirts right about now. They suited her more than her old clothes.

Balthazar's brow rose. "I'm not sure whether to address that little plan of yours, or the words you just said out loud. But by the look on your face, I won't say anything about either item." Amusement danced through his gaze as he took her measure again. "Oh, I do like this new side of you. Luc is in for a treat. Wakefield, too."

"Clothes."

"Yes, ma'am." He walked over to one of his dressers to muddle through the drawers. His gaze was wicked as he turned around and handed her a pair of boxers and a shirt. "Mine might be a bit bigger than the Sentinel's, but they'll do. Just do me a solid and let me be there when Issac sees you in these, yeah?"

Some things never changed. "Are you two still bickering like little boys?"

He pressed a hand to his chest. "Me? Never."

"Right. I'm surprised Issac even let me stay here with you." Her brother and Balthazar had a tedious relationship underlined in begrudging trust. It seemed more logical for her to wake up at Luc's house than Balthazar's, but she wasn't complaining.

"Your brothers are preoccupied with another issue at the moment." Humor danced in his gaze, making her curious.

"What other issue?"

"Oh, I'll let them explain that one to you."

"Okay." She pulled the shirt over her head while he watched and dropped the sheet to put on the shorts.

"You do remember that I have a full bath complete with all the toiletries a man or woman could possibly want, right?"

"Yes." His notorious hospitality pleased more than a few bedmates. The man was insatiable, but he treated his partners with respect and made them all feel like Gods. Or so she'd been told. As good of friends as they were, they'd never crossed that line, and they never would. Eli meant too much to them to ever even consider it.

"I miss him," Balthazar murmured, hearing her thoughts. His sad smile tugged at her heartstrings. "This new you would shock the hell out of him, but in a good way."

Her stomach knotted at his words, as a feeling of unease crept over her. "I'm not the woman he loved, B."

"Maybe not," he agreed. "But he would have loved this you, too. That man was crazy about you."

Guilt weighed on her conscious as Eli's face flashed behind her eyes. Every time she thought of him, another detail went missing. This time, it was the dark shade of his irises, a unique grey that didn't quite hold the same appeal they once did. A luscious brown stared back at her instead.

Amelia couldn't love Eli like she once did, not after everything. He would always hold a special place in her heart, but she needed someone who regarded her as a partner, not a princess, and her Eli would never be that man. Not because he was dead. Because he would insist on putting her on a pedestal where she no longer belonged. And it killed her to realize that, but the foundation of their relationship was built on her inexperience and purity, which she no longer had. Jonathan had destroyed that part of her and created a new woman. One she wasn't sure Eli could adore, at least not in the way he once did.

"Eli would want you to be happy," Balthazar murmured.

*I know.* And that only depressed her more. He was such a good man, who deserved better. But the part of her soul that forever loved him died with him that day, leaving behind a void she never thought to fill. Until Tom. He'd wormed his way inside and planted seeds of hope, suggesting that she may one day be able to love again. Assuming she got to him in time.

"Before you go gallivanting about the island, I should warn you there's a party tonight. And you're the woman of the hour."

Dread pooled in her belly, making her feel ill. "A party?"

"As that used to be your favorite past time, the others

thought it would be a good way to welcome you home. Jacque and Lara are in charge."

She sat on the bed again, hands in her lap. "What time does it start?"

"In an hour. That's hot chocolate, by the way." He gestured at the nightstand. "I even added little marshmallows."

That used to be her favorite drink, and he always prepared it from scratch with dark cocoa. A taste wouldn't kill her and might help her feel a bit better. She picked up the mug and let the rich aroma tease her nose.

"You're trying to distract me with deliciousness." Which wouldn't work. Not for long anyway.

"We're not going to decide anything on the Sentinel tonight," he added, voice low. She knew the *we* referred to the Elders, which included Balthazar. "Let us love on you tonight, Amelia. We need it almost as badly as you do."

Maybe immersing herself in her former life would help bring old parts of her to the surface. She owed it to her friends and family to try, didn't she? And Balthazar was right. She craved their love and acceptance, especially now, because she needed to know they still cared about her despite everything she'd been through and done. All she wanted for the last six years was to return home. She needed to embrace it.

"He's safe?" she asked, referring to Tom.

"Yes, and unharmed."

Balthazar never lied. He valued trust and transparency too much for it. She took a sip of the hot chocolate and moaned into the cup. It tasted like heaven and sin and flowed with purpose to her empty stomach. Issac had knocked her out for at least twelve hours, of that she was certain.

"All right, I'll go to the party, but I need proper clothing and a meal first." *And to see Tom for myself.* The challenge would be finding him, and circumventing whatever security measures the Elders had put in place.

Amusement danced through his gaze and curled his lips. If he heard her thoughts, he didn't comment. "Well, you go freshen up, and I'll take care of the rest." They used to cook together all the time, so she had no doubt he would prepare something outlandish.

She set the mug aside, stood, and pressed a kiss to his cheek. "Thank you."

He wrapped an arm around her lower back to hold her to him. "Don't thank me, Amelia. We should have come for you, and I don't think any of us will ever be able to forgive ourselves for believing you were dead all these years."

"I don't blame you," she whispered.

"You don't have to, love. We blame ourselves." He kissed her hair and rested his cheek there. "I can't begin to understand what you went through, but I'm here when you're ready to talk about it."

She swallowed. "I'm not ready yet." *And I probably never will be.* Some horrors were better left buried.

# CHAPTER FIFTEEN

## Welcome to Hydria

Tom leaned against the cement wall, hands in his pockets and legs crossed at the ankles. A group of Hydraians were having a heated argument out in the hallway beyond his locked door, but he'd given up on eavesdropping a while ago.

They'd taken his guns and knives and left him in a tiny room with one chair, a table, some food, and a bottle of water. Being as all he cared about was Amelia's wellbeing, he hadn't touched any of the items and stood waiting for someone to give him an update. No one seemed all that willing to talk to him, which he expected. It wasn't like he made a lot of immortal friends as a Sentinel.

When a female's voice rose outside the door, his attention piqued. Not Amelia, but she sounded familiar—

and furious. The knob jimmied, but stayed shut, and something loud hit the wood. He pushed off the wall and paced to the side as the thing crashed open. A familiar blonde appeared a second later, making his mouth drop.

"Stas? What the hell are you doing here?" he asked, dumbfounded.

"I told you he was fine." Wakefield's cool tones preceded him as he stepped into the room behind Stas. Her fiery green eyes narrowed at the haughty Ichorian before fixing on Tom. She gave him a once-over and seemed relieved at finding him in one piece. He returned the favor, noting her toned arms and legs, and received a warning glare from the jackass at her side. *Possessive much?* The woman was best friends with Lizzie and, therefore, like a sister to him. He'd never be able to view her outside the platonic filter. The same could not be said about Amelia.

"I want a minute alone with him," Stas murmured.

"No."

"I wasn't asking, Issac."

"And I wasn't debating, Astasiya."

She folded her arms and glowered up at the well-dressed man. Even in Hydria, he sported a suit. *Pompous ass.*

"Do you need me to persuade you to leave?" Stas asked.

Wakefield tilted his head to the side as a smile played over his lips. The adoration in his gaze was apparent as he considered her, surprising Tom. He had no idea the Ichorian had it in him to care about a woman for longer than a few hours. No wonder John wanted Stas to become a Sentinel. She was in a prime position to function as a double agent, which made her very dangerous in this situation. If she reported back to the CRF that Amelia and Tom were here, shit would hit the fan. Not that he cared really; his father deserved to be punished for his sins. He worried more about Stas becoming collateral damage, but she became that the moment she agreed to play spy with the Ichorians.

"Hmm," Wakefield murmured. He palmed her cheek and brushed a thumb over her lips. "You win this round, little complication of mine. But I plan to repay the favor later."

Stas flushed, making it clear what her boyfriend meant by that threat. Not that Tom wouldn't have inferred it by the tone. He rolled his eyes at the obvious display of possession as Wakefield kissed her to punctuate his point. *News flash, man. It's* your *sister I'm into, not the girl I love like a sister.*

"Thomas," Wakefield said when his lips were half an inch away from Stas's mouth. "Your death is already imminent, but I will ensure it is very painful if you so much as think about hurting my Aya. Understood?"

Stas slapped her boyfriend's arm before Tom could reply to that unveiled threat. "His death is *not* imminent."

"Whatever you say, love." He stepped backwards before she could hit him again and ducked out of the room with a playful grin.

*The man has lost his mind over a woman.* Sort of like how Tom had lost his over Amelia. *Well, fuck.* He never thought he'd see the day when he and Wakefield would have something in common. Other than the death of Tom's mother, of course. He never did ask Amelia about it. He didn't want to see her reaction. What if she knew about Wakefield's involvement in the murder? What would she say?

Stas interrupted his thoughts by slamming the door shut behind the Ichorian.

Tom cocked a brow. "I assume you're *Aya*?" *Great first question, buddy.* It was a weird nickname, though. He preferred Stas.

"Apparently," she grumbled before blowing out a long breath. Concern trickled into her gaze as she looked him over. "Are you okay?"

"Never been better. Why?" he asked, feigning innocence.

Her hands went to her hips, and her gaze narrowed. "Seriously? There are a bunch of pissed off Hydraians out there who want to murder you in various ways, and you're going to be all nonchalant about it?"

"Sounds about right." He figured they would want him dead. It didn't matter that he had never hurt a Hydraian or that his father called all the shots; he was guilty by association. He wondered what Amelia thought of his death sentence. Did she know? Would she care? His chest hurt at the thought of her brushing him off, but he wouldn't think less of her for it. Someone deserved to pay for his father's sins, and he seemed the prime candidate in this situation. But only to an extent. He would fight if he had to.

"Are you even listening to me?" Stas asked, interrupting his thoughts.

*No.* "Of course. Does my dad know you're here?"

"Yes."

*Shit.* "So you've told him about me and Amelia." Not a question, but a statement.

"I came in here to ask questions, not the other way around."

He waved her on. "Ask away, Sentinel Stas."

It pained him a little to be such an asshole to her, but he knew the purpose of this chat. She didn't want him to tell the others about her double agent status. If he did, they'd kill her. The fact that she felt the need to even ask him to keep quiet pissed him off. If she didn't realize how much he cared about her by now, she'd never understand. He would never put her at risk like that, but he would advise her to go home and stop this nonsense before she ended up in a body bag. The Hydraians allowing her this close to their nest meant they trusted her or, at a minimum, trusted Issac's judgment. If she didn't stop this charade soon, she'd get herself killed, or worse.

"Why did Doctor Fitzgerald move Amelia from the CRF basement?"

He blinked. That was not at all what he expected her to say. "What?" How the hell did she even know that? Did Amelia tell her?

"You heard me. Why did he move her?"

If Amelia told the Hydraians about being moved, she would have told them why, too. Which meant Stas's knowledge was based on something else. "How do you know she was moved?"

Her lips flattened. "Remember that day you picked me up from Issac's house and took me to the CRF?"

"Of course I do." One of the worst days of his life. He hadn't known whether she would be alive or dead when he got there.

"Do you remember how you stormed into your dad's office all pissed off and he walked out with you to have a chat?"

Tom went rigid at the memory. "Yes." He had wanted to kill his father that day. The bastard had taken his frustration out on Amelia and left her broken on the floor. And it was technically Tom's fault his dad was pissed to begin with, something that worsened the situation.

"I found Amelia while you two were talking. Is that why he moved her?"

He gaped at her. "So wait, you knew about Amelia?" Why didn't she say anything?

"I just said I did. Now answer my question."

"My dad moved her so you wouldn't find out about her."

Stas's gaze widened. "What?"

He dragged a hand over his face and started pacing to burn off some of his excess energy. Thinking about that night provoked his desire to punch someone, mainly his father. "After you accepted the Sentinel position, I suggested we move Amelia so you wouldn't find her. I didn't think you'd react well to it." But apparently, he'd been wrong because she hadn't cared at all.

"And you brought her to Issac?" she asked, incredulous.

He blew out a breath and gave a humorous laugh. "Yeah, well, that wasn't part of the mission at all, something you no doubt know all about."

Stas frowned at that. "Actually, I don't know anything about it. Doctor Fitzgerald—sorry, your *dad*—told me you were overseas on a covert mission, and Stark has kept me otherwise occupied." She said the latter with a scowl that told him just how much she enjoyed that.

"We were in upstate New York at my mother's cabin, but wait." He turned to study her, watching for any sign of a lie. "If you weren't briefed, then you haven't reported back that I'm here."

She held his gaze. "Doctor Fitzgerald thinks I've run off for a romantic weekend with Issac."

"Why would you lie to him?" Or was she saying that to maintain her cover? Could the Hydraians hear their conversation?

"Because I despise him." The venom in her tone was new. He'd never heard Stas speak like that, and his expression must have shown it. "Why did you bring Amelia to Issac?"

He palmed the back of his neck and considered how to answer that. Speaking the truth during an interrogation went against all his training, but this wasn't a typical situation. "I don't have an easy answer to that."

At some point, he had developed feelings for Amelia. How deep they went remained a mystery he was too afraid to solve. If he admitted loving her, he risked having his heart ripped from his chest. So he settled on caring about her, to an unknown extent. It felt safer that way.

"Want to know why I stormed into my dad's office that day?" he asked, changing the subject to something he could answer.

She studied him with an incredulous expression. "Yes."

"Because of what I found in Amelia's room. You claim to have seen her, so you must understand why that infuriated me. He beat the shit out of her because of what I did to you."

Her frown deepened. "I don't follow."

"The Arcadia, Stas. He was furious that I sent you there and thought I'd gotten you killed. While I was out checking on you, he was taking his frustration out on her, and I had no idea. When I found her like that." He had to pause to swallow the growl forming in his throat. "Well, let's just say, I lost my shit. Then you accepted his job offer, and I jumped at the chance of getting her away from him. I suggested he move her, Stark agreed, and my dad sent me along as the babysitter. It was my punishment for telling you about Ichorians."

Her lips parted in shock, a tell that all of this information was new to her. So Amelia hadn't talked to anyone, yet. Interesting detail. *Where are you, sweetheart?* he wondered, not for the first time. Being apart from her bothered him more than he wanted to admit. Having been attached at the hip for weeks had left an imprint. He missed her.

"Now tell me something," he continued, curious. "If you saw her that day, why didn't you say anything? It didn't bother you that the CRF had a female prisoner? Let alone one beaten to a pulp by the company's CEO only minutes before you arrived?" He couldn't help the hint of anger that infiltrated his tone. She hadn't reacted at all, and that puzzled him. He expected better of her.

"Oh, it bothered me a hell of a lot. And I didn't say anything because I didn't want to end up in a cell."

He blinked. "My father would never do that to you."

"Really? Considering everything he's done to me, I think he would. You know, with murdering Owen, trying to kill me with the Nizari poison, oh, and let's not forget him trying to blame that last part on Issac to manipulate me against him."

Tom gaped at her. Information overload. "Owen?" He racked his brain for a memory and frowned. "He was your friend that Lizzie didn't like, right?"

"Yes, he was also a Hydraian."

His gaze widened. "Seriously? What the fuck was he doing in New York City?" Talk about seeking a death sentence.

"You didn't know?"

"How the hell would I know that?"

"Because your dad had him killed."

He blinked. "Back up. When, how, and why?" And did she say something about the Nizari poison almost killing her? That only harmed fledglings like himself, not mortals. And no way was Stas anything but human.

"I was hoping you could tell me that."

"I have no idea. Owen wasn't causing any trouble or hurting anyone, right? The CRF only goes after rogue immortals who have harmed humans in some way. Stark should have explained that by now."

"He did, but regardless, your father killed Owen. Because of me."

"I don't understand." What did she have to do with anything? "Why would he murder someone on your behalf?"

"I imagine it was for the same reason he gave me the Nizari poison. To test me."

"Test you," he repeated. "To see if you were a fledgling?" he guessed. His dad never mentioned anything about suspecting Stas of being a fledgling, but maybe he tested all the new recruits?

"Maybe." She chewed her lip for a second and sighed. "You didn't know anything about it, did you?"

"Of course not. You think I'd let him deliberately hurt you like that?"

"Honestly? I wasn't sure."

"Wow." He laughed humorously and shook his head. "I've got nothing to say back to that, Stas. I really don't."

Man, it seemed that all the women in his life had little faith in him. Awesome. He had no idea he came off as such an asshole.

"It's hard to know who to trust," she murmured. "You have no idea who I really am or what—"

The door opened, cutting off their conversation. A man he knew all about, but had never seen in person, stepped through the threshold with his hands behind his back. His emerald gaze settled on Stas first, then Tom. With it came a wave of discomfort. Old didn't even begin to describe the Hydraian King. Oh, he resembled a thirty-five year old man with his short blonde hair and muscular physique, but the intelligence radiating from his gaze was positively ancient.

*Lucian, otherwise known as Luc.* Tom admired him as a leader, unlike Amelia's other brother. Wakefield was a pompous ass who killed for sport while Luc was an honorable man known for his fairness. The latter were traits Tom couldn't help but respect, even if they wouldn't work in his favor today.

"Tom," the Hydraian King greeted. "Could you give us a minute, Stas?"

Her gaze narrowed, but the look Luc leveled her silenced whatever she was about to say. "I know what you want to do, and I strongly advise against such recourse. For there will be consequences if you do."

"Fine," she gritted out. "But faith goes both ways, Luc. If you ever want me to join you willingly, I suggest you consider this situation very carefully."

Tom's brow rose at her boldness. Did she not realize who stood before her? He could have her killed with the flick of a wrist, and no one would argue otherwise because of her Sentinel status. Dating Wakefield had certainly bolstered her confidence, and perhaps not in a healthy way.

"I'm always analyzing the pros and cons in every situation," was Luc's curt reply. "This is no different.

Amelia might be my half-sister, but logic outweighs familial obligation. I believe you're familiar with the concept."

*Okay, I've clearly missed something.* Was this not Stas's first trip to Hydria? Did no one care about her working for the CRF? Oh, and speaking of them, why was she working for them if she hated his father? Especially as a Sentinel. Her actions were illogical. *Unless she's just a fantastic actress?*

"Fine," Stas replied. "I'll go for a walk."

"Thank you." He studied Tom while Stas escorted herself out and softly closed the door. "I think it's time you and I had a chat, fledgling."

~*~

Balthazar found Amelia a pair of jeans and a tank top, as well as underwear. She didn't know where they came from or how he knew her sizes without asking, but the clothes fit perfectly. Nothing surprised her when it came to B, and she found herself smiling as she left his house. She missed him more than she realized, and it gave her hope that seeing the others would bring more joy. But she wanted to see her brothers first.

Unlike Balthazar's home, Luc's house sat up on a hill away from the beach. He could see every inch of the small island from up here, something she knew he enjoyed and preferred. It was also in a secluded area, giving him necessary space from the others. As the leader of their race, he rarely had a moment to himself.

Warmth tightened her chest when Issac opened the door before she could knock. Relief brightened his gaze as a boyish grin curled his lips. All her frustration from the night before melted at that look. She never could stay angry with him for long, even when he deserved it.

*I'm truly home.* She fantasized about this moment so many times over the years, always dreaming of the day Issac would rescue her. She had willed him to sense her, to come for her, but he never did. Because he thought she was dead. *But he's here now.* Whether her savior or not, he would always be her big brother, and she adored him.

"You're breaking my heart all over again, love," he whispered as he pulled her into his arms. She'd obviously telegraphed some of what she felt on her face or in her thoughts.

"Sorry." She hugged him back and closed her eyes. "I just... I never thought I would see you again."

His arms tightened. "I'm here. I'll never let anyone hurt you ever again. I promise."

Amelia considered his words and frowned. Although she appreciated his intentions, she didn't want to rely on him to keep her safe. That was how she ended up in this predicament with Jonathan to begin with, by counting on the men in her life to protect her. This experience taught her the flaws in that logic.

She stepped back and held his gaze. "I am learning how to defend myself."

Tom started the process, and she wanted to continue it. Thinking of him made her heart ache. She longed to see him, but knew no one would let her. And that was part of the problem. They preferred to keep her sheltered and make all the decisions for her. She couldn't blame them, because the old Amelia preferred it that way. But that had to change. She needed them to train her, to teach her how to be independent so a monster like Jonathan never captured her again. *I'd rather die fighting than suffer his treatment again.*

Issac gave her a long, hard look and nodded. "All right."

"All right?" she repeated, startled. She'd expected an argument or at least a bit of pushback, not easy acceptance.

He grinned and cupped her cheek with his palm. "Amelia, love, I spent decades trying to teach you practical defense moves, but Eli always said there wasn't a need, and you always agreed. Remember?"

*Because Eli treated me like a delicate damsel.* She would never hate him for that, as she understood. He came from an era where a man took care of his wife, and although they never married formally, they were monogamous for centuries. Eli considered it his duty to protect her always and never wanted her to be bothered by such things. As a daughter of a Duchess, it hadn't been a difficult life to accept. *But...* "I've had a change of heart."

"I can see that." His eyes crinkled. "And I have the perfect sparring partner for you."

"You do?"

"I do." He turned as a blonde woman threw open the back door with a huff and slammed it.

"You'll never believe what Luc just said..." The newcomer's voice trailed off upon spotting them in the living area. "Oh."

Amelia's fingers fluttered to her mouth as she gasped in recognition. She *knew* her, and not because she was a fellow Hydraian. This woman had visited her in a dream. Or what she thought was a dream anyway. "You're real."

*If she existed, then that means Stark truly did disappear into mist.* She frowned. *Why didn't he mention her conversation with the blonde to anyone? Or did he tell Jonathan?* Was that the real reason they moved her to the cabin? She opened her mouth to ask the newcomer, but Issac's behavior put all of Amelia's thoughts on hold.

Adoration poured from his blue eyes as he greeted the blonde with a kiss, followed by some whispered words that made the girl blush. When he nuzzled her neck and grinned, Amelia's lips parted in wonder. *Who is this man, and what did he do to my brother?*

*This must be the woman Tom mentioned.* The one Issac had seen beyond a first date. *How did this happen?*

Tears pricked her eyes as a wave of conflicting emotions settled over her. Happiness that her brother had finally found someone, sadness that it had happened during her absence, and confusion at why he had chosen a woman under Jonathan's employ.

"Amelia, this is my Aya," Issac murmured. "But she prefers to be called Stas."

The blonde smiled up at him. "I don't think I've ever heard you use my nickname."

"That's because Aya is your nickname," he replied as he brushed his knuckles over her jaw.

"You gave her a nickname?" Amelia asked, bewildered. "You don't even call Luc by his preferred name, and he's your brother." That alone told her how he felt about this woman. *Love. My brother is in love.*

"I believe you met briefly at the CRF," Issac continued, his expression darkening. "Aya gave me your message about the butterflies. That's how I knew you were alive."

Stas cleared her throat, looking uncomfortable. "Yeah, I agreed to work as a Sentinel in hopes of finding a way to help you, but you see how well that turned out."

Amelia blinked. "You became a Sentinel to help me?" That explained the bit about Issac accepting Stas's employment situation.

Issac hugged Stas to his side and kissed her temple. "Aya's amazing, if a little reckless." The blonde elbowed him, making him grin.

Amelia swallowed, unsure what to say. Amazing didn't seem to cover it. "Thank you," she murmured, though it seemed underwhelming given the circumstances. *This woman put her life at risk for me.* She owed her more than two words, but what more could she give?

Stas snorted. "It's not like I did much. John moved you before I had a chance to even talk to you again."

Amelia nodded. "Yes, on Tom's recommendation."

"So it's true then? He helped you?" Hope lined the woman's voice, making Amelia wonder at her history with Tom.

"Yes, in more ways than one." She looked to her brother. "You put me to sleep before I had a chance to explain last night." And then he kept her in that state for nearly twenty-four hours. No wonder she woke in a daze and thought Hydria was a dream. She'd slept too long. "Which reminds me, never do that again without my express permission."

His eyebrows rose. "You've always enjoyed my dreams, Amelia."

"Yes." Which was why she could forgive him for last night. "But I need you to request permission going forward." The notion of anyone manipulating her vision after so many years of hallucinations and torment made her queasy. Issac would never harm her, and she knew that, but she needed her space. For now.

He studied her with an intense expression then slowly nodded. "Of course."

"Thank you. Now, I want to see Tom," she said, feeling stronger. "B already explained that you won't allow it, which is why I came here to talk to Luc."

"He's temporarily disposed," Issac replied in that haughty way of his. "And Balthazar is correct. We will all deny your request."

"She has a right to see him," Stas argued.

"Just this morning you agreed that he should be removed."

The girl narrowed her green eyes. "No, I said he should be given a choice of staying or leaving. Nice try, though."

He shrugged. "So the edict remains."

"It does."

"Brilliant." His sarcasm was not lost on Amelia.

"What are you two going on about? And what do you mean by *removed*?"

"Execution," Issac answered simply. "But my little complication here used her fledgling gift of verbal persuasion on the Elders and myself, making a sentence impossible."

Amelia's gaze widened. "Fledgling?"

"Yes," he replied.

*Oh, Issac.* Her brother had fallen in love with a woman he could never have, not truly. Once she died, she would be reborn a Hydraian, and a relationship between them would be rendered impossible. Politics aside, they could never physically be together. One drop of ingested blood would kill him. The risk would be too great.

Her heart splintered as she struggled for what to say. He flashed her a look that said he knew exactly where her thoughts had gone and to not comment. Did his Stas not realize the extent of this complication? Or were they both in denial?

"I won't be taking it back," Stas stated. "No one on this island can touch him."

"The Elders are waiting to see how long your compulsion lasts, specifically Lucian. You're lucky he's more fascinated by it than displeased." The light admonishment in his voice prompted the blonde to grin.

"I wanted to hear his side of the story first."

"And did you?"

"Yes, and he had nothing to do with Owen."

"Owen?" Amelia repeated. "Our Owen?"

Issac's gaze turned troubled, and he cleared his throat. "Yes. I'm not sure how to tell you this other than to be blunt... Jonathan had him killed a few weeks ago in New York City."

"What? Good heavens, why? He couldn't possibly have been a threat." She knew the Hydraian well. His infectious laugh and general joviality added to his role as social butterfly on the island. Everyone loved him.

"To test me," Stas whispered.

"Aya and Owen were close friends," Issac added. "His murder scene is actually how we met. Not exactly the most romantic of tales, is it?"

Amelia's vision started to darken at the edges. *What else have I missed all these years?* She stumbled over to the table to sit down before her legs gave out beneath her. This was too much. She rubbed the ache in her chest and considered resting her head against the table to cool it. Owen did not deserve his fate. Another mark on Jonathan's dark record.

A glass of water appeared in front of her as her brother took the seat across from her. "I know it's a lot, love," he murmured. "I'm sorry. We're going to get through this."

She nodded numbly. "Who else have we lost?" she asked, though she wasn't sure she really wanted the answer.

"Only Eli," he whispered.

She closed her eyes and breathed in slowly through her nose. That news she could handle. Her heart didn't ache the way it used to when she thought about him. Now her heart hurt for a different reason. *Tom.* They had formed a bond over these last few weeks that felt tenuous, yet strong. She wanted to explore it further, but too many obstacles had sprung up in her path. The first of which being her brothers.

"What did Tom do that has you all so displeased with him?" she wondered.

"You mean, aside from being Jonathan's progeny?"

"You, better than anyone, know not to fault a man for his parentage, Issac." It would be akin to condemning a Hydraian for the sins of his or her Ichorian father. And so many of them were immortals who lacked any semblance of humanity. A consequence of their age and customs. Her father managed to avoid it by creating a support network of family and friends that kept him grounded. But sometimes she saw that faraway glint in Aidan's eyes, a hint of insanity creeping in from too much experience. Luc possessed it as well. She wondered if it had gotten worse during her absence.

"He's his father's son, Amelia. Jonathan has molded him into a walking puppet with excellent aim."

"That's rather harsh." Even if a little accurate. Tom said himself that he had no choice but to do what his father told him to do, but he went against Jonathan's wishes by taking her to Issac. "Tell me why you suspected him of murdering Owen." She used the past tense since Stas stated he wasn't involved, but she wondered why Issac would even consider accusing him of it.

"Because he's craved his father's love and affection his entire life. Thomas would die for that man, which coincidentally, he might."

She shook her head. "You should have heard the way he spoke to him these last few weeks, Issac. That wasn't a boy seeking love, but a man rebelling."

"Or..." Issac reached for her hand and squeezed it while holding her gaze. "Or it's a man playing a game with a woman in a fragile state. A man trying to gain trust, to be invited to a place like Hydria, where he can operate as a spy and report back to his father." He let that sink in before continuing. "He's the perfect soldier for the job, darling. A fledgling with no home, nowhere to go except here, and with your approval, he might be allowed to stay."

"A game," she whispered.

No. This could not be another of Jonathan's tricks. Except, how many times did she wonder when the charade would end? How often did she question Tom's intentions? Almost daily for weeks, until he risked his life to save her. She hadn't doubted him since that afternoon at the cabin, which was only a few days ago...

*No.*

She shook her head, denying the possibility.

*I* know *him.*

But did she? The man excelled at deception and nonchalance. Would he hurt her like this?

*He held me that night.* Also part of the illusion? A way to gain her trust? It worked liked a charm. But what about the gun? She could have killed him. Unless... She never checked it for bullets. Had he removed them prior to leaving it on the nightstand? A clever stunt, indeed. And it landed her in his bed.

Issac swiped a tear away from her cheek with his

thumb, and cradled her face with his palm. "I'm speculating, but you need to be prepared, love."

She bit her lip to keep it from trembling. The possibility that it was all no more than a game to Tom made her heart hurt. Had she fallen for a master manipulator? It seemed like something Jonathan would do. He always did want to break her, and this was the perfect way to do it. Send his son in to woo her, become her confidant and lover, and betray her in the most hurtful of ways.

Another tear fell, but this one she swiped away. "If it's true," she whispered, "I want a say in his punishment." Because even if Tom was guilty, she refused to let the Elders execute him. She could never hurt him; not like that. She'd demand his safe release instead.

"But it's not true," Stas put in, frowning. "I've known him for almost seven years, Issac. He's not a bad man, and he had no idea his father killed Owen. I saw his expression today. He wasn't lying."

Issac considered the woman with a seriousness Amelia had never seen in him. *He respects her opinion*, she realized. How interesting. It usually took decades to acquire that sort of trust with her brother, but Stas had managed to secure it during their brief acquaintance.

"Perhaps," he murmured. "A decision will not be reached tonight. I can't believe I'm about to suggest this, but let's head down to the beach. I think being around your family will help, and I would prefer to avoid having Jacque flash up here with one of his expectant looks."

Amelia wished so badly to smile at that, but the pain in her chest made it difficult. An evening at a beach party did not appeal to her at all, but she owed it to her family to try. And maybe she would feel better after surrounding herself with love and support. There was only one way to find out, and later, she could think more about Tom and his potential betrayal.

*He wouldn't do that to you*, her conscious whispered. *He*

*chases away the darkness.*

She shuddered. *I have to talk to him.* It would be the only way to know for sure whether or not this was all ruse, and mentally debating it would accomplish nothing. She was finally free, and she didn't want to spend it wallowing. Jonathan would not win. Never again.

"Let's go."

# CHAPTER SIXTEEN

## New Cravings

What started as a calm affair exploded into a rave once all the formalities were finished. Amelia appreciated the diversion because it shifted the focus from her to the festivities. Jacque managed the music with Stas at his side. He appeared to be teaching her how to do something with the controls while Issac looked on with amusement.

"It's weird, isn't it?" Jayson murmured as he roasted a marshmallow over the bonfire in front of them. She'd opted to sit with the Elders instead of joining the dancers on the beach. There were too many of them, and she wanted her space. Her brother had offered to join her, but she didn't want to take him away from his new love.

"He's happy," Amelia said, smiling as her brother wrapped his arms around Stas from behind.

"It won't end well." Alik's matter-of-fact tone matched his bored expression. He sat next to Jayson with his back to the party. Typical. He did greet her with a smile earlier, though; a rarity for the Elder, and one that meant a great deal to her.

"You're doing it wrong," Luc muttered as he collapsed into a chair across from them. She'd seen him dancing with Mya and Lara a few minutes ago, his expression one of contentment, but now his narrow focus was on Jayson's marshmallow. "It's going to catch fire.

"And that's how I like it," Jayson replied as the fluff went up in flames.

Luc shook his head. "Blasphemy. Ruined a perfectly good cylinder."

"You would only care about the shape and not the taste." Jayson leaned forward to sandwich the now-black marshmallow between a graham cracker and a bar of chocolate. Not the healthiest of desserts, but the man didn't have an ounce of fat on him. None of the Elders did.

Alik was the smallest of the trio with his lean athleticism, while Luc and Jayson reminded her of rugby players. All height and muscle, short hair, and handsome faces. These were Eli's best friends, the men he loved like brothers and had known most of his life. They also happened to be the oldest of her race, hence their nickname. It felt good sitting beside them, if a little surreal.

She had thought of them often, but the little details had never left her, like Jayson's adorable dimples, the constant crease between Luc's brows, and Alik's trademark scowl. Amazing how she could recall all those traits, but the color of Eli's eyes eluded her. All she could see now was a luscious brown she knew didn't belong to him.

*Tom.*

Jayson handed her the marshmallow skewer, and she passed it to Luc. The thought of dessert turned her stomach. Despite her best intentions, Tom kept popping into her thoughts. Random comments and memories from their time together haunted her heart and mind. The way he held her after she broke down, his intoxicating kiss and addictive touch, but most of all, the sincerity in his gaze. Every time she closed her eyes, he stared back at her with that concerned look that melted her. All his actions and words didn't add up to a traitor, but Issac's comments held a touch of logic she couldn't refute.

A piece of chocolate appeared beneath her nose, pulling her back to reality. Jayson cocked a brow and waggled the treat at her. "I know you want it, Amelia," he taunted. "Dark chocolate, fresh from Argentina. Your favorite."

She smiled at his playfulness and snagged the sweet. "You haven't changed at all, Jay."

"And I never plan to, A."

The Elders had a thing about nicknames. It drove Issac mad, but she loved it. "I missed you guys," she admitted, which earned her a side hug from Jay and an air kiss from Luc. Alik's dark gaze met hers briefly in a moment of understanding before he went back to staring at the fire.

She nibbled the chocolate and fought a moan. It was the same kind Balthazar used in his hot cocoa earlier. These men knew her too well, and yet, part of her felt like an outsider despite their warmth and comfort.

*You don't feel that way around Tom.*

The chocolate soured in her mouth. Sitting here, enjoying herself while he sat God knew where felt wrong. He had been there for her in a moment when she needed him most, and she sat out here while he suffered. It wasn't fair.

A hand settled on her shoulder from behind, making her jump until she realized who it belonged to. Balthazar stared down at her with a question in his eyes. "Want to take a walk?" he asked. "Catch up a little?"

*You've been playing in my mind, B.*

The sadness in his expression answered her thought.

He brushed his thumb against her neck in a soothing gesture that made it hard to refuse him. "All right," she murmured and stood.

"Don't go too far, A." The emotion in her brother's voice tugged at her heart. Her relationship with him differed from what she had with Issac, mostly because she didn't grow up with Luc, but she loved him. Even when she disagreed with a decision, such as keeping Tom locked up. He stood as she walked over to him and engulfed her in a hug.

"I'm not going anywhere," she whispered.

"I know." He kissed her hair and held her a little longer than he used to, as if he feared she might disappear on him again. "Let's talk in the morning. I'll make waffles."

Balthazar snorted beside them. "Rubbish."

"Ignore him," Luc replied as he let her go. "Pancakes are flat and shapeless, while waffles are geometrically delicious."

Amelia smiled at the familiar debate. "Good to know not everything has changed around here."

"Pancakes can hold a variety of shapes," Balthazar argued.

"But do they form pockets for the maple syrup?"

"Not all of us are obsessed with even servings."

Luc arched a haughty brow. "That's not an answer."

"Jesus Christ," Alik muttered. "Make it stop."

Jayson chuckled and shook his head. "B, I thought you were going on a walk, man."

"Right." Balthazar extended his arm to her. "Walk with me, and I'll explain why pancakes are the superior breakfast food along the way."

She slid her arm through his and grinned. "You realize I've heard this debate a thousand times, yes?"

He looked at Luc and addressed him instead of her. "I've proven you wrong a dozen times on that front." His gaze narrowed. "You're on. Next weekend. I chose Brazil. Fine. Yes, maple syrup is allowed. Whipped cream as well.

All the toppings, Luc. That, too, and yes, I pick Jay. Deal."

"What kinky challenge did I just agree to?" Jayson asked.

"Luc will fill you in while Amelia and I take a walk."

She snorted. "You act as though I'm a blushing bride." She knew Balthazar and Luc were constantly engaged in a battle of wits, and it usually involved sexual escapades of some sort. Seemed this one involved breakfast, Brazilian women, and teams. *I don't want to know.*

"One day I'll corrupt you, love." Balthazar grinned. "Don't you worry."

"Uh huh." He'd been saying that for centuries, but never followed through. His relationship with Eli made her off limits, which suited her fine. She adored the man, but didn't want to cross the line.

They strolled arm-in-arm along the beach, away from the raging techno music and raving immortals and towards a quieter section of the island near the docks. Tourists sometimes stopped by for day visits from Athens, but there were no hotels for them to stay overnight, and the last ferry left before dinner each evening.

Automobiles and motorbikes were prohibited on the island, a way to keep the air clean according to Luc, but bicycles were available for rent. The Hydraians also sold artwork and manned two cafes for tourists who needed a bite to eat during their visit. It helped with some of the living costs in Hydria, but most of the cash flow came from those who worked full time.

Luc had a whole system in place, and everyone played their part. Her role used to involve mentoring younger Hydraians and playing hostess as needed for a variety of parties. She wondered what use she would be to her people now.

*Tom would be useful*, she thought. If Luc would give the man a chance.

"You know, I remember the day you met Eli," Balthazar murmured, cutting into her thoughts.

"Yeah?" she asked with a small grin. Amelia remembered that day, too. Her eighteenth birthday, the day she met all the Elders, including her brother Luc for the first time. Advanced technology and global transportation hadn't been invented yet. Jacque didn't exist yet, either, but more than that, Aidan wanted to keep her hidden from the supernatural world. The immortals were on the cusp of war as tensions between Ichorians and Hydraians rose. So he resided in England with Issac and their mother, a wealthy widowed Duchess, and kept her safe until the day he handed her over to the Elders.

"It was love at first sight for him," Balthazar mused. "That man would have moved the earth just to see you smile."

And there it was, the purpose for this walk. She didn't have two older brothers. She had five, and they all adored Eli. Dating anyone else would never be acceptable to any of them, especially not a man they already hated.

"It shocked the hell out of me at first, but I'm glad he found you," he continued. "You gave him three centuries of joy, Amelia. He would have wanted more time, as we all would, but I know with certainty he wouldn't want to hold you back from finding happiness." He stepped in front of her, stopping her mid-step, and stared down at her with an intent expression that caused her pulse to jump.

"Eli was your first love and every bit the man you needed once upon a time, but people change. Experiences shape our outlooks, our dreams, our cravings..." His chocolate eyes twinkled with that last part, making her snort. He never could be serious for long.

"What are you trying to tell me, B?" Because it sounded like he was hitting on her, but despite his incessant flirting, she knew he would never be interested in her that way.

"Sometimes what we need evolves into something, or someone, we least expect. Eli was your perfect match. You made each other happy and lived a full life together. But he's gone and never coming back, and even if he did, I'm not sure he would be the right man for you today. He'd lock you in a room and kill anyone who tried to walk inside without his permission, but that's not what you need." His smile was sad as he looked at her. "I've been listening, Amelia, to everything. I might not like it, but Tom is the one for you, at least for the moment. Which is why I'm going to help you."

She gaped at him. Of all the things she expected him to say, this was not one of them. "Truly?"

"Yes. He's in there." Balthazar pointed to a small utility hut off the beach, making her jaw drop. That little box was half the size of her cement prison at the CRF. Her feet were moving before she could think better of it, and Balthazar grabbed her shoulder. "Ash is in there."

Amelia froze. "You left him alone with a fire elemental?" The woman's pyrokinetic talents made her one of Hydria's greatest assets, and also terrifying.

"She's under strict orders not to kill him, and you know she takes her job seriously."

Oh, she knew all right. The woman was part of Luc's personal guard whenever he left Hydria and redefined the meaning of protection. "She'll never leave her post."

Balthazar waggled his brows and grinned. "You know how much I love a good challenge, A. Leave it to me." So much arrogance for one man, but if anyone deserved it, he did. Ash wouldn't stand a chance under his sensual assault.

"Right. Cheers, then." Because what else was there to say?

"Stay out of sight until we leave. I'll ensure the door is unlocked. Go inside, head down the stairs, and he's in the room on the left."

Her eyebrows jumped. That little shack resembled a gardening shed, not a home with rooms. "How new is this little whatever-it-is of yours?"

"Luc built it when we founded the island. It's a prison of sorts, and before you ask, you were kept in the dark because 'a lady doesn't need to know those things.'"

"I do not sound like that." Though it did sound like something she would say, at least about this aspect of Hydraian life. A prison, or the things done in a dungeon, would never appeal to her.

"Oh, but you do, love." He kissed her cheek. "The guards are scheduled to change shifts in three hours. I suggest you leave before that happens."

~ * ~

Tom paced the tiny room, hands in his pockets. Antsy didn't begin to cover his current state.

*Stas is a fledgling.* More than that, she could bend others to her will. How the hell had he missed that little detail? It didn't bode well for him that Luc had given him that information. The words came off more as a threat.

*"Once her compulsion ends, we'll decide your fate. Until then, please enjoy our hospitality."*

The Hydraian King left him with a plate of food, another bottle of water, a stack of blankets, and a pillow. Sleeping on the floor he could do, but not here. Not when his life hung in the balance. Escape seemed the logical option, but leaving Amelia felt wrong. She was perfectly safe here, yet he felt an idiotic need to stay for her.

A giggle sounded from the hallway, followed by a deep, masculine voice and a thump.

*What the hell?*

*Jesus. Are they?*

*Oh, yeah.*

Some Hydraians were about to get it on outside his door. Ridiculous. If he wanted to escape, now would be the perfect time. The door hinges were solid, but a kick at the right angle would do the job, and his guards would be too distracted to react right away. All he needed was a weapon, and they'd be toast. Of course, then he would be trapped on an island inhabited by immortals with various unworldly powers.

*Nice. Talk about a challenge.*

Except it didn't appeal as much as it should. He used to live for this shit, but Amelia changed everything. His trademark love em' and leave em' mentality didn't apply to her. She was under his skin and deep in his head, dictating all his decisions and actions. Such as the one to willingly come here. Because he could have knocked Issac and Tristan out with a pair of bullets while they were distracted by Amelia at the manor, but he chose not to. He wanted to go with her and disregarded the consequences.

A female yelped, making his eyes roll. The Hydraian guards needed better training if this was the shit they pulled during their shifts. It would be so easy to teach the immortals a lesson, but Tom refrained. The Elders already wanted him dead, no reason to further that along.

*I told you so, son,* his father's voice taunted. *Should have played ball.*

His hand curled into a fist. Tom didn't regret his decision to help Amelia, but did feel sorry for allowing hope into his heart. Somewhere along the line, doubt had crept in, and he'd wondered just what the Hydraians would do to him. Fledglings were rare, and his unique skill set could prove useful, but Luc made it clear today that he was not welcome here.

The knob jiggled, drawing him from his thoughts. He moved to the opposite side of the room to lean against the cement wall, hands in his pockets, and feigned a look of boredom as someone undid the deadbolt. The door cracked open, and Amelia's head popped through. Relief brightened her gaze when she spotted him.

"Tom." His name on her lips brightened his entire day. Hell, it brightened his existence. It took all his effort not to walk over, wrap her in his arms, and take her against the wall. But he knew she wasn't alone. No way the Elders or her brothers would let her visit unsupervised.

"Hi, sweetheart."

"Hi." She slipped inside, closed the door, leaned back

229

against it, and nibbled her lower lip. "I needed to see that you were all right." Interesting phrasing considering she didn't appear to be looking at him so much as the floor.

"I'm okay."

She nodded. "Good."

The silence between them felt heavy and uncomfortable. What happened to his confident Amelia, the one who questioned everything and loved to bicker over silly things like baseball and motorcycles? He pushed off the wall and frowned when she stiffened.

"What's wrong, Amelia?" When she didn't respond, he stepped closer and crowded her against the door. He expected it to fly open and be greeted by an irate Hydraian, but nothing happened. "Talk to me, sweetheart."

Gorgeous blue eyes peeked up at him through thick lashes. "They think you're playing a game with me," she whispered. "They think Jonathan sent you on a mission to infiltrate Hydria as a fledgling, and you're using me to do it."

"A logical assessment." He rested a forearm over her head and placed his opposite palm against the wall beside her hip. Her shiver encouraged him. "And what do you think, Amelia?" he whispered. "Am I a spy?"

"Are you?" she asked, those guileless eyes blinking up at him. "Are you playing with me?"

*Oh, I'm definitely playing with you.* Partly because he was furious that she could even ask him that, and partly because it hurt. Her words could kill him, but he wouldn't let it show. If the experiences they had shared weren't enough for her to believe in him, then they were doomed to fail. Nothing he could do would ever change her mind. He would forever be Jonathan Fitzgerald's son and share the burden of another man's sins. *Thanks, Dad.*

"What do you think, Amelia?" Because if she had to ask, she didn't trust him, and no amount of talking would fix that. "Was everything between us a lie?"

Her gaze dropped to his mouth. "I wouldn't. . ."

"You wouldn't what?" he prompted, voice low.

"I wouldn't be here if I didn't trust you."

"Then why ask?"

"Because Jonathan always wanted to break me and failed. But if this is all a charade?" Her gaze flicked up to his, and the look there cut him deep. "It'll destroy me."

"You think I could do that to you?"

"I used to," she admitted. "I thought everything was a game, all the training, you giving me a weapon, the teasing… And I think it was to an extent, but not because of Jonathan. You use cheekiness to protect yourself, but deep down, you're lonely. You don't feel like you belong anywhere because the man you admired most filled your head with lies."

*Not all of them were lies*, he thought numbly. The Hydraians really did hate him.

She palmed his cheek and sighed. "Jonathan altered us both irrevocably, but what he did to you was worse."

"I beg to differ—" Her thumb over his lips silenced him.

"Let me finish."

"Okay," he mouthed as she dropped her hand.

"I promised myself if I ever got out of that hell, I would never rely on another person for anything ever again. But you're the only one who brings me a sense of peace and comfort, and that terrifies me. I don't want to rely on you, Tom. But I can't seem to help myself."

Her words both warmed and chilled him. He removed his hand from the wall near her hip to palm her cheek and felt some of the chill dissipate when she pressed into his touch. "Leaning on someone for comfort doesn't mean you're weak, sweetheart. But I understand where you're coming from; you want to be able to protect yourself." He felt the same way, which was why these feelings for her confused him. Whenever he considered leaving the CRF, he only thought about how to look after himself, but she changed everything. A life of loneliness no longer appealed.

"You also make me feel strong," she told him. "In addition to the peace and comfort, I mean."

"Yeah?"

She nodded. "And you teach me things. It may have been a diversion at first, but I think you enjoyed training me."

His grin was automatic. "Oh, I more than enjoyed it." He fucking loved it.

"What did you enjoy most?" she asked, a smile in her voice. So much better than the sadness lurking there before. He liked playing with flirtatious Amelia.

"Everything." From the gun stance lessons to rolling around with her on the ground, he enjoyed every minute. If he died soon, those would be the memories he'd miss most. And their one explosive night together.

"All right, but what did you like teaching me most?"

He ran his thumb over her bottom lip. "Defensive moves, even though you about killed me."

"How's that?" Her mouth curled down at the edges, and he traced it with his thumb.

"'Straddle me again,'" he quoted. "Ever say that to me again, and I'll well and truly straddle you."

Arousal darkened her gaze. "I think I'd like that."

"Your brothers wouldn't." And he didn't need to piss them off any more than he already had. Though, it might be worth it in this case.

"They don't need to know, and Balthazar won't tell them."

"Balthazar?" he repeated, frowning.

"He distracted the guard for me."

"Really?" An Elder helped her get to him? "Why would he do that?"

"Because he thinks you're good for me, even though he doesn't like it."

He didn't know how to interpret that. Luc made it sound like his death was imminent, but that could have been his interrogation technique. Tom hadn't spilled all his knowledge, but he'd provided enough to indicate his worth. He never mentioned Stas's double agent status, though he now suspected she was a triple agent and reporting CRF details to Issac. An interesting twist of events.

Amelia brushed her lips over his in an impatient gesture that amused him. "Did you come here to check on me, or because you need me to help you forget again?"

"Can't it be both?" Her impish expression made it difficult to remember why her suggestion was a bad idea.

"This isn't a very romantic venue." *There's gotta be a better reason.*

"I don't want romance." She hooked her thumb in his belt loop and gave it a tug. "I need you." Those words on her lips were pure sin.

"Careful, sweetheart." *Or I'll be tempted to take you up on what you're offering.* This might be his last night alive. Might as well enjoy it.

"I don't want careful, either."

"What do you want?" he whispered, needing to hear her say it. There could be no misunderstandings between them. Only truths. She pressed her mouth against his, and he pulled back. "Tell me what you want, Amelia."

"Kiss me."

"Is that all you want?" He spoke the words against her lips.

She shivered and tugged on his jeans again. "No. I want to well and truly straddle you. Without clothes."

He palmed the back of her neck and pulled her in for a kiss filled with pent up heat and yearning. It'd been a long fucking day, and he wanted nothing more than to lose himself in her. But he needed her to know what that meant. This wouldn't be like the other night, and he demonstrated that with his tongue. He memorized every inch of her mouth in dominating sweeps, and she melted. Oh, she'd straddle him all right, but not in the way she thought.

"This is going to be hard and fast, Amelia." It came out in a harsh whisper against her neck. He punctuated the warning with a tender bite at the base of her throat, and she responded by arching into him. He grinned against her tender skin. It seemed she liked that. Good. Because there would be no slow burn tonight. They didn't have time.

He fisted his hand in the hem of her tank top, while his opposite palm tightened around her neck to force her attention up to him. "You still want to straddle me, sweetheart?"

"Oh, yes." Her flushed cheeks and thoroughly kissed lips nearly undid him. But it was her words that sent him over the edge. He ripped her top over her head and flicked her bra to the floor.

Her fingertips danced along the top of his pants, beneath his shirt, and he swore electricity trailed her every move. His cock hardened against his zipper, begging her to go a little lower and give it a stroke, but she kept her touch light and taunting. He paid her back by taking her nipple into his mouth and sucking. Hard. Her hands flew to his hair, his jeans forgotten. He gave the abused peak a little nibble, and her head flew backwards against the door on a deep moan.

"Take off my pants, Amelia." He followed the order with another bite before taking her other nipple into his mouth.

She tossed her head back and forth, her hands trembling and tightening in his hair rather than going where he wanted them. He grinned against her breast. This wasn't defiance, but a woman too lost in pleasure to think clearly. He took hold of her wrist and lowered her palm to his upper thigh then up the center of his jeans. Some of the lust induced fog must have cleared because she grabbed the denim and held on. He rewarded her with a lick that made her groan his name.

His balls tightened as she went for his zipper first, then

popped off the button, and pushed the fabric down to his knees. He finished the job and kicked it away as he pulled off his shirt.

She eyed the bulge in his boxer shorts and licked her lips. "I really want to taste you again."

"Fuck." Tom fisted his hand in her hair and kissed her sinful lips into submission. He needed to be deep inside her, to memorize every inch of her slick heat with his cock. Then they could taste each other. Her jeans disappeared follow by her panties and his boxers, all while he fucked her mouth with his tongue.

She locked her arms around his shoulders and held him as if she couldn't get close enough. Clingy women usually turned him off, but he loved Amelia's desperation because it rivaled his own. He adored this woman, would give up his life for her, and very likely was by staying here when she'd offered him the perfect chance to escape. But all he wanted was her. She intoxicated him on a level he didn't know existed, and he loved it. Maybe even loved her.

He grabbed her hips and lifted her up against the wall. Her legs wrapped around his waist as he settled his hard length against her damp center. This was how he wanted her to straddle him. Always. He slid his palm to her ass and shifted back before thrusting into her waiting heat.

"Harder," she demanded and dug her nails into his shoulders to encourage him.

He wrapped his free hand around her nape and placed a bruising kiss on her lips. She nipped back at him, making him grin. "What happened to my sweet, compliant Amelia?"

"She met you."

Oh, he liked that. "I wouldn't have it any other way."

"Good. Now start moving."

"Yes, ma'am." He drove deep and captured her mouth as she screamed.

Her wet, eager body hugged him, sending electricity zipping up and down his spine. If she kept moving like that, he wouldn't be able to last long despite his unworldly control. Amelia undid him with her strong spirit and feisty energy, and all he could do was lose himself in her. Her screams turned to cries of approval as he increased the pace and swiveled his hips in a way that stimulated her clit.

When her legs started to tremble around him, he knew she was close and gave her one final deep thrust to send her over the edge into bliss. She convulsed around him, squeezing his cock in the most amazing way, leaving him no choice but to follow her into ecstasy. His knees shook from the force of his orgasm, making him lean harder into her against the wall and intensify his hold.

"Amelia," he breathed, burying his head in her neck. She hugged him back with a ferocity that completed him. No one had ever held him with so much adoration and care. Not that he'd ever let anyone get this close, but Amelia was different.

One look from her was all it took to get under his skin. He thought of her often and chalked it up to worrying about her treatment. But it went so much deeper than that. Her soul spoke to his. Suggesting his father move her had nothing to do with Stas, and everything to do with keeping Amelia safe. He hadn't wanted to babysit her because he feared their inherent connection. And all the training was a way of making her stronger because he craved an equal.

He pressed a kiss to her throat and slid his hands to her waist to pull her away from the door. His pile of blankets would have to do, because he wanted to love on her for hours. He went to his knees with her legs still wrapped around him and laid over her on the bed of blankets without breaking contact between their hips. She met his lazy kiss with a sensuous one of her own, tracing his lips with her tongue and sliding it in his mouth for a luxuriating taste. He cradled her face between his palms and moved slowly inside her, cherishing their deep connection.

Her lips curled into a smile, but froze when a flourish

of footsteps came from the hallway.

*Oh, shit.*

He pulled away and threw a blanket over her just as the door crashed open.

# CHAPTER SEVENTEEN

## Kiss of Death

Tom stayed on his knees, with his hands folded in his lap, naked.

*Well, this isn't awkward at all.*

Three sets of eyes stared down at him, only one of them making him truly uncomfortable. "Stas," he greeted.

Her wide gaze swung back and forth between him and Amelia. Then understanding colored her expression, and she jumped in front of her fuming boyfriend. "Issac, don't."

"As if I could," Wakefield seethed. "This is not cute, Amelia."

Tom frowned at his harsh tone. "Don't talk to her to her like that," he said at the same time someone else said something very similar in his voice. He glanced to his left and met the gaze of his identical twin. *Holy shit.* "You shifted."

"Nice try, sweetheart," Amelia replied in a voice that sounded exactly like his own. "She doesn't need to see this, Wakefield. Take her away."

Tom gaped at her then realized what she was doing. "Oh, hell no. She's lying."

His identical twin rolled his eyes. *Note to self. Never roll my eyes again because I look like an idiot.* "Give me a gun, and I'll prove who's lying."

Wakefield tried to step forward, just to be forced back by Stas. "Don't touch or hurt him, Issac."

"Trust me when I say, you do not want to do this to me, Astasiya. Not right now."

Stas remained unmoved, hands on his chest, and acted as a barrier between them. To Wakefield's credit, he didn't try to remove her, though every line of his suit clad body was tense and ready to fight.

The third member of their party leaned against the wall with his arms crossed, his green eyes darting between the two Toms with a curious expression. Seemed the Hydraian King was mildly amused. *No doubt planning my colorful execution.* Except there were two Toms to choose from, which put Amelia's life in serious danger. No fucking way would he let her suffer for him.

"Okay, that's enough." Tom grabbed a blanket, wrapped it around his waist, and stood to meet Wakefield's gaze. "I'll prove it's me." And vividly recalled the night he accidentally sent Stas to the Conclave. Her face had resembled a white sheet as she left the Arcadia. He'd wanted to approach her, but the Ichorian at her side had made that impossible.

Wakefield narrowed his gaze then nodded. "He's Tom."

"What? No. I'm Tom."

"Nice try, sweetheart," the real Tom murmured, echoing her words from a few minutes prior. "I'm glad to see your gift works, again, though."

Amelia shifted back to herself with a sigh and hugged the blankets to her chest while staying on the ground. "Please don't hurt him. I made my own bed. Quite literally, I suppose."

"Don't hurt him?" Wakefield repeated. "Dear sister, this man—and I use that term lightly—has fantasized about murdering me several times in my presence. Why am I not to return the favor?"

Tom snorted. "Might as well finish what you started, right, Wakefield?"

He gave him an affronted look. "And what the bloody hell is that supposed to mean?"

"You know damn well what it means." And it pissed him off that the Ichorian pretended otherwise.

"I assure you, I do not." He folded his arms and cocked a brow. "Do enlighten me, Sentinel."

"Oh, you want to talk about it?" Because he sure as shit didn't. That night haunted him. He'd wanted to go home for months, to seek the comfort of his mother's arms and beg her not to send him back to that awful place, only to find her slaughtered on his bed. The image flashed behind his eyes of its own accord, and his hands curled into fists. Only a handful of Ichorians knew about Anna, one of whom was standing before him pretending not to have a damn clue about that night.

"Why are you showing me this?" Wakefield asked, his brow furrowed.

"Ring any bells?" he forced out through clenched teeth. "Or did that night mean nothing to you?" Just another merciless killing for no fucking reason. That was why he hated Ichorians. They lacked humanity and heart.

Surprise lit Wakefield's features. "You think I did this?"

"I know you did."

"Do you? And how is that, Thomas? Were you there?"

"No, but I saw what you did afterwards."

"I see. And Jonathan named me as the culprit. How

fitting."

Tom took a step forward and froze when Luc pushed off the wall. Right. Two on one, unarmed and naked, not a fair fight. Time to reign in the emotions a bit. "You're right to want to kill me, Wakefield. Because if you don't, I'll kill you."

Amelia's gasp struck him like an arrow through the heart. He never had a chance to explain his side, or tell her why her brother deserved to die, and now he'd leave her without answers. Because the glower Wakefield leveled him was one he'd seen countless times. His minutes were numbered.

"Would you like to know how I recall the events of that evening, or would you prefer to die with your ignorance?"

Amelia jumped up and placed herself between them. "I'm begging you not to do this, Issac. He's not working for his father. I know he's not."

"Alik," was Wakefield's reply.

A chill slithered down Tom's spine as the shorter Elder sauntered into the room. The Hydraian was a legend. He could bring a room of people to their knees with a single thought, and not blink an eye. Tom had never seen a photo of the infamous immortal, but recognized his dark traits and placid expression. Death would be preferable over an evening with this guy, but it seemed Wakefield had other plans.

"Amelia," Alik murmured. "Would you mind accompanying me into the hallway?"

"I'm not going anywhere."

Alik sighed and stepped forward to take hold of her arm, making Tom want to intervene, but one glance from the man told him that would be the wrong move.

"I said no," Amelia argued.

"I heard you," Alik replied as he gently nudged her over a few paces. "So we'll stay here while Wakefield and the Sentinel continue their chat."

"You can't do this," Amelia whispered. "I'll never forgive any of you."

"Time forgives all transgressions," Luc stated. "Trust me."

Tears filled her eyes, breaking Tom's heart. As if the woman hadn't been through enough, now she had to watch his trial? No. He wouldn't allow it. "Just get whatever it is you plan to do over with," he said, focusing on Wakefield. "For her."

Stas's shoulders stiffened. "Issac, don't—"

"Thomas, for the record, I did not kill your mother. I was on the opposite side of the state at a military school saving the life of a young fledgling who was the spitting image of his father. Perhaps you'll dream of it."

The crack of a bullet and Amelia's scream preceded the pain. He always wondered what it would feel like to die.

*It turns out you don't feel anything at all.*

His eyes closed on that thought, and the world fell silent around him.

~*~

Amelia collapsed, her hands at her mouth, and her heart shattering in her chest. Watching Tom fall to a lifeless heap on the floor was worse than anything Jonathan or Anita had ever done to her. It hurt more than Eli's death. He at least lived a full life, but Tom? His life had been cut short by the man she called her brother.

*How could you, Luc? I trusted you.*

Her body shook in a way she knew too well. Darkness was calling, and this time she'd let it consume her. What was the point? Her so-called family had betrayed her in the cruelest of ways. It appeared Jonathan would win after all.

*I'm broken.*

The conversation floated around her, but she felt too numb to care. Their words meant nothing to her.

They would never understand.

They never cared.

Revenge won every time.

"It seems Stas's command wore off," Luc remarked. His voice made her cringe. She didn't want to hear him ever again. When she saw the gun in his hands, she tried to jump in the way, but Alik held her back.

*I hate them.*

"Why are you glaring at me like that?" Luc asked.

"This is not what we agreed on," Issac replied flatly. "You quite literally jumped the gun."

"Stas commanded you not to hurt him again, which left me as the viable option. Or have you forgotten that Amelia is my sister as well? Also, logic dictates that as the Hydraian King, it's my duty to handle fledgling issues as I see fit. And so I did."

Amelia wanted to cry, but couldn't. It took too much energy to call on tears. All she needed was to crawl into the dark place and never come out. She created it all those years ago and hid there often during experiments. It seemed she'd crafted a forever home for her conscious. Maybe it would kill her. She wasn't sure she cared. A sad reality considering how hard she'd fought these last few years.

*Tom wouldn't want you to do this*, her conscious chided.

*Well, he's not here to care, is he?*

She shivered, feeling so cold and alone. Tom's warmth was a million miles away. Her heart ached without him. *I'm so weak.* All that talk about making her stronger had been a lie. She promised never to rely on another person again, but he'd anchored her in inexplicable ways. All the ghosts his presence chased away came roaring back, badgering around in her head and pulling her deeper into that hole of nothingness.

"Jesus Christ!" A deep voice crashed through the waves of her mind. She swam farther away while the conversation flowed above the dark water. "What the fuck were you thinking shooting him in front of her?"

Warmth flowed over her, but it felt foreign and wrong. *Not Tom.* She struggled to get away, but something strong wrapped around her and flooded heat through her veins. It hurt, yet numbed at the same time. She fought like hell to push it away, but the power broke through and forced her back into reality. Her eyelids felt heavy as they opened, her mouth dry. Eventually, her focus returned, and Balthazar's worried expression filled her view.

*How did I get in his lap?*

Then it hit her like a punch to the chest. "No."

"Oh, yes. Sorry, love, but you needed me."

She tried to slap him, but her arms refused to move. "Bloody bastard," she settled on saying instead, despising that he'd used his gift for emotional manipulation on her. "I hate you."

"I know." He looked contrite as he brushed a lock of sweaty hair from her forehead. "He's going to be okay, Amelia."

"He's dead," she replied, voice flat. Inside, she wanted to scream, but Balthazar had muted everything on the surface. It was like sitting inside a dense fog of foreign emotion with all her true feelings locked up inside a vault. And she didn't have the key.

"He's a fledgling, A. He's going to wake up in twelve hours with a headache and a new set of immortal genes."

Luc peered down at her over Balthazar's shoulder. "We didn't behead him or set him on fire, and I used a normal bullet, Amelia. A direct shot to the head provides the least amount of pain. He'll wake up Hydraian tomorrow."

She glowered at the Hydraian King. "You're a right bastard."

"One who just did his baby sister a huge favor. A mortal death was the sentence we agreed upon. When he wakes up, he'll be one of us. A useful addition, if I do say so myself."

"You should have fucking explained that to her prior to pulling the trigger," Balthazar growled in a voice she didn't usually associate with him. When those chocolate eyes met hers, they were filled with fear and understanding. He knew how close she'd been to crossing a line she wouldn't have come back from.

"Yes, well, the plan was for me to kill him. Not Lucian." Issac crouched beside her and brushed his knuckles over her cheek. "I'm sorry, love. I still don't care much for him, and likely never will, but I would never intentionally hurt you or Aya."

"I'm still fucking pissed at you." Stas's voice came from the other side of the room, and she sounded furious. "All of you. Except B."

Balthazar smirked. "Hear that, Wakefield? Your competition is the only one she likes right now. Should I use that to my advantage?" He waggled his eyebrows at Issac, making Amelia groan. She did not want to be in the middle of this discussion. Balthazar let her go as she squirmed away to lie beside Tom's lifeless form. He seemed peaceful enough, and someone had placed a pillow beneath his head.

"Lucian, may I borrow your firearm?" Issac asked. "I would like to give Balthazar a headache."

"No," Stas said, arms folded. "No more guns. No more shooting. No more *anything*."

Issac sighed, "Aya—"

"No. You just killed my friend. Sorry, not you, but Luc. But don't you see? Tom didn't get a choice in becoming a Hydraian. You took that from him, and that's not okay. If you *ever* do that to me, any of you, I promise you will live to regret it. Life is not something you just take on a whim or for some idiotic form of punishment. It's not a game. Especially not to me." She stormed out of the room without a backwards glance.

"Fuck," Issac muttered, palming the back of his neck.

Balthazar whistled. "Yeah, good luck fixing that."

"As always, your commentary is not helpful." Issac started after Stas, but stopped to study Amelia. The pain radiating from his sapphire gaze made her feel a little better. He should feel bad, because if Luc hadn't pulled the trigger, he would have done it. But she hated the conflict in his gaze. He didn't know who to choose. She would never stand in the way of love, especially for him.

"Go after her," she told him. "I'll be okay." And she wouldn't stay angry with him. Something told her Stas would punish him enough for it.

He stared at Balthazar, and the Elder gave him a nod. Then Issac disappeared out the door. They had such a bizarre relationship, bickering one minute and friends the next.

A hand settled on her shoulder, making her flinch. Luc stared down at her with a mixture of emotions in his eyes. "When Tom wakes in the morning, ask him what we talked about today. Then let me know if what I did was truly as wrong as you and Stas seem to think it was." With that, he left. Alik, who had stood silently in the corner, followed her brothers without a word.

"Right then, leave me to clean everything up." Balthazar stood and wiped his palms on his trousers. "Let's move Tom to my guest room. He'll be more comfortable there in the morning, and you can stay with him."

"Did you know what they planned to do?" she asked.

"Yes." He held out a hand to help her stand, and she accepted.

"Why didn't you tell me?"

"You know why, Amelia."

*Elder business.* They rarely made decisions for Hydraians, but when they did, their edicts stayed private unless otherwise appropriate. "But you helped me sneak in here to see him."

"Yes, to give him an opportunity to choose his fate, and he chose you."

She didn't understand. "What?"

"Think about it, love. You being here gave him the

perfect chance to escape, but he didn't. And why didn't he? Because he wanted to be with you more than he wanted his freedom. Some might call that love."

She gaped at him. "It was all a test?"

"No, it was a choice. Had he chosen to escape, we would have let him leave. But he chose to stay, so Luc made him immortal. Now, can we head back to my house? Digging into your emotional psyche was exhausting, and I'd like to get some sleep."

*Oh.* She worried her lower lip. "About what you saw…"

"Don't. You're not ready to go there yet, A." He palmed her cheek. "But when you are, I'm here, okay?"

She nodded. "All right."

"Let's get him to my house, rest, and regroup in the morning over breakfast. I'll make pancakes, too. You can flaunt them in front of Luc as revenge."

"I'd like to do a lot more than throw pancakes at my big brother right now."

"Take his advice and talk to Tom tomorrow. You might be more forgiving afterwards."

"Doubtful."

He shrugged. "Then you can take Luc a plate of pancakes and force him to eat them."

She shook her head, bemused. "You and your breakfast food."

"He's the one obsessed with waffles."

"Uh huh."

Balthazar secured the blanket around Tom before lifting him with a gentleness she didn't expect. He didn't appear dead so much as asleep. A good thing because it implied Luc had told the truth about the bullet. Tom's body still functioned on a psychic level, keeping his organs and bodily functions intact, while his immortal genes took over. There were those who swore the heart still beat a little during the process. She might have to listen for it later.

Balthazar cast her an amused glance. "Not that I mind, but can you maybe throw on some clothes before we walk out of here? Don't want to cause too much of a scene between you and the dead fledgling."

She took in her bare legs and realized someone had dressed her in Tom's shirt at some point. *Right.* Because she'd been naked in a blanket when they walked into the room. Her years as a laboratory rat kept her from feeling too embarrassed by that fact. It was the love-making fresh between her thighs that made her face heat. No way any of them had missed that detail. Especially Balthazar.

Not wanting to wear her own clothes, she pulled on Tom's boxers, gathered their trousers and other items, and followed B out the door.

*At least he's alive.*

~*~

Tom squinted into the semi-darkness and willed the truck parked on his head to move, but it refused. The weight centered between his eyes and spread in agonizing lines through the rest of his skull.

*Shit.* Talk about a hangover. Except he couldn't remember the last time he touched alcohol. Intoxication could get him killed in his line of work.

He frowned.

*Killed.*

He shot straight up out of the bed and regretted it the moment his head started to spin.

"Fuck," he muttered, touching the middle of his forehead. Smooth skin met his inspection, but he could swear something had hit him there.

"Tom?" Amelia's husky voice went straight to his balls. She yawned and stretched on the bed he'd just jumped out of and blinked sleepy eyes up at him.

*What the hell happened last night?* Because the sun outside told him it was late morning. He fought to remember, but a thick haze filled his memory. Something about fucking her against the wall and wanting to make love to her on the pile of blankets in a room that did not resemble this one in the slightest.

Dark wood furniture, a four-poster bed, and a balcony with a beach view stared back at him.

"What the hell happened last night?" he asked.

Amelia cleared her throat. "Er, you don't remember?"

He examined the pajama pants covering his legs. "Whose pants am I wearing?" Because they sure as hell didn't belong to him.

"Balthazar procured them for you. We're in his guest room. Apparently, a woman named Eliza is staying in my old home." His cock stirred at the sight of her stretching her arms over head. Her breasts looked fantastic in that thin tank top.

"I don't really mind, though," she continued. "It would be weird to stay there, and from what I understand, she needs it more than I do."

He touched his forehead again and grimaced. Did he hit it against something? Maybe that's what woke him. No. Adrenaline woke him with an odd jolt, and the headache followed. He caught Amelia admiring him and cocked a brow.

"You've seen me shirtless before, sweetheart. Not that I mind you gawking, of course."

She grinned. "You have no idea, do you?"

"Mmm, no idea about what?" he murmured, as he crawled over her on the bed. A different part of him was starting to ache, and he had the perfect solution.

Mischief lit her blue gaze. "Oh, this is quite fun."

"Is it?" He settled his hips between her legs and allowed her to feel the full weight of his arousal.

"You know," a deep voice intruded, "I'm all for exhibitionism. Voyeurism, too, of course, but I'm afraid not everyone in the house right now shares my liberal views."

Tom glanced over his shoulder to find Balthazar leaning against the door with his arms crossed. He met the Elder before the Hydraian King's interrogation. *Was that yesterday? Why is everything so damn foggy?*

"Because Luc shot you in the head," the mind reader replied. "Welcome to Hydria—officially I mean. The pancakes are ready." He pushed off the door jam and left with a wicked gleam in his eyes. Tom stared at the empty space for a solid minute before returning his focus to Amelia.

"I'm a Hydraian?" He didn't feel any different. Just well-rested with a killer headache.

"Are you mad?" she whispered.

"Mad?" he replied. "Why would I be mad?"

"Because my brother took away your mortality without asking?"

"Not exactly." He frowned. "He asked me for my opinions on becoming a Hydraian during his interrogation. I thought he wanted to know about my feelings towards his kind, not because he planned to turn me. What does this mean? Why am I not dead?"

*And why don't I feel any different?* He should have two supernatural talents, like Amelia's shifting and knowledge transfer. But he didn't sense anything unique. *Am I broken?*

"Luc said your mortal death was your punishment, though I still don't know why he needed to punish you to begin with, and he considers you a Hydraian. A useful one, if I remember correctly."

That made him grin. Tom had mentioned his potential to the Hydraian King several times during their discussion. Not to beg for his life, but to give the practical reasons why the Elders shouldn't kill him. He gave up a few CRF details, but kept the important ones close to his chest. Some of the memories from last night tumbled through his thoughts, making his eyes widen. "You shifted."

Amelia's cheeks flushed a pretty pink. "I did."

"Into my twin."

She nodded, biting her lip. "Your trick the other night, although cruel, worked. I didn't even think twice about it. I just shifted."

His lips curled. "So I helped?"

"Maybe," she conceded, her pupils dilating. "Want to help me...?" her voice trailed off into a frown. "Never mind. Issac's here. He's filling my head with butterflies."

"Do I even want to know what that means?"

"I believe he's apologizing for last night. Which reminds me,"—her gaze narrowed—"when were you going to tell me about your intentions towards my brother? Who, by the way, did *not* kill your mother."

His blood ran cold, and whatever was left of his erection died. He didn't want to talk about this. Not with her. She would never understand.

He rolled off the bed. "Is my shirt lying around somewhere? Or one that I can borrow?"

"Seriously? You're going to change the subject and walk away?" She jumped out of the covers to stand in front of him with her hands on her hips. "We need to talk about this."

"Why?"

"Because you wrongly think my brother killed your mum and never bothered to mention it."

He folded his arms. "Yeah? And when would have been a good time to bring it up?"

"You had the last several weeks to do it."

"To what point? So I could see the same self-righteous look you're giving me now? No, thank you." He tried to walk around her, but she stepped into his path.

"He's my brother, so of course I'll defend him, but in this case, it's because he's innocent. He said as much last night." She placed her palm over his heart. "But this isn't about him so much as it's about us, Tom. This will never work if we don't talk to each other."

*Us.* What a strange and amazing word. Tom had nothing against monogamy or relationships, but never considered having one due to his line of work. There was the occasional girlfriend in college, though they all stopped coming around after realizing his career aspirations were his first and only love. But with Amelia, he liked the sound of *us*.

"Is that what we are? A couple?" he wondered, voice soft. "Is that what you want?"

She studied him for a moment, silent. Then swallowed. "When Luc shot you, I..." She paused to clear her throat. "I didn't handle it well. You told me leaning on someone doesn't mean I'm weak, but I was last night. This bond, or whatever this is, terrifies me." Her lids lowered as she peered up at him. "But losing you terrifies me more. I stayed with you all night, worrying that you may never wake up even though I knew you would. How do you define that?"

*You don't.* There were no words for it, only feelings. He wrapped his hand around her nape and pulled her in for a long, devastating kiss. Her arms went around his shoulders as she lifted onto her toes to get closer to him. He left her panting against him when he pulled back to stare down into her gorgeous eyes.

"You were right the other night," he admitted. "I've always been alone. I'm not used to having someone I can confide in or trust. This isn't going to be easy, sweetheart."

"Nothing worth having ever is," she whispered.

He nuzzled her nose. "I want this—you—more than anything I've ever wanted. And it terrifies me, too. That's why I didn't mention your brother. I didn't want to lose you."

"You won't," she promised. "But you do need to talk to him."

He groaned. "I knew you were going to say that." Tom would rather have all his teeth pulled than talk to Wakefield.

"Tell me why you think he killed your mum?"

"Because Jonathan told him I did," a cultured voice

said from the doorway. Apparently, the bedrooms in Balthazar's home weren't considered private. "Amelia, could you give Thomas and me a moment?"

*Oh, good. Looks like we'll have that chat now then.* If his supernatural talents could appear now, he would love that. They might come in handy while talking to Amelia's big brother.

*Will you be okay?* Amelia's eyes seemed to ask.

He sighed. What choice did he have? Amelia's comments about last night had brought back his memory of Wakefield's final words.

*"I was on the opposite side of the state at a military school saving the life of a young fledgling who was the spitting image of his father."*

That night forever haunted him. The phone call from his mother telling him to run, being cornered by a hoard of Ichorians who wanted him dead, and a man saving him from the shadows. His father claimed to be the savior, but Tom never understood why he couldn't picture his face clearly. Everything else was so vivid, except the one who saved him. He'd been in shock, his father said. That was also how he explained the memory gap between leaving the school and arriving at the cabin too late to save his mom. Hearing Wakefield's words made him wonder if it hadn't been shock so much as someone fucking with his vision.

"Tom?" Amelia whispered, waiting for an answer to her unspoken question.

He let her go with a nod and stepped out onto stone paved balcony. The humid air did little for the heat climbing up his neck, though the pant-wearing Ichorian beside him seemed perfectly fine.

"Do you not own shorts or something?" Tom wondered.

Wakefield eyed his khaki slacks and polo shirt. "This is acceptable island attire."

"If you say so, buddy." He folded his arms onto the railing and admired the Aegean Sea. The clear water rolled in smooth waves over the black sand beach below, giving the scene a peaceful atmosphere that appealed to his tormented soul. He could see why the Hydraians chose this place. It might not be economically sound, but something could be said about tranquility.

"I used to admire your father a great deal, Thomas. Aidan considered him part of the family, despite being Sired by a different Ichorian."

Tom knew the story. His father had been reborn too weak according to his maker, and he'd left him for dead. Being able to force truths from people wasn't exactly a competitive skill among the Ichorian community, but Aidan took him in anyway and gave him the means to defend himself.

"As a result, I considered him family. Amelia, too," Wakefield continued. "So when he called me that day and requested my assistance to save his son, I agreed without question." He leaned against the railing, his back to the ocean and his gaze on Tom. "Imagine my surprise when I found a twelve-year-old soldier fending off Ichorians twice his size. They would have won, of course, though today I think you'd put up a good fight."

"Careful, Wakefield, that almost sounds like a compliment."

He smirked. "It is. I don't have to like a man to admire his skill. But my point is, my only dealing with Anna's death was delivering you to her cabin that night. Your father was the one covered in her blood, presumably after trying to save her life, but I always wondered as to the veracity of his retelling. And I find it particularly convenient that he blamed her death on me. If you want my opinion, I'd say he was trying to drive a wedge between you and the only allies you could ever potentially depend upon."

*To leave me forever alone and dependent on him.* A perfect manipulation. How many other lies had his father told throughout the years? Luc's acceptance of him in Hydria proved one of the biggest threats false, and now this? Tom shook his head. *What a mind fuck.*

A commotion from inside the house drew his attention. "What's going on?"

Issac frowned, his gaze distant. "I'm not quite sure. They appear to be crowded around the television and watching a news report. Something about a foiled terrorist attack in upstate New York at what appears to be a hospital."

Ice dripped through his veins. "What part of New York?"

He said the name and blinked. "Is that your mother's hometown? It's near the cabin."

"No. That's where my aunt lives, and that hospital is where she works. I need a phone."

# CHAPTER EIGHTEEN

## Family Bonds

"Two hours and fifty-seven minutes? I'm disappointed, son. Have you forgotten your training already?"

Tom ignored his father's jibe and got to the point. "What have you done?"

John tsked. "Now, Tom, it's not about what I've done, but what I'm going to do. Unless you cooperate."

His hands fisted, but he kept his voice calm. "What do you want?"

"The asset, of course."

The tension in the room was palpable as all eyes fell on the phone in the center of the dining room table. Tom had put his father on speakerphone, not because anyone requested it, but because he wanted to be transparent. Trust was earned, and he had a lot of making up to do.

Allowing the Elders, Stas, and Amelia to hear this conversation was just the beginning. Everyone stood in a circle around the table, but no one spoke except Tom.

"Yeah, that's not going to happen, John," he said, replying to his father's request. "She's gone."

Silence. Then, "And where did she go?"

"Home."

"If that were true, I would have received, at a minimum, a call from at least one of her brothers—or perhaps her father. Try again."

Wakefield and Luc both shrugged, as if to say *man's got a point*. Which he did, but he failed to factor in that they cared more about seeing Amelia than they did revenge. And from what Tom had gathered about both men, they were the type to think things through before reacting. Otherwise, they would have killed Tom without a second thought.

A moan sounded over the line, followed by a crack. "Quiet," his father snapped. "Can't you see I'm having a conversation? Though I must say, Rosalie, it's not going in your favor. Seems Tom prefers his new plaything over you."

Cold rage replaced his nonchalant demeanor. "Rosalie has nothing to do with this."

"Well, it was her or Lizzie, and the latter would upset Stas. But really, son, this is your doing. Had you just gotten this fling out of your system and returned home, none of this would have been necessary. Alas, here we are."

"You're a dead man," Tom seethed, meaning every word.

"Ah, there it is! I wondered when the real you would come out to play. Excellent. Shall we get to the point, then?"

*Prick.* He wanted to get to the point ten minutes ago. "Yes."

"Sorry, what was that? I didn't quite hear you."

*I'm going to fucking kill you.* "Yes, sir."

Tom pictured his father's triumphant grin and fought not to break something. "Very good, then. I propose an exchange, your only living relative on your mother's side for the asset."

A bullet through the heart would hurt less, but he refused to let it show. John loved a good game of chess, and he'd trained his son to be a master. "All you want is the asset for Rosalie? Fine. Done. But I get my freedom."

Luc smirked, clearly catching on to his strategy, while Issac cocked a brow and Amelia flashed him an affronted look. He tucked her closer to his side and kissed the concerned lines of her forehead. As if he'd ever give her up.

"So you admit she's with you?" Arrogance underlined John's tone.

"Where else would she be?"

"You said she was home."

"I lied. I can do that over the phone, you know." His father's powers only worked in person, a fact he seemed hellbent to change despite it being that way for over a millennia. He may have created a small army, but Ichorian gifts didn't evolve over time. Not naturally anyway. Tom wouldn't be surprised if some of the CRF's research was devoted to enhancing immortal gifts.

"When and where do you want the asset?" he asked, voice bored.

"You're willing to trade?"

"Yes." He kept the answer simple and flat on purpose to inspire curiosity.

"I expected more of a fight," John replied, his disappointment clear.

"The asset for Rosalie and my freedom. You're giving me the better end of the deal, so why would I argue with that?"

He pictured his father frowning as he considered. "And where will you go?"

"Well now, John, that's the whole point of having my

freedom. I won't have to answer to you or anyone ever again."

Silence. "I see."

"So we have a deal then?" Tom prompted.

"No."

He grinned. "No?"

"I'll release Rosalie if you agree to come home and undergo rehabilitation. Willingly."

*Checkmate.* "But you just said—"

"I know what I said, and I changed my mind. Your willing rehabilitation and the asset for your aunt's release, or no deal."

"So you want me and the asset? That seems a hefty price for one relative." It killed him to say it, especially knowing she could hear him. But he had to play this part or John would bulldoze him. "Especially a relative who will die in a few years while I live for eternity."

"Fair point," John conceded. "I guess I need to sweeten the deal by throwing in a person I know you care about with immortal genetics, then. Like, say, Lizzie? Of course, I don't know how immortal she is, but I'm sure the scientists would enjoy testing her limits, don't you think?"

Ice coated his spine, making him freeze. Stas met his gaze with a look of fury and horror, all mixed into one. He had to clear the cotton from his throat to speak. "You have my attention."

"Do I? Good." The smile in his father's voice made him want to shoot something. "So I leave Lizzie alone, for now, and release your aunt—"

"Unharmed," Tom amended.

"Sure, no more harmed than she already is," John continued, "and you turn yourself and the asset in. I think that sounds like a splendid trade."

Tom stared at the phone, unsure of what to do. So much for his checkmate. A motion in his peripheral brought his attention to Luc who gave him a nod.

*Yes to what? The deal?*

Luc nodded again, clearly reading the questions from his eyes. He followed it with a hurry up motion, and Balthazar mimicked it beside him.

*You want me to agree?* he asked the mind reader.

He moved his head in the affirmative.

*I'm not handing her over.*

Balthazar gave him a look that said *no shit* and gestured impatiently at the phone.

"Have I lost you, son?" Jonathan asked, victory evident in his tone. "Or would you like to hear a demonstration of what I intend to do to Lizzie? Your aunt probably won't survive it, but you don't seem to care anyway."

*Fucking prick.* "I'll do it."

"Sorry, what was that?"

Oh, he would rip his father apart when he saw him. "I agree to your terms, sir."

"Very good. Now how far away are you from your mother's cabin?"

Luc held up the number seven and mouthed *hours.*

"I need at least seven hours to get there."

"You have six. Bring the asset, and come alone."

"Who the hell would I bring?"

His father laughed. "Fair point. See you soon, son."

Tom pressed the end button with a little too much force, picked up the phone, and threw it at the wall. It shattered into a dozen pieces.

"You know, untraceable mobiles are not cheap," Jayson said conversationally from his position in the kitchen. "And I happened to like that particular model."

"Because you don't have ten more just like it at your house," Balthazar replied.

"I was talking about quality, not quantity, and it's the principle of the thing. You don't break other people's stuff. It's impolite."

"Yeah, and how many beds have—?"

"Enough." The authority in Luc's voice captured everyone's attention. "Tom, tell me about Lizzie."

"Yes, what he said," Stas echoed, her expression dark.

"Right." He cleared his throat. "I don't know a lot. My father implied once that she could be biologically related to me about a decade ago when he found us in a rather compromising position." At Stas's raised eyebrows, he clarified. "She tried to kiss me. Nothing happened."

She nodded for him to continue.

"Anyway, I assumed he had an affair with Lillian until I found some CRF files on Lizzie a few months back. I didn't realize it was her at first, just someone called test subject four-seven, but one of the researchers slipped her name. When I asked my dad about it, he told me it wasn't anything to worry about, that he would keep me apprised of any developments." *Whatever the fuck that meant.* "All I gathered is she has immortal genetics of some kind inside of her, and I don't think they were put there through normal means."

"I always wondered at her kinship," Wakefield murmured. "Elizabeth resembles neither of her parents, and she has a uniqueness to her."

"Why did you never mention this to me?" Stas asked.

"It was not pertinent at the time, love. Nor was it related to anything of consequence, just a nagging thought."

His answer seemed to placate her because those green eyes landed on Tom. "So are you saying Lizzie—my best friend—isn't human?"

"She's something other than mortal, and I'm pretty sure the CRF is still experimenting on her despite her not being in the lab. My father mentioned something about her needing the monthly dose once to George. I didn't think much of it at the time, but now I wonder if he meant a medical treatment of some kind."

Luc scratched his chin. "Interesting. Any idea how many people are aware of the study?"

"Knowing my dad, he's the only one with all the knowledge and he's only given pieces to others." John never divulged enough to give up his position, a power play to keep himself in charge. "He wouldn't even tell me about it, and he considered me his heir." Her records were all classified at the highest level, above what Tom's used to be, and the technicians refused to talk about her files. He tried a few times with no luck.

Luc nodded. "An intelligent strategy that makes him more useful alive. The question becomes, how valuable is Lizzie Watkins?"

Tom bristled. "If you think I'll sit by and let her suffer in John's hands, then think again. She might not mean anything to you, and I might be a shitty friend, but I love that woman like my own flesh and blood, and I will not sacrifice her life for my freedom."

"What he said," Stas growled.

"Easy, love," Wakefield murmured as he wrapped an arm around her shoulders. "I believe Lucian is trying to determine whether or not the Hydraians should look into Elizabeth's case."

"Correct. And from what I'm hearing, she's valuable to Tom and Stas, making her of interest to me. I would offer her asylum, but Tom's comments regarding her monthly dose concerns me. Until we learn more, I can't help her."

"What do you propose?" Wakefield asked, eyes narrowing.

"We keep Stas in play at the CRF while someone else infiltrates Lizzie's life in a more intimate capacity."

"Uh, hello?" Stas waved her hand. "I'm her roommate and best friend."

"You're also not staying on as a Sentinel. Given recent events, it's too dangerous," Wakefield added.

Tom nodded his agreement. *Stole the words right out of my mouth, buddy.*

"She's my best friend, Issac. It's my decision."

"Did you hear what Jonathan threatened to do to Elizabeth just now? He'll do worse to you, Aya. Especially if he thinks it will control me or Thomas to do his bidding.

With Amelia being home, the environment is too unstable. Jonathan—"

"I have an idea regarding that," Luc cut in. "A solution that keeps Stas safe, or at least as safe as she's been, and protects Amelia and Tom. Also, it'll keep Jonathan alive, for now."

Tom frowned. "Why do you want to keep him alive?" He assumed they would want to slaughter him. Brutally. Or at least torture the|man for what he did. The boy in him who once loved his father unconditionally ached at the thought, but the man he'd become understood John deserved to be punished. Even if it hurt.

"I want to know who Jonathan is working for," Luc replied.

"My father works for himself." He was too egotistical and arrogant to report to anyone else.

"Really? So how did your father acquire the wealth to build the Catastrophic Relief Foundation?" Luc paused for effect before continuing. "He went from relying on Aidan's financial assistance to opening his own humanitarian organization in less than a year. Then he miraculously created a secret army of superhuman soldiers to fight Ichorians and Hydraians overnight. That's quite an achievement for a man whose only gift is to force truths. I'd like to know how he managed that."

The CRF was created prior to Tom's birth, so he didn't know much about it. "I thought Aidan loaned him the funds for it, like he did Wakefield."

Wakefield snorted. "Is that how he explained my history as an entrepreneur? How quaint."

*Another lie then? Fantastic.* "Okay, but my father never mentioned working for anyone other than himself."

"Which is why I sadly still need him alive," Luc replied. "And I need him comfortable, so he keeps his guard down."

*Okay, I'll bite.* "You obviously have a plan in mind. So what do you suggest?"

Luc grinned. "I thought you'd never ask. Let's start by talking about your new Hydraian gifts and how to use them."

\* \* \*

The cabin hadn't changed. Tranquil, secluded, and haunted by memories. Tom shivered at the thought of stepping inside. He wanted to burn the place to the ground and never return. And if Luc's plan worked, he would be allowed to do just that.

"You okay?" Amelia whispered.

He swallowed and nodded. She stood beside him in jeans and a tank top, while he wore his favorite leather jacket to hide all his weapons. His father would ask him to hand them over, but by then, it would be too late.

Wakefield leaned against a tree about a hundred yards away, hands in his slacks. He would disappear when his father arrived, as would Tristan, Mateo, and the Hydraians who opted to join their mission. Jacque had teleported everyone in without breaking a sweat. A true testament to his potential. Tom caught him walking along the roof and admiring the night sky.

His entire sense of time was fucked up thanks to his immortal rebirth and all the traveling. But he felt more alive than he'd ever been, especially now that he understood his abilities. Amelia's analogy the other night proved to be accurate. Using his gifts were as natural as walking, except without the toddler learning curve. He hadn't noticed them earlier, because they were second nature to him and just enhancements of skills he already owned as a human. The plan hinged on his new gifts, which should have unnerved him, but didn't.

Tom only had one concern: Wards.

Wards, or cryptic symbols, were what kept the CRF headquarters safe in a city of Ichorians, though he never did understand how they worked or where they came from. All he knew was they blocked supernatural gifts and kept immortals from entering the CRF compound without being invited. His father's researchers were trying to figure out how to apply the wards in a mobile capacity, but hadn't solved that puzzle yet. At least, Tom hoped that was still the case, because if they had discovered how to apply wards to a person rather than a building, then this entire plan would fail.

When Tom mentioned it to Luc, the big man had shrugged and said, *"Then we'll move on to Plan B."* But they didn't have time to discuss what that actually meant.

"Alik says they're coming," Amelia murmured, breaking into his thoughts.

"I had no idea he was a telepath until Luc explained his plan today." Tom knew about the whole mental torture thing, but never looked into his other power. It didn't really matter when compared to his ability to take out a room full of people with one thought.

"He doesn't use it unless he has to."

"Well, that's good I suppose. So what can Jayson do? Aside from control metal, I mean." He seemed to be the carefree one of the Elders, but held an unmistakable air of danger around him. There was a reason the four Hydraians had lived so long and were considered royalty among their kind. Each of them carried deadly gifts that made them difficult to kill. But of all the Elders, Jayson's records at the CRF held the least information, and Tom always wondered why.

She grinned. "You don't know?"

"There are not a lot of records on him, other than he's old and has an affinity for metal. His appearance varies in all the notes as well."

"And there's a reason for that. He can alter visual perception and memory, which is why no one can recall what he looks like, unless he allows it."

Tom frowned. "So his gift is similar to your brother?"

"Not really. Jayson only controls the visual memory of

265

his own physical appearance, not the surroundings. He more or less influences how someone remembers him, but doesn't change the surroundings or where they met."

"In other words, he's the perfect spy," Tom mused.

"Yes, he—" Tires rolling over gravel cut off the rest of Amelia's reply. Three four-wheelers headed down the drive toward them. Tom kept his stance lose with his hands in his pockets, while Amelia shifted from foot to foot beside him.

"You ready?" he asked.

"Yep." Confidence underlined that single word, making pride blossom in his chest.

"I so want to kiss you right now."

"And do you want to straddle me as well?"

*Minx.* He swallowed his grin. The last thing he wanted was to appear amused as his father approached. John would expect repentance and submission, not excitement. The flirtation in Amelia's voice didn't show in her expression, only determination. His father would interpret it as defiance, which worked well for their plans.

"Hello, son," John greeted as he strolled up the drive in one of his signature suits. Half a dozen Sentinels flanked him on each side, all of them former friends. Stark was notably missing, which meant Stas's role in their plan had worked.

"Sir," Tom replied. *I see your arrogance has taken over the unit.* None of them had their weapons drawn. His father must have told them it wouldn't be necessary. *Mistake number one.*

"Ah, I'm almost disappointed to see the cocky demeanor go, but it is the first step in your rehabilitation."

*Fucking prick.* He couldn't wait to begin their charade, but he needed to see his aunt first. "Where's Rosalie?"

"Right. Our trade." John motioned over his shoulder, and Blake broke rank to return to one of the four-wheelers. His blue eyes flicked to Tom before opening the back door. Rosalie's appearance sent a jolt of shock to his system. He expected her in a similar state to Amelia, but instead, she was dolled up for a date with her black dress, heels, and stylish updo.

*Something isn't right here...*

She sauntered up to his father's side and placed a hand on his shoulder. "Hello, Tom." His stomach turned over at the smile she flashed him. So familiar, yet with a touch of cruelty. Did his father engineer an identical twin to take her place? This sophisticated woman didn't resemble the down-to-earth aunt he knew.

"What is this? We had a deal, my life and the asset for Rosalie." And this look-a-like was clearly not his aunt.

"And I'm upholding that deal to an extent. We agreed on her release, of which she's free, but choosing to stand by my side." John gazed at the stranger beside him. "Would you like to tell him, or shall I?" he asked.

"Oh, I think you should. You're his father after all." Her voice sent a chill down Tom's spine. *She sounds like Rosalie.*

"Indeed." Dark brown eyes, the same color as his own, locked on Tom. "Rosalie and I have an understanding of sorts. It started around the time I met your mother and has continued, well, through today, obviously. She's helped me keep an eye on you, and before you, your mother."

Tom couldn't speak, but maintained a studiously blank expression. Clearly, John wanted to tell a story, and the evil glint in his eyes implied he wanted it to hurt. A form of punishment, no doubt.

"You know, I liked your mother. Sweet woman and gorgeous, too, but she decided to do something I didn't quite agree with. She planned to give you to the Hydraians, which for obvious reasons was not in your best interest, and I therefore had to deal with the issue."

Tom's jaw hurt from squeezing it so tightly. There were no words. His father hadn't finished yet, but the purpose of this lecture was clear. He wanted to explain how Anna died. The real story. And it seemed Tom's aunt was involved, which would force him to change the part of the plan where he saved Rosalie's life. She might be his blood relative, but if she willingly worked with his father in any capacity against his mother, he would have no choice but to leave her in John's hands.

*Please tell me he's lying, Rosalie. Tell me this is all a cruel joke.* But the adoration on her face as she listened to John's retelling lent truth to his words. Was this really his aunt? The woman he trusted? The woman he considered giving his life up for only hours before?

*What a fool I've been.*

"You were too young to understand at the time," John continued, "but I'm sure you see now why she had to die. As for Rosalie, she was the one who informed me of your mother's plans and helped me fix the problem. It was perfect really, as she took over the mother-role in your life, but remained loyal to me. The perfect way to keep you in line until this most recent mission. I suspected something was going on with the asset, of course. That's why I had Rosalie arrange dinner with you. Had I realized all hell would break lose, I would have gone about it in a different way."

"Not your fault, darling," his aunt cooed. "We both underestimated his loyalty."

Tom couldn't decide who he wanted to shoot more, John or Rosalie. The smile in her eyes made her the ideal candidate for a bullet to the head, not that he had the heart to follow through. But Jesus Christ, he wanted to do damage. She voluntarily distracted him so Amelia could be tortured? And she betrayed her own sister to his father? Those sins alone were unforgivable. Fuck trying to save her. She dug her own grave with John and, from the looks of it, was quite happy about it.

*Jesus.* How had he missed the obvious connection between his aunt and father? Every time he saw her, she commented about how alike he was to John. He didn't even realize they'd stayed in touch, let alone knew each other well. But she mentioned him every time they spoke. Like a hypnotic chant reminding him to stay in line, but in a different way from his dad.

*Fuck.*

It took all his energy not to react and keep his breathing even. Inside, a beast raged, but outside, he maintained his calm demeanor. The same could not be said about Amelia, who he could see bristling in his peripheral. His father must have noticed as well because he switched focus to her.

"You cost me a brilliant researcher, Amelia. Now we'll have to find someone else for the position, but we can offer you for their employee orientation. I wonder if Anita's replacement will think of any new tests? Hmm, this actually might be a good thing, a fresh pair of eyes is just what we need on your case. I would apologize for your future pain, but really, dear, you only have yourself to blame."

Amelia smiled. "I mean this sincerely when I say, go fuck yourself, Jonathan."

In all their time together, Tom had only heard her use "*arse*" and "*bloody hell.*" Never "fuck." She said it with such arrogance and vigor that he couldn't help but feel a trickle of satisfaction.

*That's my woman.* And she'd just stood up to his father's threats instead of cowering. It provided the distraction he needed to regather his focus. Reacting to his father's reveal would do nothing to move their plan forward, and he needed Amelia safe once and for all. He could digest the reality of his mother's death later and, one day, seek his revenge. But today was not that day. There were too many other players in this game for him to call checkmate now.

"So the threat against Rosalie was a lure to bring me home. Well played, sir." Tom kept his voice calm, with a touch of boredom.

"I appreciate the sentiment, though, Tom." Rosalie gave him an indulgent smile, the same she gave him as a teenager when he confided in her about his studies. "I care about you, too, you know. We're just trying to do what's best for you here."

He couldn't respond to her. The betrayal was too new, too deep, and it threatened his focus. He leaned on his inherent ability to ignore his inner turmoil, something his father had beat into him as a child. *Good job, John. You trained me well.*

"As to my mother," Tom continued, "you were probably right. The Hydraians would never accept me." He put a little power behind those words, focusing them on John, and willed for him to believe his sincerity. "No one would. That's why I'm here, Dad. You're the only one who cares about me. I have nowhere to go." He stressed the helplessness while weaving in notes of persuasion. *Trust my words.* It seemed all those years of finding ways to lie had turned into a unique talent, one Luc found particularly useful in this scenario. Tom's gift wasn't the same as Stas's ability to compel so much as a way to twist lies into words others mistook as truths.

"There's just one thing," Tom continued. "I don't think we need Amelia. She can't shift anymore, and she's pretty fucking unstable. I considered delivering her back to her brother for fun, but obviously, I decided against it. So, instead, I suggest we dispose of her properly and be done with the mess. It solves the problem of Stas ever finding out, and Wakefield as well."

The words nearly killed him, but they were part of the plan. He put his compulsion behind each statement, encouraging John to accept the veracity of his sentiments. The Sentinels and Rosalie were included in the web of lies, while he exempted all the others in their vicinity. Those in the cars couldn't hear him, and he didn't want to mistakenly set off one of the immortals. It amazed him how easy the gift came to him; all he had to do was think about it, and the psychic threads snapped into place.

"So none of the immortals are aware she's alive?" John

asked.

A pointed question, which meant Tom couldn't lie. But he could evade. "What immortals would I have told, sir? And would any of them have allowed me to return with the asset in exchange for my mortal aunt?" His talent naturally weaved through each word, setting the statements in stone. *I speak the truth, John.*

His father nodded. "Yes, where would you go? I'm glad you've come to your senses, son. Of course, rehabilitation will still be required, and there are those in your unit who would see you punished."

"Of course." *I'd like to see them try.* "Can I shoot her now?"

Surprise filtered through John's features. "You want to kill her?"

Another direct query that required evasion. "Why not? Wouldn't it be a good way to start my therapy or, at a minimum, serve as a punishment for fucking up again?" *Say yes, John.*

"Tom..." The plea in Amelia's voice made him cringe. It was part of the act, but did she have to sound so hurt? She stared at his profile while he refused to acknowledge her.

His father scratched his chin, thoughtful as he studied them. "It could be a reasonable start, yes. Tell me, how would you feel about killing her?"

*Ah, finally something he could answer honestly.* "The very thought of hurting her makes me want to tear my heart from my chest and burn it."

"She's well and truly in your head, son. How did that happen?"

"We spent a lot of time together." *And I loved every fucking minute, even when she insulted my precious Yankees.* "I developed feelings for her as a result."

"And you realize those feelings are wrong now?" his father asked, curiosity evident in his expression.

This would be tricky. "I've realized what needs to be

done about them, yes."

"You don't mean that," Amelia implored, playing her role. "Please, look at me."

He folded his arms and cocked a brow at his father. "We need to end this, sir. And I need to be the one to take her down. It's the only way I'll be able to prove my worth and rejoin your ranks." Compliance was his father's weakness. He wanted everyone to bow down and call him master, and Tom did just that both with his words and body language. It lowered the asshole's defenses and allowed Tom's gift for lie manipulation to settle in and take effect.

"You have all the samples you need to further your research. Keeping her alive is a waste of space and resources, sir. Let me kill her and prove my loyalty once and for all."

"It would be a good lesson in loyalty," John replied, considering. "And it would help with the Stas issue and enable me to pursue a business deal with Issac. But I've always been hesitant with having Amelia in custody. Hmm." He stepped forward and waved off the Sentinels who tried to follow. "Do you have anything to add, dear? Care to beg for your life?"

"What kind of life would it be?" Amelia's broken voice sounded so different from her confidence of minutes ago that Tom almost risked a glance at her. But he knew if he did, he wouldn't be able to pull this off. Aiming a gun at her would be hard enough without meeting her gaze.

"A painful one." John almost sounded contrite, but then he smiled. "I don't think I'm ready to give her up yet, even if it is the logical thing to do."

*Check*, Tom thought as his father took another step forward. He lifted his hand to cup Amelia's cheek in a false act of tenderness. "But Tom does bring up an excellent point about loyalty. Maybe I can replace you with another Hydraian?"

"I hope you burn in hell," Amelia seethed, her entire

demeanor changing as she grabbed the hand against her cheek and let loose her secondary gift. Just like they planned.

John had expected her to be defenseless without her ability to shift, but Tom had reminded her before they arrived that experience was a powerful weapon. And she unleashed it on his father now, pushing six years of pain and suffering into one forceful tendril of information. It brought the CEO to his knees with an agonized shriek, and the Sentinels reacted. They leapt forward to pull John to safety while Tom drew his weapon, aimed it at Amelia, and pulled the trigger. Twice. One bullet to the head, and a second to the heart. Or at least that's what everyone else would see thanks to Wakefield's intervention.

In reality, both bullets went into a nearby tree, the sound muted by Tristan. Having two Ichorians on standby with sensory gifts was certainly useful, as was Tom's new gift for perfect aim. It hadn't surprised him to learn that his secondary Hydraian talent revolved around his ability to shoot. All he had to do was focus on his target, and he'd never miss. He couldn't wait to explore that one more later as Luc suggested it went beyond guns. *You could throw a knife with perfect accuracy every time as well.*

Shrugging off the possibilities, Tom holstered the weapon and went to his knees beside his wheezing father. "Dad? Talk to me." He allowed a semblance of panic to enter his voice, despite feeling victorious inside.

"What the fuck, man?" Blake cried after realizing Tom had shot Amelia. She lay off to the side, staring blankly into space. Her brother had agreed that sending her into a temporary comatose state would help with the charade.

"Shit, man," Charlie added. "You used incendiary bullets."

"Did you not see her trying to kill John?" Tom asked, irritated as he watched the CEO slowly recover. *You deserve so much worse for your sins.* "What the fuck was I supposed to do?"

273

"Use normal bullets like the rest of us?" Blake suggested, his tone incredulous. "You *killed* her."

"I did what needed to be done," Tom argued as he studied his father's expression. Awe and understanding had entered his dead eyes. He lifted his hand to weakly touch Tom's arm and gave it a soft pat before letting it fall to the ground. Amelia obviously hadn't given him the full dose of knowledge because he seemed to be recovering quickly. *Not nearly enough suffering.*

"Welcome home, son," his father managed on a wheeze.

*And there it is. Checkmate.*

# CHAPTER NINETEEN

# Hello, Death, My Old Friend

"Well done, son." The satisfaction in his father's gaze when he looked up from Amelia's presumed corpse confirmed that Wakefield's manipulation had worked. An invisible weight fell off Tom's shoulders. Step one was complete, which meant no wards were in play. Good. On to step two.

All the Sentinels and Rosalie wore similar expressions to his father, except Blake. His old friend's lips were flat, and his shoulders tense. Hopefully, the Sentinel kept his feelings to himself, because the plan hinged on all the pawns moving to the right spaces on the board.

"Let's put her in the cabin and burn it," Tom suggested.

"Eager to be rid of your past, son?"

"Yes." *And that includes you, asshole.*

Pride curled the edges of his father's mouth. "Excellent. Yes, the cabin will do."

"You're going to burn it?" Rosalie asked, hesitation leaking into her expression for the first time. *About fucking time.* Would have been nice if she hesitated like that the night his mother died, but something told him she didn't. His father had clearly seduced her, which—yuck. Thinking about their relationship, whatever it entailed, made Tom want to hurl. Better to divert his focus.

"I can manage the asset," he said and lifted Amelia with ease.

"Let's put her in your old room," John suggested, a taunt in his voice. The bastard knew how much Tom hated that room, and to add a dead body to it would only make it worse.

He swallowed the growl growing in his throat and managed a, "Yes, sir."

"Wait, we can't burn it down," Rosalie was saying as Tom moved towards the cabin. John followed with Sentinels Blake and Charlie at his back. The others remained outside to guard the perimeter, and what excellent scouts they were proving to be, what with being surrounded by immortals.

The fact that not a single one of the CRF's men detected the dozen or so Hydraians and Ichorians lurking outside said a lot about their training and technology. Of course, Wakefield had his progeny Mateo to take care of the latter. Apparently, the Ichorian had an affinity for cybernetics and could hack into anything, with or without a computer. Fascinating talent.

Tom didn't look around as he walked through the cabin. He felt fine until he entered the bedroom and noticed the blood stained floors. The bodies were gone, but their murder scene remained. His grip on Amelia tightened as his mother's death came roaring back and smacked him between the eyes.

*Dad covered in blood.*
*Mom ripped to shreds on my bed.*
*Toys coated in red.*
*Ruined photos.*
*An expression of horror in mom's eyes.*
*Something isn't quite right with Dad.*

He shuddered. Everything was so vivid, so clear, so real. That moment changed him irrevocably. It haunted his essence, reminding him every day of the dangers in this world. Except that night was a lie. Another story his father told him to strike fear in his heart and mold his outlook to match his own. And he used this place to taunt him. Another form of manipulation to keep him under control and obedient.

John Fitzgerald redefined the meaning of monster. He told him the Hydraians would shun him, but they welcomed him. He cited Wakefield as Anna's executioner, but more or less admitted tonight that he lied. He vowed that Amelia would remain unharmed, but beat her when Wakefield pissed him off. He sent Tom on hundreds of missions, both as a child and an adult, all of which could have gotten him killed or worse, and never batted an eye.

*I'm the queen on his chess board*, Tom realized. A powerful piece for him to dictate about, but sacrifice as needed. There was no love between them, only a history of violence. And John considered himself the king.

Tom laid Amelia on the bed and pulled a blanket over her head to hide the missing wound before turning to meet his father's amused gaze. Another manipulative game of torment meant to add fractures to his son's psyche, but for the first time, Tom saw the scene clearly. His mother's death had been a mercy, a way for her to escape this world. And Tom's death would be the same.

"You can't burn this place down," Rosalie repeated from the doorway beside John. "This is my family's cabin."

"Actually, it belongs to Tom," his father corrected.

277

"And this place holds no value, right, son?"

"No value at all," Tom agreed, realizing he meant it. The cabin's dark hold over his past morphed into a new strength, one founded on truth. He spent years fighting the wrong demons, when the real one stood in front of him all along. His father.

"Don't I get a say in any of this?" Rosalie asked.

John's lips flattened as he refocused on her. "No, I'm afraid you don't, my dear." He cupped her face in a loving gesture that made Tom's stomach turn over. "You've been so useful to me all these years, but Tom and I are about to enter a new era of our lives that doesn't quite apply to you. Tom no longer requires a mother figure, and I suspect he'll have no interest in confiding in you now that he knows your role in Anna's death, so you're rather worthless to me, aren't you?"

"What are you saying?" she asked, eyes wide.

John's sigh was all hot air. "You see, dear, this is why I have no patience for mortal women. It doesn't matter how I say it; you'll never understand. Give Anna my regards." The crack of the gun startled Tom. He'd been so focused on his aunt that he missed the weapon at his father's waist. Blood pooled from Rosalie's torso as a single tear fell from her wide eyes. She crumpled to the floor with a gurgling sound that must have irritated his father because he promptly shot her in the head.

Bile rose in Tom's throat at the sight, and it took all his effort to maintain his nonchalance. He focused his breathing in the same way he did when sighting a target through his scope and forced his limbs to still. Breaking now would ruin everything, and he was so close to succeeding. Rosalie chose her fate by getting in bed with his father, and she'd paid the ultimate price.

"I believe our deal was for you to release Rosalie, sir." The words felt foreign in his mouth and tasted bitter on his tongue. He wanted to rant and rave and knock the shit out of his father. But Luc's reminder that they needed him alive shouted in the forefront of his mind. It took him a minute to realize the voice he heard belonged to Alik, not himself. As if he needed the reminder.

"Well, yes, and I did. She's been released from her mortality." John exchanged his weapon for a handkerchief and wiped a spot of blood on his shirt. "Well, that's ruined. Sentinel Charlie, can you go start a fire in the kitchen?"

"Yes, sir." The young blond man scampered off to do his master's bidding.

John dropped the soiled handkerchief on Rosalie's corpse and focused on Tom. "Shall we go then?"

"If I may, *sir*, when did we start assassinating women?" Sentinel Blake asked, expression livid. Tom tried to warn him with a glare that he ignored. Not good. "Because I didn't sign on for this shit. The asset I can let go, because you put her out of her misery, but the mortal? That's over the line."

John fixed his tie before turning to address the Sentinel in the doorway. "I'm not sure I like your tone, Sentinel. Have you forgotten who you're speaking to?"

The final part of the plan required Tom to make it to the front door without incident, and it seemed his old friend Blake was about to throw a wrench in it.

"Not someone I respect, that's for damn sure." The Sentinel narrowed his gaze at Tom. "You know, man, I had a begrudging respect for you standing up for your beliefs, but you crawling home with your tail between your legs has got to be one of the most pathetic things I've ever seen. You killed the asset without batting an eye. I've never been so disgusted in my life."

*Okay, ouch.* "Just doing what I was created to do, Sentinel." *Now if you could start moving and stop talking before you fuck all this up, that'd be awesome.*

His father nodded in agreement. "Sentinel Blake, if you have an issue with how things operate here, I'll be happy to entertain your resignation."

*Oh, shit.* "Let's—"

"You have it," Sentinel Blake said, cutting Tom off.

*Fuck.* Time to improvise. Tom drew his weapon and aimed it at Blake. He made sure it was the same one he used earlier on Amelia so everyone would know it held incendiary bullets. All part of the original plan that appeared to be taking a trip to hell in a hand basket.

"How about we go outside and talk about this, Sentinel. Preferably before the house burns down." *Because I need to get to the front door.*

Blake pointed his gun at Tom's head. "I'm fine here."

"Gentlemen," his father chided, "we're wasting precious time."

"Why, you have another woman to kill?" Blake sneered. Tom understood the man's anger, but he'd seriously chosen the wrong time to display it.

Sentinel Charlie whistled from the hallway. "Yo! Fire's going. Let's go!"

Tom raised his brows. "Sentinel, do you really want to die like this?"

"It's here or outside. We both know that's the only way out." A hint of sadness echoed in Blake's gaze.

He opened his mouth to reply when all hell broke loose. Gunfire broke out, not in the bedroom, but the hallway, and Blake reacted. John shouted just as a bullet hit Tom square in the chest. It fucking burned and knocked him into the bed. He dropped his pistol in shock and clutched his jacket.

*Jesus Christ*, it hurt. His blood was on fire, burning a path from his heart outwards, and shooting pain to his limbs. A scream lodged in his throat, but refused to escape, as his vision blurred. His father's face appeared, stark horror filling his expression.

"Thomas!" he shouted, but it sounded so distant. Like a faraway dream.

*I'm dying*, Tom realized. *I'm truly fucking dying.* And he hadn't had a chance to tell Amelia how he felt. Her eyes filled his vision, those gorgeous blue irises, blinking innocently down at him as a smile curled her full lips. God, he would miss that expression. His biggest regret would be never seeing it again.

"Son, my son," his father's voice echoed in his mind. The sadness lingering there would haunt him in the afterlife, because for a brief moment, it made him wonder if it was possible. *Does John Fitzgerald actually care?*

Darkness swallowed him, leaving him with his last cognizant thoughts of a man he vowed to hate, who may have loved him after all.

*O*ne *Week Later…*

Amelia floated on her back in the pool with her eyes on the stars, wearing a wistful expression. This was her new favorite spot. She said it gave her a sense of peace that reminded her of the dark place, but with bright spots to keep her grounded.

"Still pissed at me?" a snarky voice asked from the pool deck.

Tom scowled. "Yes."

Alik shrugged and snagged the chair beside him. "Good thing we have eternity to fix that."

"If you tell me it was the only way one more fucking time, I'm going to shoot you. And we both know I won't miss."

"I'll have you on your knees before you can even think to grab your gun," Alik returned. "But seriously, consider it an initiation. We've all fucked with each other at one point or another. You just got tagged team by three of us at once."

*Wakefield, Tristan, and Alik.* One screwed with his vision, the second obscured his hearing, and Alik set his insides on fire. All to make him and everyone else in the cabin think he'd actually been shot by an incendiary bullet. If it hadn't been on fire, the trick may not have worked, but his father and the Sentinels didn't have time to examine him too closely. Then Jacque had popped in, grabbed Tom and Amelia, and whisked them to Hydria.

*"We needed them to think it was real,"* Wakefield had explained the next morning. Tom would have believed him if it wasn't for the smirk at the end.

*"You improvised, so we improvised,"* was Tristan's version of an apology.

Alik just said, *"Welcome to Hydria."*

"I had the situation handled," Tom said now, not for the first time.

"Probably," Alik agreed. He sat forward, legs splayed, and braced his forearms on his thighs. "But here's the thing. You're one of us now, and we take care of our own. That's the beauty of being a Hydraian. We watch out for each other, which means we'll never just drop you off in the middle of a fight and expect you to figure it out on your own. Same goes for a flaming cabin in the middle of the woods. You're not alone anymore, kid. Deal with it."

Tom arched an eyebrow and focused on the part he felt comfortable commenting on. "I'm not a kid."

"You are to me," he replied then nodded at the beauty in the pool. "But maybe not to her."

Tom met Amelia's glittering gaze with a smile. *Definitely not to her.*

Alik hopped up, took a step, and paused. "Oh, by the way..."

"Yes?" Tom asked, meeting the Elder's burning stare.

"Hurt her, and what we did to you last week will feel like a happy dream. You understand?"

*Well, that makes four.* The other Elders had threatened

him earlier in the week, in a variety of ways. All about Amelia. "She's lucky to have so many people who care about her," Tom replied. "I wouldn't have it any other way."

Alik tilted his head in acknowledgement and left.

"He likes you," Amelia said as she folded her elbows on the side of the pool.

"He has a funny way of showing it," he muttered.

"Alik doesn't talk a lot, but he just gave you a lecture about family and what it means here. That means he likes you."

"So you missed the threat before he left?"

She smiled. "Oh no, I heard that, too. Another sign that he likes you since he cares enough to let you know."

"Right, because that's exactly how I took it." *Not.*

Amelia pulled herself out of the pool and straddled him over the chair. Water pooled between them, but he didn't care. She could get him wet anytime, anywhere she liked. He brushed her damp strands from her face and palmed her cheek.

"I'm not used to this," he admitted. Not the half-naked woman on his lap or the arousal straining the zipper of his jeans, but the feeling of family. Of love. "I don't know how to accept it or, really, how to allow it." Relying on others to help him out of situations felt so foreign to him. He understood Alik's lecture on principle, but applying it took a strength Tom wasn't sure he possessed.

"We'll learn together." Amelia brushed her lips against his. "You're not the only one who has trouble trusting, Tom."

"I trust you," he admitted. She was the reason he stayed in Hydria, because fending for himself would never be an issue. But he didn't want to leave her.

She smiled. "You can say love, you know. I won't shy away."

He chuckled and grabbed her ribs to give them a tickle. "That's where my arrogance went. I wonder who stole it."

She squirmed and squealed. "Tom!"

He didn't stop tickling her until she was under him on the lounge chair and he had her straddling him the way he wanted. Settling between her bare thighs was heaven personified. Until a cough broke the moment. He glanced over to find Wakefield and Stas standing on the pool deck, dressed in black.

"Oh, good, this will make five threats," he muttered as he pushed off Amelia and helped her stand. She fixed her blue string bikini, before picking up a towel to wrap around herself.

"Hi," Amelia greeted, her cheeks flushed. She opened her mouth to say more, but paused when Stas threw her arms around Tom's neck and buried her face in his shoulder. He returned the hug while flashing a *what the fuck* look at Wakefield.

"We've just come from your memorial service," he explained. "I think it felt a little too real."

Stas nodded, her shoulders shaking.

"My memorial service?" Tom asked. He supposed a funeral wouldn't work without a proper body to mourn. "Bet John had fun milking that."

"Oh, he's opening several Fitzgerald funds in your honor." Wakefield smirked. "And he's requested an official business partnership with Wakefield Pharmaceuticals."

"No, shit. What did you say?"

"I agreed under the pretense of trying to please Aya, which it is to an extent as I intend to use my resources to dig into Elizabeth's welfare. If Jonathan truly is experimenting on her, then I imagine he may be interested in acquiring certain inoculations or medications, of which I own several."

Stas pulled back to stare into Tom's eyes. Her concern unnerved him. "I really am fine, Stas."

"I know. Yes, I know." She shook her head and finally let him go, taking a step back. Wakefield draped his arm around her as she sniffled. "But Lizzie doesn't... And I can't help her. No one will let me bring her here."

It broke a piece of him to see Stas so upset, but Lizzie mourning him was what really took a toll on his heart. He wished there was another way, but they had to keep her in the dark to keep her safe. For now.

"She thinks you died overseas. John made up this whole crazy story, and he included Blake in it. Said you both were true heroes." She bit her lip and shook her head. "He's a fucking bastard."

"Blake is undergoing rehabilitation," Wakefield added. "Your father is making an example out of him, claiming he set you up then killed you."

Tom's hands curled into fists at his sides. "You could have saved him."

"Not without announcing our presence, and you know that. We needed Jonathan to believe you and Amelia were dead for this to work. Blake is a sacrifice."

"He doesn't deserve it."

"Perhaps not, but blaming ourselves is counterproductive. Jonathan is the one to blame here, and he will pay." The promise underlining Wakefield's voice did little to dispel the tension lining Tom's shoulders.

"Sometimes I think killing the bastard would be easier," he growled.

"Absolutely it would, but waiting will make his death more meaningful. We need to know who is pulling his strings and what he did to Elizabeth."

"And that's where I come in," Jayson announced as he stepped onto the pool deck with a suitcase. He dropped the luggage and folded his arms.

Wakefield gave him the man nod. "How was Brazil?"

"Fabulous." Jayson's satisfied expression was one all men recognized. *Someone had a good time.*

"Who won the challenge?" Amelia asked.

"Come now, A. You know I don't kiss and tell."

Amelia rolled her eyes. "Fine. Be that way."

Jayson blew her a kiss before looking at Tom. "Any questions about the house before I head to New York?" He'd offered to let them borrow his home, which came equipped with the swimming pool, while he was out of town. It served as the perfect housing solution while they built their own place down the beach, but that didn't mean Tom approved of the reason behind it.

The notion of relying on someone else to protect his oldest friend grated his nerves. But he didn't have a choice. It was this or announce his reincarnation, which would spoil everything. And as Luc noted, Jayson's abilities made him the best man for the job.

"Trust," Amelia whispered, wrapping her arm around him. "Jay knows what he's doing."

The Elder slid on a pair of shades despite the late hour and resembled a fallen angel in his suit and tie and disheveled hair. "Don't worry, kid," he said to Tom. "Miss Watkins is in good hands."

"Are they all going to call me that?" Tom muttered, referring to the kid part.

Amelia smiled. "Consider it an endearment."

"Like arse?"

"Yes, exactly like that."

"Whatever you say, asset." He kissed her temple and hugged her close.

Wakefield pulled a few items from his jacket pocket and handed them to the Elder. "Mateo set it all up, including your new residence in her building."

Jayson flipped through the documents and grinned. "Jayson Masters. Indeed, I am."

"The other items you requested are already in the flat, including the knives."

The Elder nodded. "Then I'm all set." He regarded Amelia and Tom. "Stay out of my bedroom. You two aren't ready for that level of experimentation yet." With that sound advice, he picked up his bags and disappeared.

"Okay, never mind. That's where my arrogance went,"

Tom remarked, playing on his earlier statement.

Amelia shook her head. "Jay redefines arrogance."

"Are you sure about this?" Stas asked, gaze on her Ichorian. "He seems a bit much for Lizzie, don't you think?"

"Oh, I'm certain Elizabeth can hold her own. In fact, I'm looking forward to it." He shifted focus to Amelia. "On a similar topic of amusement, I hear Aidan is scheduled to visit tomorrow. Do you plan to introduce him to the Sentinel?"

Tom pictured shooting Wakefield in the face and smiled when the Ichorian flinched. *Thanks for that reminder, jackass.* Meeting a lover's father was hard enough with normal people, let alone an ancient Ichorian with the gift for omniscience. Talk about nerve-racking.

"Yes, he mentioned something about Osiris being preoccupied and it being a good time to visit." Amelia's excitement was palpable. She had spoken to her father a few times over the last week, but hadn't seen him yet. "I can't wait to see him, and he promised to bring Clara with him."

Stas scowled at the name, making Wakefield chuckle. "Don't worry, Aya. We won't be here."

"I didn't say anything."

"No, but you did turn a lovely shade of green," he teased.

She attempted to push the Ichorian into the pool, but he lifted her into his arms on a laugh as she struggled.

"This suit would not fare well in the chlorine, darling."

"I beg to differ." She used an impressive move that almost sent them both into the water, but Wakefield countered it and wrapped his arms around her in an impenetrable hold. Tom felt a begrudging surge of respect for the man. Those moves weren't luck on either part, which indicated Wakefield had an understanding of martial arts. Interesting.

He nuzzled Stas's neck and hugged her close. "When

do you to return to work, love?"

"In about twelve hours," she muttered, still squirming.

"Brilliant. How about a jaunt down the beach and a quick dip?"

"I would like that." Stas's smile was unlike any Tom had ever seen from her. *He really makes her happy. How did I miss that before?*

"I want to have a conversation with you when I return, Thomas. Don't go anywhere."

And just like that, he didn't care how happy the Ichorian made his friend and went back to hating the bastard.

"Oh, I'm looking forward to it," he replied, voice thick with sarcasm. Wakefield responded by blacking out his vision for a split second as he and Stas left. "Your brother's an ass, and I don't mean that endearingly."

Amelia giggled and slipped her arms around his waist. "You'll change your mind someday."

"Doubtful."

"You changed your mind about me."

"Did I?" He smiled down at her. "And what did I change my mind about?"

"You trust me."

"And I didn't trust you before?"

"You didn't trust *anyone* before."

"Hmm…" She had him there. "You know what else I didn't feel before you?"

She shook her head. "No. What?"

He nibbled her earlobe and whispered, "Love."

"And you feel that now?"

He nodded. "For you, I do."

Her smile took his breath away. "Truly?"

"Truly," he repeated with a grin. Her accent amused him, especially when she used odd words like *truly*. He tucked a damp strand behind her ear and allowed some seriousness to leak through. Actions were his preference over spoken endearments, but there were some moments that required words, and this was one of them.

"You make me feel, Amelia. You're my home." There was no other way to describe it. He never had a sanctuary or a place he felt safe, until her.

She went onto her toes to kiss him and sighed against his lips. "You're my home, too."

"I know."

She smacked his arm with a laugh and rolled her eyes. "I see your arrogance is back."

"It never left, sweetheart."

"Yeah?" She pulled back to look him up and down. "Straddle me again."

His gaze narrowed. "Are you asking me to spar with you while wearing nothing but a towel and a skimpy bikini?" Because he definitely approved of that idea.

"Maybe."

"Be certain, Amelia."

She bit her lip and grinned. The minx. "You'll have to catch me first."

"A chase, followed by sparring?" God clearly invented this woman for him, and only him.

"Only if you think you're up for it." She dropped the towel and jumped in the pool with an excited squeal that went straight to his groin.

"Oh, game on, sweetheart."

# IMMORTAL CURSE SERIES
## What's Next

Dear Reader,

Amelia and Tom's journey was a particularly difficult story to write due to their dark emotions and the underlying depressive themes. But watching them grow together as a couple, and build each other up after years of torment and pain was a gratifying experience. I hope you enjoyed reading their story. They will be key characters in future novels, so you will see them again, and their love will continue to expand throughout the series.

Up next is Blood Heart, starring Jayson and Lizzie. I suspect there will be a lot of heat, chemistry, and heartache. The poor girl has been lied to her entire life. I doubt she'll be too happy when she learns the truth. I'm so excited for their story, and I hope you are too.

Angel Bonds, book four, will star Issac and Stas again as they continue to strengthen and test their relationship. That's all I can say for now as I don't want to give anything away.

Please keep in touch. I have a monthly newsletter, and I'm active on Facebook, Instagram, and Twitter. My reader group, Foss's Night Owls, is where you can find me often.

Thanks again for reading!

Cheers,
-Lexi

# ACKNOWLEDGMENTS

There are so many people who helped make this book possible, starting with my husband, Matt, who tolerates my very long working hours and constant daydreaming. Special thanks to my critique partners, Elaine and Nathalie, who keep me honest and help me craft the best work possible.

Thank you, Louise and Melissa, for keeping me organized and helping me navigate social media. I'd be lost without you!

To my sprinting buddies, LK and Fiona, thank you for helping me write faster. To my beta readers Allison, Dodie, Laura and Louise, thank you for your time and feedback, and for reviewing all my revisions.

Jenny, thank you for helping me on such short notice and giving Forbidden Bonds the attention it needed. Allison, Cheryl, Pam, Tara and Tracey, thank you for being amazing friends and proofreading for me. And to Jacy, thank you for fixing all my punctuation mistakes, pointing out my overused words, and correcting all my grammar errors.

It takes a dedicated team to produce a book, and an army to market it. Special thanks to my Famous Owls, you all rock! And thank you to Claudia, Catie and Julie for producing such an amazing cover.

None of this could be possible without my ARC Team, Enticing Journeys, Itsy Bitsy, Jennifer R. Promotions, Love Kissed Promotions, Pure Textuality PR and Quill & Ink Book Tours. Thank you, Thank you, Thank you!

But most importantly, thank you readers for allowing me to entertain you. Your trust and faith in me keeps me going. Thank you!

# ABOUT THE AUTHOR

Lexi C. Foss is a writer lost in the IT world. She lives in Atlanta, Georgia with her husband and their furry children. When not writing, she's busy crossing items off her travel bucket list. Many of the places she's visited can be seen in her writing, including the mythical world of Hydria which is based on Hydra in the Greek islands. She's quirky, consumes way too much coffee, and loves to swim. Cheers!

# ALSO BY LEXI C. FOSS

**Immortal Curse Series**
Blood Laws
Forbidden Bonds
Blood Heart
Elder Bonds
Angel Bonds
Blood Bonds

**Blood Alliance Series**
Chastely Bitten

**Dark Provenance Series**
Daughter of Death
Heiress of Bael
Divinity of Acheron

**Mershano Empire Series**
The Prince's Game
The Charmer's Gambit
The Rebel's Redemption
The Devil's Denial